The Blackening Pond

Also by Fadette Marie
NORTHERN GIRL

The Blackening Pond

FADETTE MARIE

teampublishing

First published in Great Britain
in 2014 by Team Publishing

A CIP catalogue record for this book
is available from the British Library.

ISBN 9780956770516

Typeset in 11/14pt Sabon by Falcon Oast Graphic Art Ltd.
Printed and bound in Great Britain by
CPI Group (UK) Ltd, Croydon, CR0 4YY

For you Jean,
my unceasingly entertaining cousin,
on this your 80th year

I wish you health,
I wish you wealth,
I wish you gold in store,
I wish you heaven after death,
What could I wish you more.
                               Gran

Chapter 1

Evenwood, County Durham – 1947

'Upset! Of course I'm bloody upset!' Jessie stared hard at her mother for asking such a stupid question. 'Comes back here, bold as brass, with his bloody French bride in tow, *and* a bairn!'

'Well, ah never liked 'im anyway,' Maude remarked, unable to resist a satisfied smirk.

'You never liked him 'cause yer were scared shitless that ah was goin' ter marry him. Then where would yer have been, eh? No one ter skivvy for yer, this place would be a hovel without me. Huh, ye're filthy, that's what you are!'

'Yer can call me what yer like, but face it, 'ees not comin' back. Yer've lost 'im and good riddance, Tom bloody Dawson, that's what ah say.'

'Oh, ye're not human, you!' With a jerk of her head, Jessie got up from the cluttered table, rushed to the front door and *slam*, she was gone.

Eyes tight closed, Jessie stood for a few seconds, her back pressed to the door. The thought of her life panning out before her in this hovel made her sick to the stomach. Well, she wasn't going to take this lying down. She'd go over to Hannah Dawson's and see for herself just what was so special about this ... this foreign piece, that her blue-eyed, can't-put-a-foot-wrong son had married.

Over at Hannah's, the fire burned brightly in the grate. The reflections of the flames danced on the blackened surround of the fireplace, with the power to hypnotize if you had the time to sit around looking at it. And right now, Jeannie sat in front of it, toasting fork in hand and cursing for all she was worth. Not that her curse vocabulary was that polished at her tender years.

Oh, how she wished that she were old enough to know all the best swear words – especially now, when the toast had landed, for the third time, on the fire and was as black as the coal it rested on.

Exasperated, she called up the stairs, 'Maddie! Maddie! Can you come down and prong this blinkin' bread on to the fork for me? It keeps fallin' inter the bloomin' fire and me gran'll do 'er nut if she sees how much bread ah've wasted.'

Maddie put down her pen, pushed her half-written letter to one side, and smiled.

'Coming!' she called. It was just as well that Jeannie's

mother was at work and unable to hear her daughter's language, she thought, with some sympathy for poor Rene, who she knew had tried very hard to improve Jeannie's speech.

Even moving the five miles out of the village to the town of Bishop Auckland hadn't helped very much, although Maddie had noticed that Jeannie was very careful not to use swear words in front of her mam or her grandma Hannah. But she obviously thought that she could get away with it in Maddie's presence, no doubt imagining that being French, Maddie wouldn't know what these words meant.

But Maddie *did* know, and found it very amusing, but she would never dream of mentioning anything to Jeannie's mother or grandmother.

'Look!' Jeannie exclaimed, as Maddie came into the living room. 'The blinkin' bread is in the fire! Great-grandda Elliott is never goin' ter get his breakfast at this rate!'

'Let me see,' said Maddie, holding out her hand for the fork.

After threading the fork firmly through a slice of bread, Maddie gave it back. 'Try it now. Just try to keep your hand still, Jeannie,' she smiled, 'and you will see it will work zis time.'

'Thanks, Maddie, yer can go back ter writing ter yer mam and dad now if yer like.'

Amused at how grown-up Jeannie had become over

these last few weeks since her great-grandda had been staying at the house, she said, '*Merci*, Jeannie, I will tell your *grandpère* that you will bring his toast very soon, eh?' She raised her eyebrows for confirmation.

'Ah'll bring some for you as well, if you like,' the child said, confident that she knew how to do it now.

'No, thank you, I will eat later wiz—'

The loud knock on the back door stopped Maddie mid-sentence.

'Oh damn and blast, who's that now?' said Jeannie, about to get up from the fireplace.

'No . . . no, Jeannie.' Maddie raised her hand. 'You stay there and do your *grandpère*'s toast, I will get it.'

When Maddie opened the door, it was to be confronted by the back of an unfamiliar slim figure topped by a mass of dark mid-length curls. And when the figure turned to face her, Maddie stuttered, unnerved by the cold brown eyes boring straight into her own. 'Hello, are you looking for someone?'

'Oh, I'm looking for someone all right,' the girl said, looking her up and down with what Maddie perceived to be distaste.

When there was no follow-up with the name of who she might be looking for, Maddie, disturbed and wishing to get rid of this rude girl, said quickly, 'Well, Hannah is in ze village shopping right now . . . so you must call later.' She started to close the door but the girl, not taking her eyes from Maddie's, put her foot against it, and leaning right in until their faces almost touched, she said, 'Tell Hannah . . . Jessie called.'

The second that she turned away, Maddie slammed the door shut, took a deep breath and stood there with her hand over her mouth.

'Who was that?' Jeannie asked, without looking up from spreading Gran's home-made marmalade on the now perfect toast.

'It was a very rude girl called Jessie, that's who it was!'

'Oh, she used ter be our Tom's girlfriend,' Jeannie said nonchalantly as she poured her grandda's milk into a mug.

'So, that's her.' Maddie felt a bit wobbly and had to sit down for a moment.

As soon as she felt she was far enough away from Hannah's house, Jessie stopped to catch her breath. Shaking with anger and jealousy, she fumbled to get a cigarette from her bag and light it.

She inhaled deeply, and slumped against the wall surrounding one of the row of identical back yards in the street. Only two puffs later she had made a decision. She threw the cigarette to the ground, crushing it with a determined twist of her foot, and disappeared among the strings of washing that criss-crossed the back street like a badly made spider's web.

*

'Are yer comin' up ter have a mug of milk with me and Grandda?' Jeannie called down to Maddie from halfway up the stairs, while balancing a plate of toast and three mugs on a tray that was far too small.

'*Oui* . . . yes, I am coming up to finish my letter,' Maddie said as she mounted the stairs. Her mind was very much on this girl Jessie now.

She'd known that Tom had had a girlfriend before he'd gone to war, but had understood that it was all over long before she met him. And yet, here was this girl looking like thunder and knocking on Tom's mother's door . . .

'Are yer goin' over to the house after breakfast?' Jeannie's interruption brought her sharply back to the present moment.

'Er, yes I am, but Tom is there painting ze doors right now, so I will go later when zey have time to dry a little.'

'I'll come and help if yer like,' said Jeannie, always wanting to be involved in everything. 'After all, the quicker yer get it done up, the quicker yer can move into it! Eee, it's goin' ter be grand, Maddie, when it's all finished like,' she said, once again sounding much older than her eleven years. The two girls, each deep in their own thoughts, sipped their milk, while Great-grandda Elliott sat there silently eating his toast and thinking how lucky he was to have had two such lovely girls to keep him company while he'd been under the weather.

The peaceful moment was suddenly broken by his daughter Hannah's voice coming from somewhere downstairs.

'Here, Jeannie! Can yer come down and give uz a hand?' Hannah was struggling to get her shopping inside and the pushchair into the living room.

'Comin', Gran!' Jeannie called as she swung down the stairs, gripping the banister on one side and the stair rail on the other.

'Shush! Don't make so much racket, pet, she's just gone off to sleep.' Hannah nodded towards little Francine in the pushchair. 'Is her mam upstairs?' she whispered.

'Yes.' Jeannie's whisper was loud enough for Maddie to hear. 'She's writin' to 'er mam and dad and keepin' Great-grandda company while he's havin' his breakfast.'

'Has he eaten anything, pet?' Hannah sounded worried.

'Well, if yer'd seen the way he devoured his toast, yer'd think there was nowt wrong with him.'

'Oh, ah'm pleased about that 'cause—'

'Jessie called round while yer were out,' Jeannie interrupted.

'Jessie! What did *she* want?'

Jeannie seemed deep in thought now. 'Don't know . . . It was Maddie that answered the door and she looked a bit funny when she came back in, ah've got ter say.'

Without taking her coat off, Hannah started to unpack the shopping. More to herself than to Jeannie, she said, 'This doesn't bode well. There's trouble afoot, ah just know it.'

Upstairs, her face cupped in her hand, Maddie was sitting at the dressing table and staring at the sheets of paper spread out before her. Great-grandda Elliott, watching with a kindly smile on his face, commented, 'Eee, lass, yer've got enough paper there ter be writin' a book!'

Maddie leaned back in the chair, stretching her arms above her head. 'Yes, well, I have so much to tell Maman and Papa. They ask me so many questions in their last letter, so I must answer zem all.' She nodded her head in agreement with herself.

When she thought now about how she and Tom had first met in France and she could speak hardly any English and he no French, she realized how far she had come since then and felt quietly proud of herself. In the short space of time that she'd been in England, by listening to the wireless and concentrating hard to understand what she read in newspapers, she had picked up so much more of the language. She knew that she had amazed not only herself but the whole family.

As if reading her thoughts, Great-grandda Elliott suddenly piped up, 'Ay, yer English is getting quite good, pet. Ah'm that proud of yer 'cause it can't have been easy, with nobody round here able ter speak French like!' Pulling himself further up in his bed, he leaned towards her and whispered, 'That lot down there think ah'm losing me marbles, but ah notice things, yer know, and ah'm very fond of you. They all are . . .' He stopped, suddenly changing tack, before the tears he could see welling in Maddie's eyes had time to fall. He flapped his hand and demanded, in a feigned stern voice, 'Now go and get me a cup of tea, will yer, ah'm parched here. This milk our Jeannie brought up is no good ter me. Why it's a bairn's drink, man!'

Maddie smiled, checking her tears. 'You are so cheeky, *Grandpère*, but I am so pleased zat you are here.'

'Go on with yer, and don't dilly-dally down there, mind,' he answered, on a cough, which was meant to disguise any possibility of tears leaking from his own eyes.

When she left the room, Great-grandda leaned back on his pillows, thinking, Ay, she's a grand lass, but it grieves uz to see her so sad. The sooner ah'm well enough ter go back to me own house the better. It must be hard on our Hannah and Jack an' all, making up beds downstairs every night, what with Maddie, Tom and the bairn here too. Well, they'll be movin' out and into their own home soon as it's done. Maybe Maddie'll settle better when they're in their own place.

He had to admit that Tom had done well to get that derelict house. Never thought ah'd see the day that our

Tom would take on such responsibilities, and so willingly. Must love that lass one heck of a lot, that's all ah can think.

Jeannie broke in on his thoughts, calling up the stairs, 'Yer cup of tea is on its way, Great-grandda, just puttin' yer milk in!'

'Ah'll have a couple of them nice biscuits that ah had the other day an' all . . . and where's Maddie?' he called, slipping back to his usual gruff ways.

'She's gone off ter post her letter, so yer'll have ter make do with me,' came the equally gruff reply.

Pleased with herself at having got the tea up the stairs without spilling too much into the saucer, Jeannie said, 'Here yer are, Great-grandda, and there'll be no drips ter fall on yer pyjamas this time . . . so nowt fer yer to moan about!' She put on her best stern face.

'When's our Rene comin' ter pick yer up?' Great-grandda asked, as Jeannie carefully steadied the rattling cup and saucer in his hands.

'Well, as it's Saturday she'll probably finish work a bit later. She'll be here about half past six, I expect . . . Why? Are yer wantin' rid of me like?' She laughed.

'Never, pet . . . no, never.' He looked solemn for a moment, then with a grin he added, 'Anyway, who would skivvy for me if you weren't here, what with yer mam at work and our Tom busy every weekend doin' up his house. And then there's our Hannah always doin' stuff for everybody else, and as for yer grandda Jack, well by the time he's got all that coal dust washed off himself there's nowt of him left ter skivvy for anybody!'

'Ay, Great-grandda, you are funny. We all look after yer, yer know that fine well, so stop yer mitherin'. Here, sup yer tea, so ah can take the cup back down.' She held on to the saucer while he took the cup. Once he'd drained it, he handed it to her, saying, 'Right, get yerself down there now and leave uz in peace. Ah'm in need of a bit sleep.'

'OK,' Jeannie sighed, 'ah'll go about me duties now, if ye're quite finished orderin' uz about!'

As she turned to leave he watched her go, and even when she had closed the door behind her he kept his gaze on it a moment longer. Then, with a contented sigh, he shuffled down the bed until his head rested on the pillows.

Maddie came out of the post office, licked the stamp and stuck it on the envelope containing her letter to France. She kissed the envelope, then dropped it into the postbox and went to retrieve her bike from where she'd propped it up against the wall.

She straightened the bicycle ready to straddle it, but with a sudden clank and jangle the chain fell unceremoniously to the ground. Just then, the tail of a dark-coloured coat disappeared off to the left, into an adjoining road.

'*Mon Dieu!*' Wondering what to do, Maddie stood there despairingly, both hands to her head.

'Maddie! Maddie, what is it?'

Maddie turned towards the familiar voice. Running towards her, Rene said breathlessly, 'I saw you from the bus! What happened?' Without a word, Maddie pointed to the chain.

'Not to worry, pet,' Rene said consolingly. 'It was a cheap bike anyway, all that Tom could afford at the time, but he plans to get you a better one so don't fret, love. We'll get it home together.'

'But Rene! Someone must have done zis!' Maddie had pulled back from Rene's supporting arm.

'No . . . no, pet! Who on earth round here would do something like that?'

'You don't understand, Rene. Strange things have been happening before, and I'm sure I heard someone running away . . . down there.' She pointed to the corner of the post office building.

Rene wasn't convinced that the two things were connected. 'OK, pet. Well, it's fortunate that I had taken the afternoon off work . . . Surprise for Jeannie, thought I'd take her out somewhere, I hardly see her these days.' She smiled. 'Anyway, let's get the bike home. Probably just a children's prank, eh?'

But Maddie knew that whoever she'd heard running was no child.

Chapter 2

Marck, France

'Martine!' Maman called up the stairs. 'Do you remember the bracelet that Tante Lucy bought for Madeleine?'

'Yes, the gold one, to thank her for the clothes she had altered for her.'

'Well, Madeleine says in her letter that she was certain she had taken it to England with her but she can't find it anywhere, and could we look for it here.'

'Well, I can't imagine she would have left it lying around, that bracelet is very precious to her. She'll be devastated if she's lost it!' Martine came running down the stairs. 'What else does she say, Maman?'

'She tries to sound excited about the little cottage that they are doing up, but I know Madeleine ... She is hiding something, probably how homesick she's feeling. I know that it's only been a short while, but the pain doesn't get any less.'

Knowing that her mother was referring not only to Madeleine but to her own pain as well, Martine put her arms around her. 'Oh Maman, we all miss her, you know.'

'You are a good girl, Martine.' Maman patted her eldest daughter's hand. 'But,' she sighed, 'I guess that one day you will all be leaving . . . and that's how it should be.'

'Oh, I understand how you feel, Maman, but Simone, Dominic and me . . . well, we won't be leaving so abruptly. We will make sure that you have more time to get used to the idea.' She squeezed her *maman*'s hand. 'Poor Madeleine didn't really have a choice but to do things in the way that she did, it was all so quick. Once the decision was made, so much happened in such a short space of time.'

If only we'd dealt with the news of Madeleine's pregnancy differently, Martine thought for the umpteenth time.

'It was the shock, Maman. We should have all talked together, as a family. We should have made Papa sit down and talk with us instead of letting him stew like that on his own,' she said now, but her *maman* interrupted.

'Oh, I know all that. I did try but there was just no talking to your *papa* at that time. As you well know, Martine, he couldn't come to terms with his little girl becoming pregnant. I'm afraid that your *papa* and I allowed the shame and disappointment to cloud our judgement. If we had only reacted differently, Madeleine probably wouldn't be in this situation now . . .'

'You say, "this situation", Maman, but she does love Tom, you know.'

'I know she does, but she would never have run away if she'd felt that we, her family, would stand by her. I can't forgive myself for that.'

'Oh Maman, I'm sure Madeleine has forgiven all that by now.'

Martine put out a consoling arm but her mother, obviously needing to get these things off her chest, continued regardless. 'And then by the time we'd found Tom's address in England and sent Dominic over there to meet Tom's family and tell him of Madeleine's pregnancy, well, Madeleine . . . thinking that she had shamed us all and that we would be better off without her, had already run away to Boulogne, hoping to find solace with her friend Nicole. Imagine that!' She looked at Martine through her silently flowing tears. 'Imagine having to go all that way to find someone who might care enough to help, when she was surrounded by her family, who couldn't.'

'I know,' Martine said, still holding on to her mother's hand. 'But it's done now and we can't change it. Madeleine knows how much we all love her.'

Still her *maman* continued, and Martine let her talk.

'Poor Madeleine. As she was the youngest of the four of you, we always tried to protect her, almost as if she were still a child. It must have been such a shock to discover in Boulogne that Nicole's *maman*, Ginette, had been running a brothel all those years.' She looked at her daughter. 'You knew about that, didn't you, Martine?'

Martine nodded. 'Yes, well, maybe we did overprotect her. But Madeleine is quite grown up in some ways, probably more so than any of us give her credit for. Instead of just trying to warn her away from her friendship with Nicole when she came to stay with me in Boulogne, I should have told her the reason why. But she would have taken no notice even if she'd known the truth, of that I'm sure. She continued to meet up with Nicole behind my back anyway, so what could I do?'

'It was a terrible time,' Maman agreed. 'But it turns out that Nicole is a lovely girl, and her *maman* too, so who are we to judge? And when I think now of how Nicole and Ginette must have suffered at the hands of those ignorant monsters who dragged them to the market square and sheared their hair like that!'

Martine felt sick at the memories her *maman* had evoked of this dark period in their lives. 'And believing them to have serviced the *Germans* during the war!'

'Huh! Well, there were plenty of women doing that who were supposedly loving wives!'

This observation brought Martine up short. She

16

couldn't believe that this was the same strong-principled *maman* standing up, even if indirectly, for a prostitute and her daughter. *Mon Dieu*, how this war has changed everyone, she thought.

But she also knew that her mother was aware that if it hadn't been for Nicole and Ginette, Madeleine probably wouldn't have survived the trip to Boulogne. She couldn't have been there at a worse time, with over-excited mobs roaming the streets, looking for revenge on anyone they considered to be a collaborator. It had been pure luck that she'd been saved from the hair shearing at all . . . and only by mere seconds.

Dominic had been in the north-east of England, on his mission to tell Tom of Madeleine's pregnancy, when the telegram arrived saying that Madeleine had run away.

He and Tom had dropped everything to rush down to Dover, and crossed the Channel to search for her in France.

They knew that Madeleine must have been beside herself to have run away. Their great worry now was that she might be contemplating one of the greatest of Catholic sins, in order to rid herself of the baby that was causing her family so much shame.

They had found Madeleine tied to a chair, semi-conscious and face down, in the market square in Boulogne, while the mob cut off the hair of Nicole and her mother. Even though Nicole had shouted to the baying onlookers that Maddie was pregnant, not one had taken pity. When Tom had picked up his beautiful Madeleine like a rag doll in his arms, he hadn't expected either her or their unborn baby to survive.

None of the family had ever told Maman the full extent of Madeleine's experience in Boulogne, and Martine wasn't about to now. But, if there was one good thing to come out of it all, it was that Tom, far from shirking the predicament he'd found himself in, had chosen to stand by his very young girlfriend.

Having come so close to losing her, he knew that he loved Maddie more than enough to give up what he'd thought would be an unfettered lifestyle back home in England after the war. He wanted to be by her side, and to take on the responsibilities of a husband and father.

And he wasn't the only one to be giving up the life he had planned. Madeleine would be leaving her family and friends, moving away from everything she had known and understood all through her eighteen years of life.

'Martine . . . !'

Martine jumped. 'Oh sorry, Maman, I was miles away.' She'd been so caught up in her thoughts that she'd not heard her mother speak.

Looking over her mother's shoulder at the letter she held in her hand, she asked in a lighter tone, 'What else does this little sister of mine have to say?'

'Here,' Maman handed her the letter, 'that's why I

was calling, so that you can read it for yourself.' As Martine took the letter she pretended not to notice the tears in her mother's eyes.

Just as she settled down to read it, the door burst open and in barged her brother Dominic and his girl-friend Yvette, both looking happy, breathless and fresh-faced. Oblivious to anyone else, they continued to giggle and tease each other.

'Shush!' Martine looked at her younger brother. 'I'm trying to read.'

Ignoring Martine's huffy attitude, he asked, 'Where's Simone then?'

'She's still at work of course!' she said even more huffily now, flapping her hand to get him to go away. Then, as if suddenly remembering her manners, Martine smiled at Yvette, who looked embarrassed. The younger girl whispered, 'Sorry!' and immediately shoved Dominic into the kitchen.

'Mmm, lovely smell in here, Maman. What delectable dish are we being served today then?' Dominic grinned mischievously at his mother as he put an arm around her.

'Boiled beef, with a tomato purée.' She looked to Yvette to check that she liked that idea.

'Sounds delicious,' she said. Just the smell wafting through the kitchen was enough to get her juices flowing, and she went to fetch the cutlery from the drawer.

'Martine seems a bit serious today?' said Dominic, pulling a comically serious face.

His mother was busily peeling potatoes at the sink. 'She's reading a letter from Madeleine and we are worried about her. As much as she loves Tom, I don't think she is settling very well in England.'

'Oh?' Dominic was pacing around the kitchen. 'Well, we all knew it would take time . . . Do you think that if we planned a little trip for her to come back and visit us, maybe . . . ?'

'But it's been such a short time, and England is her home now.' Maman seemed uncertain.

'Oh, you know what I mean Maman! Dominic hadn't intended to sound snappy, but Yvette cast a frown in his direction anyway.

'Well, she would need money to get here, and it will be a very tiring two-day journey from the north of England. And it's too soon to bring little Francine all this way.'

Even as she was saying this, Maman felt that she'd give anything to see her daughter and granddaughter again.

But Dominic, ignoring the difficulties of the journey, was only concerned with getting his youngest sister, whom he'd missed terribly, back home for a visit. 'Well, what if we all contribute some money to pay for her and Tom and Francine to come over?'

'Yes,' chipped in Yvette, 'let's do that! I can help too.'

Maman smiled at this lovely girlfriend of Dominic's, so pretty, with her red lipstick and her glossy, symmetrically cut dark hair. But more than that, having spent many weekends with them since Dominic had first set eyes on her, on a draughty station platform, she had become part of the family.

'That is very kind of you, Yvette. We will see, eh?' she patted her hand affectionately.

As soon as Simone came in from work at the pharmacy, there were discussions as to whether it would be a good idea to suggest to Madeleine she came home for a visit. All three of the siblings had agreed immediately, so Maman took a pen and paper from the bureau in the hall and wrote to Madeleine, telling her that the family were offering to pay for the three of them to visit, as soon as she liked. And with her heart less heavy, she rushed out to post the letter.

But she hadn't reckoned with Papa.

Later that evening, he came in from his workshop, tired and hungry, after a particularly wearisome day of constructing a heavy oak wardrobe. When he had taken off his blue carpenter's overalls, from which the aroma of oak sawdust wafted pleasantly around the kitchen, and he was confronted with the news that they had written to Madeleine inviting her to come home for a while, his usual calm countenance was transformed.

With the family seated at the dining table, he asked, without looking up, 'What on earth made you think that this would be a good idea?' Shocked, no one answered immediately, so he continued, but louder now. 'Have *any* of you thought,' he looked at each in turn, 'that bringing her back here so soon would probably make her even more unsettled than she is already?'

No one had anticipated this outburst from Papa. He could often be faulted for taking little interest in family arrangements, so no one had thought of consulting him before writing the letter. But the fact was, he was probably right.

'Well, it's done now!' Maman snapped back, not only annoyed with herself for having been so hasty in writing the letter but embarrassed now at this display in front of Yvette. She banged down a plate of food in front of each of them and ran through to the kitchen.

Simone and Martine threw down their serviettes, glared at their *papa* and followed Maman.

'Well! This is a fine situation,' Papa said, with a quick glance at Dominic, before picking up his knife and fork.

Yvette scraped her chair back across the tiles. 'I will go and join the others.' Dominic nodded his approval, picked up his cutlery and began to eat.

Evenwood

'Pet! Ah know that yer want ter see yer mam and dad, but we're right in the middle of doin' the house up. Ah thought yer were really lookin' forward to movin' out of me mam's and into our own place?'

'I am, Tom, of course I am, but my family . . . zey are offering to pay for us to go!'

Hardly able to contain herself, she held up the letter.

Tom felt torn. He knew how much a visit home to France would mean to Maddie. But he also knew that he would have to take time off work, which he could ill afford. Apart from that, Maddie would be unsettled for a long time afterwards, always looking forward to the next time, and the next . . . No, he was going to have to put his foot down, firmly. He'd tried to be patient and understanding, knowing how much she missed her family, but this . . . Well, it was just too soon!

'Look, pet. Why don't we hang on just another few months, till we get ourselves sorted, then I'll gladly come with you, eh?'

Maddie's whole demeanour changed. Her shoulders dropped, and she sat down on the nearest chair. 'But Tom?'

'There's no "but Tom", pet. We just can't do it at the moment. Surely you can see that?'

'Oh . . . I can see all right. You just want to stay here to be close to zat . . . zat Jessie girl, I suppose!'

'Hey! Hey! Come on, pet!' He couldn't understand why she should mention Jessie out of the blue like that – after all, she never cropped up in conversation. A bit wary now, he asked, 'What's Jessie got to do with anything anyway?'

'She obviously thinks she has everything to do wiz everything! Coming round here, pretending to look for Hannah! Well, I think she was looking for you!'

Any other time, Maddie's animated French accent would have made Tom smile with adoration. But not this time. This time Tom was angry: what the hell could Jessie want that would warrant a visit to the house? If he knew anything about her, she was probably out to stir things in some way. And quite apart from that, what on earth were Maddie's family thinking of, unsettling her like this? They obviously hadn't thought this through properly.

Unceremoniously he plonked the kettle on the fire. 'What's all this about Jessie comin' round? No one told me.'

Maddie made no answer, and on seeing him take two cups from the cupboard she got up from the chair. 'Don't bozzer to make tea for me ... I am going upstairs for a while.'

As she turned her tear-stained face towards him, he felt his heart would break. Feeling her loneliness as she mounted the stairs and unable to bear the thought of leaving her to fret on her own, he took the kettle from the fire and followed her to the bedroom.

When Hannah came bustling in with her usual bag of

shopping and saw Tom come down the stairs, she asked, 'Where is everybody? Is Maddie out with the bairn?'

'No, Mam, she's been having a bit of a lie-down, while Francine was sleeping. They're both awake now like.' He picked up the kettle and pushed it back on the fire.

'Has she said anything about Jessie?' Hannah asked, as she unloaded her shopping.

'Well yes, as a matter of fact she did, but ah think ah've put her mind at rest now.' Tom sounded more confident than he actually felt, then asked suddenly, 'Why d'yer ask?'

'Well, it's just that little unexplained things seem to keep happenin' to Maddie, and ah think she's convinced herself that somehow Jessie's behind it.'

'What . . . yer mean like the chain fallin' off her bike, and losin' her bracelet?'

Yes . . . and a few other things, like stuff turnin' up in places other than where she thinks she put them.'

Tom hesitated a moment. 'And you . . . what do you think, Mam?'

'Ah can't see how Jessie could have anything to do with the stuff in the house. There's no way she could get in without being seen, for a start. And then ah can't see why she'd want to be bothered with petty stuff like this, after all this time.'

'Exactly! Ah darn't say anythin' ter Maddie, but ah think maybe her mind's workin' overtime. After all, the bike was old, and ah dare say her bracelet will turn up in France. She could have easily forgotten it, in the turmoil before we left. And as for misplacing stuff . . . well, we all do it all the time. Ah think the poor lass is so homesick at the moment, she can't concentrate properly.'

Tom took the kettle off the fire and poured the boiling water into the teapot.

Deep in thought as he watched the tea leaves swirling around while he stirred, he added, 'Given time, she'll be all right, you'll see.'

'Well, ah hope ye're right, lad . . . ah really do.'

Frowning slightly, Hannah continued to put the shopping away, while Tom poured the tea into the three teacups lined up on the table. He looked up to see Maddie coming down the stairs, with a bright-eyed Francine in her arms. 'Ay, there ye are, me two lovely lasses! Come on, pet,' he winked at Maddie, 'and get this cup of tea down yer.'

Chapter 3

Tom and Maddie's house, two months later

Maddie waited anxiously for Tom to come home from work. She'd gone over and over in her head how she was going to break the news to him, and as she watched him walk towards their very own front door, hands in pockets and whistling happily to himself, she still hadn't found the words.

'Hello, pet.' Tom kissed her on the cheek as he came in. 'How are my lovely girls then? Francine asleep, is she?' He glanced up the stairs to where he knew she'd be. Without waiting for an answer, he walked into the kitchen and, seeing the steaming pans, turned to Maddie and smiled. 'Something smells good and I'm starvin'.' He lifted one of the lids and sniffed. 'Oh lovely, mince beef with onions 'n' gravy.'

'Yes, wiz mash and peas.' Maddie tried to keep her voice light as she drained the peas into a colander.

'Yorkshire puddin', dare I ask?'

'Of course!'

He grinned, patting her playfully on the backside as he went past to pull out a chair from under the kitchen table. As he sat there tugging at his boots, he asked, 'What've you been up to today then, pet?'

Maddie felt her face flush. 'Here, let me help you! She grabbed the heel of his boot and tugged, thus evading his question. This conversation had better wait until after they'd eaten, she'd decided.

Tom ate hungrily, chatting about work, while Maddie only picked at her food.

They cleared the table and then stood side by side on the doorstep, while Tom drew heavily on the stub of his Woodbine.

'By, that was a lovely dinner yer made tonight.' Tom smiled his appreciation and Maddie half smiled, looking up to the sky.

'No stars tonight, pet, too cloudy for that.' Tom cupped Maddie's upturned face in his hands, his eyes crinkling with affection. 'Yer've been very quiet. Is anything amiss?'

Maddie shuddered.

'Ay, come on, lass, let's get in the warm.' Tom led her in from the doorstep.

'Sit down, Tom,' Maddie said seriously.

'Oooh, this sounds ominous,' Tom laughed.

No amount of blinking would stop the tears. As if she

were listening to someone else far away in the distance, the words came tumbling from her mouth. 'I'm pregnant, Tom.'

The resulting silence seemed to go on for ever. Maddie tried to speak, but at that moment no further words would come.

'How long?' Tom asked, finally.

'Long enough for me to know . . .' Maddie replied, before adding more precisely, 'two months or so.'

Tom considered for a moment. 'Trouble is, we've spent all our money on doin' this house up.'

Maddie, feeling sick, rushed to the front door, sobbing. 'Do you think I don't know zat? Why do you think I have been so nervous to tell you?'

Tom leapt up from his chair. 'Don't run off, pet . . . Come here.' He pulled her towards him. 'It's not the end of the world, other people manage and we will too.' He smiled now. 'Here, dry your eyes.' He handed her a crumpled handkerchief from his pocket. Seeing her hesitation, he smiled again and said reassuringly, 'It *is* clean!'

When Maddie, wiping her eyes, smiled in response, he pulled her closer.

'Sorry, pet, it was just the shock. I thought we'd always been so careful.'

'What does that matter NOW Tom?' Maddie was feeling irritable. 'We have to decide what we are going to do!'

'We are going to sit down calmly and talk about it, then we are going to get on with our lives, that's what we are going to do. There's another seven months yet, so plenty of time to get a bit of money together, eh, pet?' He patted her leg affectionately, and she took his hand and held on to it.

'Zer is something else I need to say, Tom.'

'OK, fire away then, pet,' Tom said, a slight frown forming on his brow.

'I want to go home to have ze baby.'

'Home? You mean to France?' His tone had changed totally.

'Yes, Tom, I want to go to my parents . . . my family.'

Bishop Auckland

Since they'd moved into the flat above the shop, Rene and her lively young daughter, Jeannie, had become immune to the sounds of the buses and cars passing just below their upstairs window.

On their first night there, they'd been kept awake by the constant chatter down on the street below, not to mention the banging of car doors. There had been nothing of that sort in the little mining village of Evenwood. But there was no way that Rene was going to complain about it; after all, hadn't she spent the last few years trying to get herself and Jeannie out of the village, in the hope that they could better themselves? And here she was, manageress of Bella's, one of the most upmarket fashion shops in the town, *and* with a flat thrown in. All she had to find was money for electric, food and incidentals, of which there weren't that many readily available anyway with the rationing still in force, so she considered herself to be in clover.

Even Jeannie, who hadn't wanted to move at all, seemed to have settled happily into her new school. And the fact that she'd been allowed to stay at her gran's back in the village on a Saturday, while her mam was at work, had helped them both enormously. Rene knew how much Jeannie loved spending time with Maddie and little Francine. Almost since the day that Tom and his new wife, Maddie, had made the arduous journey from France with the tiny form bundled up in an enormous shawl, Jeannie had discarded her dolls, much preferring the real thing.

At first, Maddie, in a strange country and hardly able to speak the language, had been terrified to let Francine out of her sight. But as time had gone on and she'd come to know and trust Tom's family, she had allowed Jeannie to take Francine out in the pushchair up and down the terraced street at the back of Hannah's house, but no further.

Rene's heart ached, even now, when she pictured the look of bewilderment and terror on Maddie's face, on the day of her arrival in Evenwood. To have walked into a room full of strangers, albeit Tom's family, and with that precious little bundle cradled in her arms, must have been the worst kind of nightmare for a timid girl like her, and after such a long and gruelling journey too! She wouldn't even hand the baby over to get her coat off at first.

In fact it wasn't until Tom, at Rene's suggestion, had surprised her with the photograph of the derelict house that she had begun to relax a little. The house, detached and situated at the edge of the village, would be perfect, he'd thought, for him and his little family.

Rene remembered now how Maddie's eyes had lit up when she'd realized that they wouldn't always be living in the cramped conditions of her mother-in-law's house.

Maddie had had no idea of Tom's plans for them, and Rene could see that her love for him had grown even more as she came to realize just how hard it must have been for someone of his nature, who'd always been keen on having fun rather than worrying about respon- sibilities, to gather the money together in order to rent this house. They both knew that he must have worked lots of extra hours. Even though he was paid a bit more now that he'd been moved up to foreman, with his own gang of brickies to look after on that new site in Bishop Auckland, he still didn't earn a great deal.

Rene placed the kettle she'd just filled onto the hob, sat down, kicked off her shoes and smoothed her grey skirt over her knees, waiting for the water to boil. Mam had been such a help too in not asking for any rent, she thought. 'Just a bit towards the food will do,' was what she'd said to Tom, knowing that he'd been saving like mad in the months leading up to Maddie and Francine's arrival. As far as Rene knew, she still wouldn't accept any rent from them. Trying in her way to help them with the new house, no doubt. And really, the sooner they got the house sorted and were able to move out, the better.

Rene poured the boiling water into the teapot, instinctively stirring the swirling tea leaves while she continued to mull things over. Francine, coming up to a year now, was growing by the minute. She was practically walking, and into everything. Far too much for Mam, she thought.

The fact that the house was derelict and in need of much work hadn't seemed to deter Maddie at all. She and Tom had worked back-breakingly hard, stripping off all the old wallpaper, which was stained from all the years of the previous old boy's pipe smoking. Occasionally, in certain rooms, the air still seemed awash with traces of tobacco smells, lingering discreetly to remind you that a life had been lived there before. Even the immaculate new wallpaper and shiny new paint couldn't always disguise it.

None of that had fazed Maddie; in fact, everything should be wonderful, they should be happy, but Rene wasn't so sure that they were. She was thinking that no matter how much Maddie loved the little house. homesickness still loomed heavily over almost everything she did. And worse than that, she had become convinced that someone was playing nasty tricks on her, or was out to get her in some way . . .

With a cup of tea in front of her, Rene sat in quiet contemplation, elbow pressed to the table.

'Mam, Mam!' Rene's peace was abruptly shattered by her daughter's urgent calling. She looked up to see Jeannie pushing the door open with her bottom and entering the room backwards, with what appeared to be an enormous bundle of rags in her arms.

Speechless, Rene watched as with great aplomb Jeannie dropped the bundle onto the table and stood back proudly. 'What d'yer think of that lot then?'

'What is this? And more to the point, where did you get it?' Rene didn't know whether to laugh or cry as she selected what appeared to be a good-quality length of cloth from the heap.

'It's mat-ee-rial, Mam . . . you know, for makin' stuff with!'

'Making what, exactly?' Rene hardly dared ask.

'Clothes! Clothes for me, and for Francine, even you if you like!'

'Oh Jeannie.' Her mam did laugh now. 'And who do you think is going to make these clothes?'

'Maddie, of course! She's really good at sewin' and

did yer know, our Tom's goin' ter get her a sewin' machine some day!'

'Well, it *will* only be "some day" as you put it, because Tom hasn't got the money just now to buy something like a sewing machine. They need a lot of other things before that. Anyway, Maddie hasn't got the time for making clothes right now, pet. She's too busy with the house.'

Rene looked at her daughter's face and felt a pang of sympathy at the disappointment she saw there.

'But Mam! It's just what she needs at the moment, and ah'm sure that Mrs Hurd, along the road from Gran, will let her borrow her machine if we ask her nicely. She's too old ter be sewin' now, she can't even see ter thread a needle!' Jeannie's eyes were wide and pleading, and not ready to let the subject drop, she continued, 'It's just what she needs, so she's not thinkin' about goin' home all the time.'

'Oh pet! You've really thought this out, haven't you.' Rene smiled down on her, and the sight of the shining ringlets and the yellow ribbon, which by this time of day was always hanging by a thread, led to her thinking how lucky she was to have such a caring daughter, even if she did get up to mischief from time to time. But that train of thought was soon eliminated when, with a sudden jerk of her head, she enquired, trying not to sound too suspicious, 'Where did all this come from, Jeannie?'

'Ee-an's dad gave it to me.'

'Ian Mortimer's dad?'

'Yes . . . yer know that Ee-an's dad works in text-tiles and stuff?'

'Yes, textiles . . . I do know about that.' Rene looked puzzled.

'He gets all these samples, so I asked if ah could have some, and he gave me all these!' With arms outstretched to emphasize the huge amount of fabric she'd been given, Jeannie continued, 'And he dropped me off outside the door, on his way ter takin' Ee-an ter the dentist.' She pulled an awesome face at the word 'dentist'. But her eyes lit up with enthusiasm when she added, 'Oh, and he said that the next time ah go over to Ee-an's for me tea, I'm ter bring you with me.' Then, as casually as you like, she added, 'Ah told him that yer get a bit lonely sometimes.'

Before Rene could utter a single word, Jeannie was jumping around with her legs crossed. 'Ah need the toilet,' she announced urgently, and rushed out through the door, leaving Rene open-mouthed to digest this final gem of information.

Suddenly feeling hot and flustered, if not hugely humiliated and totally incredulous at what Jeannie had just told her, she took a deep breath, flopped down into the armchair and counted to ten.

'She actually told him I was lonely . . . *lonely*! Whatever will that girl get up to next!'

Chapter 4

Marck

The two sisters looked closely at their mother, and Simone said quietly, 'You mean Madeleine is not coming?'

'No, not right now. She is going to get her new home together first, then maybe come in a few months' time.' Even as she said this, a shiver passed through her body.

'Something is not quite right, Maman.' Martine spoke for both of them, while Simone nodded in agreement.

Maman didn't want to dwell on her own feeling of unease – after all, it could be nothing – so she asked now, in a more cheerful tone, 'Have you any idea if Madeleine keeps in touch with Nicole, in Boulogne?'

'Yes, she does,' said Martine, 'and her *maman*, Ginette, often writes a few lines at the end of Nicole's letters. Why do you ask?'

'Oh . . . well, I was just thinking, wouldn't it be a lovely surprise if we invited them to come and stay with us when Madeleine does come home?'

'What a fantastic idea!' Simone was always excited at the prospect of having new people around. But these two would be particularly exciting, if all that she'd heard was true.

She'd listened, agog, to all that her brother Dominic had divulged on his and Tom's return from their search for Madeleine, after she'd run away to Boulogne last year. Just hearing the story, she'd almost tasted the sweat from the bodies of the vigilantes as they'd tied Madeleine to a chair, and felt Madeleine's terror as she saw what was happening to her friends. Even so, Simone being Simone, she had realized that she still felt a little envious at the romantic aspect of Tom's ferocious rescue of her sister.

Just how Madeleine could have been mistaken for a prostitute, never mind someone who'd given her services to the *Germans* during the war, neither she nor the family would ever understand! If only Tom had written to her, as he'd promised, when he'd gone back to England, then she could have told him about the pregnancy and she would probably never have felt the need to run away. But who could blame him, Simone thought, on returning home from such a dreadful war, for wanting to get on with his life, in his own country, with his family and everything he knew.

Apart from hearing nothing from Tom, Madeleine had been unable to bear the shame of being pregnant and unmarried, and seeing the worry and disappointment on her family's faces every day had finally clinched it. As far as she was concerned, she'd let them all down really badly, and in her mind the best thing she could do, for everyone's sake, was to leave.

Madeleine's parents knew nothing about her friend Nicole in Boulogne. Madeleine had met her during her wartime visits to her sister Martine, who was living and working there.

Simone understood that Madeleine had felt deserted by everyone she loved. That was why, after much deliberation and with no idea of what she was letting herself in for, she'd taken the decision to sneak out of the house in the middle of the night, cycle to the station and get on a train to Boulogne, where she would find Nicole. Once there, she'd been welcomed and looked after by Nicole and her mother Ginette, with few questions asked.

The fact that Madeleine and her unborn baby had survived the attacks by those savages was a miracle. The only good thing to have come out of her suffering was that Tom, having come so close to losing Madeleine and in such a vicious way, had realized that he couldn't bear to go back to England without her, and he'd asked her to marry him, even before she'd recovered from her injuries.

Filled with gratitude, and admiration for how he'd rushed all the way over from England to rescue her, Madeleine had accepted readily, without giving too much thought to what it might mean to live in England. In fact, she was so grateful to be alive and still carrying her baby that *where* she would live had paled into insignificance. The only thing that she did ask of Tom was that she stayed in France until the baby was born.

The thought of baby Francine brought a brief smile to Simone's face, until she remembered the tears of all the family, as they stood, freezing in the wind, in the port of Calais, waving goodbye to the three of them. With no idea when they would see each other again, they had watched and waved from the docks, with Maman to the fore, until the ship was no more than a dot on the horizon in the choppy waters of the English Channel.

Tom, Madeleine and Francine were bound for a new life in England, and Maman was desolate.

'Simone!' Maman walked into the kitchen, interrupting Simone's thoughts. 'Why don't you go find Martine and put a letter together, inviting Nicole and her mother to come to stay with us when Madeleine is here. I think it will do her good to be surrounded by people other than all of us. Maybe it will help lessen the intensity of the family, and make it easier for her to break free when she has to leave again. Although we don't yet know exactly when Madeleine will be here, I would like to know if they would be willing to come, *and*,' she smiled at Simone now, 'I find I am curious, as I know you are, and would like to meet them.'

Boulogne

Holding the letter tightly in her hands, Nicole was impatient to give her mother the news. But her *maman* was still on the telephone trying to cancel, once and for all, yet another of her long-standing clients.

Nicole was so proud of her mother for keeping her word to bring an end to her old way of life. After all, she had saved enough money over the years, and Nicole was more than happy to look for what she classed as proper work, now that she'd left her job at the *boulangerie*.

She sat down at what used to be the reception desk, and supporting her chin on the palm of her hand, she waited.

'Yes, Nicole?' said her *maman*, finally replacing the receiver.

'It's the Pelletiers, they've asked if we would like to go and stay with them to surprise Madeleine when she comes back home for a visit.'

Nicole was beside herself with excitement. She had so much to tell Madeleine.

'Well, we still have a lot to do here, and we've just come back from quite a long holiday.'

'I know. Maman, but that was for us. This would be for Madeleine . . . she needs us!'

Ginette smiled at this thoughtful daughter of hers, all worries fading of how guilty she'd felt over the years, in running her not-so-normal business, along with trying to be a good mother to Nicole.

When she looked at her now, she knew that she must have done something right in this unconventional life of hers. Nicole certainly didn't seem to bear any resentment towards her. In fact the opposite was true: they had become very close of late, for which Ginette was thrilled, and she had great plans for their new life together.

'Oh come on, Maman!' Nicole broke into her thoughts. 'You and I had a fantastic time together, and I think it did us both a lot of good . . . And look!' She grabbed a handful of her hair. 'Our hair is growing back!'

'Yes, it is, darling.' Ginette's eyes clouded for a moment. But immediately shunning the memories, she said on a decisive sigh, 'OK, when do the Pelletiers want us?'

'They say they will let us know.' Nicole's smile was wide. 'They wanted to ask us well in advance, to allow us time to decide and to organize things, but . . .' Nicole's smile faded slightly now as she added, 'Madeleine's *maman* must be worried about her, to be arranging this so early . . . strange, very strange.'

Chapter 5

Bishop Auckland

'Does it matter all that much, Mam?'

'Of course it matters, Jeannie. Whatever were you thinking, to tell Ian's dad that I'm lonely?'

'Well, you are sometimes, Mam, I can tell, and I just thought . . .'

Rene was not only cross but embarrassed at the idea of this man, who would be picking them up any minute now, feeling sorry for her.

She checked her face and hair in the mirror.

'You look lovely, Mam.' Jeannie smiled in all sincerity.

When they heard the knock on the shop door downstairs, both visibly jumped. Jeannie ran down the carpeted stairs, closely followed by Rene, who composed herself briefly before opening the door.

The silence can't have been more than a couple of

seconds, as she and the pleasant-looking man outside exchanged glances. Ian looked blankly from his dad to Jeannie, while his dad, eyebrows raised, held out his hand to Rene. 'Hello, I'm Robert . . . or Rob if you prefer,' he said with a smile.

Jeannie looked up at her mam, and gave her a nudge.

'Hello . . . I'm Rene.' She took his hand and shook it briefly. Disconcerted as a tinge of a shiver passed through her, she said, 'Please come in, I'll run up and get my coat.'

Hearing a titter as he walked further into the shop, Rob looked over to where Ian and Jeannie were huddled in a corner, by the curtained fitting rooms. And from the whispering that was going on, he guessed that they were in collusion over something or other as usual.

'Told you they'd like each other,' Jeannie whispered to Ian.

'Well, they've only just met, how do you know?' Ian whispered back a bit too loudly.

'Shush! I can just tell.' Jeannie shrugged her shoulders.

'What's all that giggling about, you two?' Rob asked, catching Rene's eye as she came down the stairs.

'Oh, I've given up asking what they whisper about, they're always at it!' Rene feigned an exasperated frown. 'By the way, thank you for all the lovely fabrics you gave to Jeannie.' She was smiling now.

'Well, she was insisting that they would be put to

good use, by her uncle Tom's wife ... Maddie, is it?'

'Yes. Her family in France call her by her proper name, Madeleine, but she seems not to mind being referred to as Maddie here. The poor girl is still coming to terms with the big changes in her life since her move to England. I'm afraid that the village was a huge shock to her. She's only just managing to speak English, never mind trying to understand the miners' dialect in Evenwood!'

'Yes, well, I can relate to that,' Rob said, grinning. 'It was difficult enough for me when I first came to the village, and that was only from the south of England.'

'But now that you've moved into Bishop it should be a little easier, not so many pitmen.' Rene locked the front door carefully.

'Oh yes,' he answered, opening the car door for her. 'I only had a few weeks in Evenwood before my house was ready here in Bishop Auckland, and, thank God, I can understand *you* very well ... You don't seem to have much of an accent, even though you were brought up in the village, by what I understand from Jeannie.' He raised his eyebrows as he glanced at the culprit.

'No, well, rightly or wrongly, I struggled against it from the start, I think, even though my dad's a coal miner and I was surrounded by those poor men who do that godforsaken job. I can't imagine how horrendous it must be, extracting coal, day in day out. But it's still there, underneath – the dialect I mean,' she added more lightly now. 'And I do lapse every now and then, much to my family's amusement. I tried with Jeannie too, and had hoped that your Ian's presence might help her to speak more clearly, but so far it's not very evident, I'm afraid.'

'Blinkin' heck! You two haven't stopped talkin' since we got out of the shop!' Jeannie piped up from the back seat of the car.

Rob and Rene exchanged glances, and laughed. 'You see what I mean!' Rene said with a sigh of resignation as she relaxed into the passenger seat.

Before they'd reached his house, Rene had learned about his family, and discovered that his wife, Isabelle, had been killed by a bomb that had fallen right on the munitions factory where she was working. When he'd felt that he could grieve no more, he'd become desperate, and like so many others had needed to put the war and all its consequences behind him. He'd known that as long as he stayed in the south, he would be haunted by the memories, stifled even. For a while he had sensed Isabelle's presence everywhere he turned. So, as much for Ian's sake as his own, he'd created a position for himself as far north as he could sensibly go, and keep the business ticking over at the same time.

He in turn had found out that Rene's husband had not returned from the war.

Jeannie had been surprised to hear her mam mention her dad at all. Especially since Grandma Hannah had once told her, when she'd asked why her mam didn't talk about Daddy, that she didn't talk about him out loud because she preferred to talk to him in her own mind.

Both Ian and Jeannie were quietly agog in the back of the car, neither having ever heard their parent talk so much in such a short time.

Rene looked in awe at the house in front of her. Rob had turned the car into a fenced-off enclosure leading to the main entrance, and Rene had been expecting another two or three vehicles to be stood next to it. But no, it was on its own, surrounded by trees and garden laid mostly to lawn. Rob had parked right in front of the imposing Georgian-style house, where there were two steps leading to the front door. He walked round to open the passenger door for Rene, who, looking up at the red-brick façade, stumbled in her high heels as she walked awkwardly up the roughly gravelled path. 'Wrong shoes.' She smiled, red-faced, as Rob fumbled in his pocket for the key. 'Yes, sorry about the path, Rene, it's just until I get the paving slabs laid.'

He put the key in the door, and as it opened, he turned, put out his hand and drew her inside. 'After you.'

She walked in, and her eyes were stretched at the realization that this entrance hall was wider than her kitchen.

As she went slowly down the passageway, taking in

the exquisite décor and ambiance of the place, Ian came running past, dragging Jeannie behind him. 'I'm just going out the back, to show Jeannie the bike I've been doing up, Dad,' he called over his shoulder, and they were gone.

As soon as they got outside Ian let out a wild whoop, exclaiming, 'This is better than we thought ... They like each other!'

Jeannie hadn't seen her mam like this before. Although pleased, she couldn't help but wonder, as she'd more or less forced her into this, if her mother was just being polite to Ian's dad. Well, she'd have to wait until they got home to find out.

'Jeannie,' Ian said breathlessly, 'did you hear me?'

'Yes, I heard you, Ee-an, but we'd better not celebrate just yet. Let's get back in to keep an eye on them, see if we can tell if they *really* like each other?'

'OK. But come and have a quick look at my bike first then, just in case they ask about it.'

Inside, Rene was being offered a glass of sherry. She couldn't remember the last time she'd drunk sherry, the war had put paid to things like that.

She watched as Rob lifted the lid off a pan that was gently simmering on the hob.

'How unusual to see a man making a ... stew?' she said. 'Well, cooking at all for that matter!'

'Aha!' he answered, his face beaming with mischief. 'A man on his own round here ... a vulnerable man like me,' he said with a smirk, 'well, there's no shortage of help from the ladies. So yes, I did make the stew, but with very strict instructions as to exactly when to add what. It is all written down on this precious piece of paper . . . and I must not on any account deviate from what this paper tells me. That's what I was told, in no uncertain terms.' He showed her the paper and she laughed out loud.

How many times had she laughed over these past few years? she wondered. Not many. And here she was with this comparative stranger, laughing, genuinely laughing.

Feeling comfortable sitting here in these beautiful surroundings, she glanced at her glass of sherry. Was that the reason she could laugh so freely? From her chair she had a view down the length of the well-appointed long room, and through the door to the kitchen. She found herself staring at the back of the man standing at the hob, who, while carefully stirring the stew, stopped intermittently to take a sip from his glass, and suddenly her stomach gave the slightest of flutters. Startled by this, she immediately averted her eyes and forced her mind to something else.

'What a remarkable room!' she called through to the kitchen, while taking in the tasteful furnishings. She was drawn to the oak-framed mirror that hung above the fireplace, so big that it almost covered the width of the chimney breast. The glass-fronted cabinet amused her with its delicate china tea service filling the top two shelves. She really couldn't imagine a man of Rob's muscular build ever drinking from those tiny teacups. Perhaps his wife had chosen them . . .

'Yes, it is, isn't it,' he called, in answer to her comment on the room. Still at the cooker, he tasted the juice formed from the delicious-smelling contents of the pan and decided to add a little more seasoning. 'And to think that not so long ago it was a series of small rooms, one of them being the parlour,' he said, in a tone which conveyed to her how amusing he found the idea of having a parlour.

So Rene answered in the same vein, 'Oh, doesn't everyone have one of those?'

He laughed, put the lid loosely on to the stew pan, then came back to join her. 'Yes, I suppose they do, and you are sitting in it! And next to what was the parlour, about where I am standing now, was the dining room, with a small kitchen beyond. Very pokey. So I had all the inner walls knocked down until I felt I could breathe. And the result is what you see now.' He looked pleased with himself as she gazed around appreciatively. She had never even imagined a room like this, never mind been in one.

She got up, and walked towards the wood fire, burning low on the stone hearth and bordered by two iron dogs. Seeing the wicker basket beside the fireplace, full to the brim with logs, she curbed the urge to pick one out and throw it on to the fire. If she knew anything about carpets, these colourful ones beneath her feet were probably Persian.

She wasn't so much in awe of the fact that he could afford to do all this; it was his taste, which showed itself in every piece of furniture and in how the colours blended so beautifully, that impressed her. The armchairs, covered in a warm rust-coloured fabric, picked out perfectly one of the colours in the rugs, and she was amazed that there hadn't been a woman's influence in the design and decorating of the room. She guessed that his involvement in the fabric industry had given him a good eye for colour. She still wasn't sure exactly what his job was, but she felt that now wasn't the right time to ask. It could wait, she decided.

The squeals coming from Jeannie and Ian, who had tipped a bag of marbles on to the rug further down the room and were competing furiously, brought her back with a thump. When Rob came over suggesting that the youngsters might wash their hands before tea, Rene stood there open-mouthed at how the pair of them got up from the floor to do as they were bidden, without fuss or grumbles. Suddenly she wondered if Jeannie had perceived her as lonely because it was almost always her, on her own, correcting her daughter. Maybe she needed variety in who was issuing the rules . . .

'Penny for them?' Rob was standing next to her, bottle of sherry poised.

'Oh . . . sorry!'

'Are you going to stay in that little world of your own or are you going to join me in a top-up?'

'Just a small amount then.' Rene held out her glass.

'Tea will be ready by the time the "bairns", as they call them round here, get themselves down from the bathroom,' he said, grinning.

Rene held her glass towards him. 'Cheers, and thank you so much for inviting me.'

'Not at all. I was worried that you wouldn't come.'

'Worried?'

'Yes . . . worried.' Rob held up his glass now. 'Here's to a lovely friendship.'

'A lovely friendship.' Rene lifted her glass again, and, unsure as to what degree her face had flushed, her hand went to her cheek.

Chapter 6

Evenwood

Maddie shook her head violently. 'No! No, Hannah! I know that I switched the wireless off before I went to ze shop! Someone is watching me, zey *must* be!' Maddie was insistent. The sheer desperation in her eyes almost convinced Hannah, but not quite.

'Sit yerself down, pet, and ah'll make us a nice cup of tea,' Hannah said, trying to sound sympathetic rather than worried, as she most definitely was.

Maddie seemed to be having these strange ideas more and more frequently.

'I know zat you think I'm mad, Hannah, but you must believe me. I worry for Francine also. What if somebody is coming into ze house, not just when I am out but also when I am here?'

'Listen, pet, no one is coming into the house. The house isn't big enough for somebody to be sneakin' around without you knowin', now is it?' Hannah placed a reassuring hand on Maddie's shoulder. 'What does Tom say about all this?'

'Oh well, nothing happens when he is here, it is only when I am alone wiz Francine. For example, only ze ozer day, I put Francine's clothes to dry outside, and when I went to get zem later, zey were already folded in ze basket!'

'Aw, pet! If somebody else had taken them off the line, surely they wouldn't have bothered to fold them . . . would they?'

Maddie pondered on that thought for a moment. 'Oh, I know how it looks, but zis is somebody very clever . . . or very ill in ze head.' She jabbed her finger to the side of her head to emphasize the point.

'My, my, you are in a state, pet!' Hannah was shocked at how real this all seemed to be in Maddie's mind. She'd have a talk with Tom later, maybe he could encourage her to see the doctor.

'Tell you what, pet, why don't you go and have a lie-down for a bit . . . Ah'll mind the bairn for an hour or so. Ah could take her up the village and do me shoppin' at the same time.'

Maddie hesitated a moment before answering, 'But what if someone comes in when . . . ?' Seeing Hannah's worried look, she stopped mid-sentence, realizing how silly all this must sound, and with a sudden change of tone she said instead, 'Well, I am tired, Francine didn't sleep too well last night, so yes, thank you, Hannah, zat would be lovely. I will get ze pushchair out for you, and would you mind getting Francine's coat from the airing cupboard? It was so damp outside zis morning, so I put it in there to dry when we came home.' Hannah was already mounting the stairs on her way to the airing cupboard, when Maddie's agitated voice brought her hurrying back.

'What is it, pet?'

'Ze coat! Francine's coat! It is here, in the cupboard under ze kitchen sink!'

'That's all right, pet, you just forgot to take it up.' Hannah laughed. 'My God, if you knew the times ah did things like that at home!'

'No, Hannah! I took the coat up to the cupboard as soon as I came in . . .'

Maddie had finished the sentence quietly, almost as if she knew that there was no point in trying to convince her any further.

Feeling slightly nonplussed now, Hannah put the coat on Francine, who, oblivious to what was going on, had played happily with the squeaky teddy that Jeannie had passed on to her.

If Hannah was being honest, she was afraid for Maddie. This kind of worry was the last thing she needed, her being pregnant and all.

Somebody very clever, or very ill in the head. Maddie's words came back to Hannah as she pushed

Francine towards the village. Jessie was clever, wily even, and there was no doubt that she could be ruthless. But no . . . what would she stand to gain from doing anything like that? And anyway, how would she get into the house?

No, she decided, this has got to be down to poor Maddie, homesick, pregnant and tired. All that was enough to play tricks on anybody'smind.

'Shut up! Just shut up, Mother, will you! Ah don't want to hear it!'

'Ah was only sayin', our Jessie, that that French piece of Tom's isn't lookin' too good these days. Looks like she hasn't slept for weeks!'

'Serves her right for havin' that bastard bairn then, doesn't it.' Jessie couldn't help herself.

'Ah know how yer feel, lass, 'specially now that she's expectin' another.'

Incensed by the sly smirk on Maude's face, Jessie shouted, 'Don't you dare tell me how I feel! How could some cold biddy like you possibly know how ah feel?' She grabbed her bag and coat, and was out of the door almost before her mother had taken a breath.

Stopping to get a cigarette out of her bag, Jessie lit it and marched on, muttering to herself all the way along the road, 'Well, ah'll get me revenge, see if ah don't. Huh, givin' her another bairn like that! Ah might have stood a chance with him if he'd only had one bairn ter contend with,' she told herself, 'but the stupid sod's gone and given her another.'

She stopped, leaned against one of the many red-brick walls surrounding the back yards and dragged heavily on her cigarette. She looked disdainfully around her. The back-to-back terraced brick houses had pathetic little yards leading out to narrow back streets, which were forever hung out with washing. She couldn't remember how many times she'd decided she was going to get out of it all, for good.

She would never have enough money to move away, she knew that. If her fate was to be stuck here in the same village as him, she was buggered if she was going to witness all this happiness of his without putting a spanner in the works. And as for his bloody sister, she thought, unable to control the fierceness of her jealousy, well ah've hardly set eyes on *her* since she moved to Bishop, stuck-up cow that she is!

Once again she'd gravitated to the vicinity of Tom's house, and there in the distance she could see Hannah struggling to push the pushchair along the stony garden path from the cottage to the main street.

Jessie jumped back, out of sight.

Once Hannah had passed by, she ran towards the cottage, where she squeezed herself through a hidden gap in the straggly beech hedge along the side of the house. In the garden now, she glanced at the upstairs dormer window and smirked to herself. On seeing the curtains closed, she guessed that the French piece was having a lie-down.

She crept round to the back, where hidden from view by an overgrown conifer was the old coal hatch. She remembered, as a kid, watching the coal man chuck the coal through, and it fell in a heap into a floor space inside a small larder-sized room which was also accessed from the inside, via a latched door.

Jessie crouched down and felt around in the undergrowth close to the wall of the house. Once she had the screwdriver in her hand she squeezed herself between the conifer and the wall, where she went to work on the hatch.

She wedged the screwdriver into the crack at the base of the hatch door, right where the rotting wood had been worn into a screwdriver-sized hole, and forced it open.

She doubted either Tom, or *her* inside, had ever had reason to look at the hatch from the outside, hidden away behind the tree as it was. And she knew that the coal hole hadn't been used for years, even the old boy who lived there before hadn't stored coal in it laterly. And from the inside, what with no electric light in there, she doubted that *they'd* have taken any notice of the hatch, tucked away in the dark like that. The only thing in there was the bike belonging to the French piece. She could see that the chain was back on it but the whole thing looked to be in need of attention, so she was quite confident that no one would have reason to go in there, at least not while Tom was at work.

But when Jessie, in her quest for revenge on Tom, had been figuring out the best way to get to him, it had come to her: like a light being switched on, a vision of the hatch. Knowing how feeble most coal-hatch doors were, this was too good an opportunity to miss.

She removed her high-heeled shoes and laid them on the grass between the tree and the wall, before carefully hoisting herself up and through the hole. When she lowered herself down, her feet made contact with the rough concrete floor, where the cracks held tiny jagged fragments of leftover coal.

Once inside, she crouched for a moment, listening . . . Hearing nothing, she straightened up, and taking no chances, even though it was hidden, she pulled the hatch door to behind her, until it was wedged just enough to stay closed.

Deftly feeling her way along the brick wall in the dark, her fingers eventually touched the latch on the inner door, which led to a small scullery, just off the kitchen. The rattle of the latch as she touched it brought her to a stop. Eyes tight closed, she waited for a second or two, hardly breathing, and listened.

With no sounds of movement at the other side of the door, she exhaled, then carefully and slowly lifted the latch, opening the door only slightly at first. A moment later she opened the door wider, and she was in.

Chapter 7

The sun was shining, and there was a light breeze blowing. She still needed a coat but Hannah's heart was lifted by the brightness of the day, and whenever, as now, she took 'the French bairn', as the villagers had come to think of her, to the shops, she was spoilt by everyone who saw her. And Francine in return had not disappointed. As she smiled and giggled at everyone in sight, her wispy blonde hair, held in a topknot with a ribbon usually matching the colour of her clothes, and her big inquisitive blue eyes framed by the darkest of lashes had even the hardest-faced villagers entranced.

'It takes me twice as long ter do me shopping, mind, but it's worth it just to see the smile on everybody's face when they meet her,' Hannah had said to her friend Mrs Parkin, who'd been out on the doorstep awaiting Hannah's return from the shops just so she could have a cuddle with the bairn.

Feeling happy with herself as she approached the

cottage, having tired out the now dozing little Francine, she was toying with the idea of peeling a few vegetables ready for their supper tonight . . . when her reverie was abruptly broken by an almighty scream coming from the house.

'Oh my God!' Hannah rushed inside, only to find Maddie crouched down in a corner of the kitchen.

'What? What is it, hinny?' Hannah rushed to her side.

'Zat! It ees zat!' She pointed a shaky finger at the running tap and the overflowing kitchen sink.

Hannah hurried over, turned the tap off, pulled the plug out and threw a couple of towels down on to the lino, to stop the water from reaching the new sitting-room carpet.

'There now, pet, it'll be all right now.' She crouched down beside her. 'And once we've wiped up the mess on the floor, it'll be as good as new. It's only water. You'll see, it'll all be back to normal in no time.' Hannah tried desperately to conceal the fear that she was feeling on Maddie's behalf. Seeing her so het up over a running tap, she found herself thinking, This can't be normal.

'No, no! Hannah, you do not understand. I did not do zis!'

'Come on, pet, nobody's goin' ter be upset with yer for leavin' a tap runnin'.'

'Hannah, *please* listen to me! I did not leave ze tap running. I went upstairs straight away when you left here!'

'Well, how's it happened then, pet?' Hannah looked around as if to check whether anyone else was there. 'You didn't pour a glass of water ter take up with yer, and maybe leave the tap running?' Hannah ventured.

'What? And put ze plug in as well?' Maddie shrugged in disbelief at Hannah saying such a thing, and said quietly, 'Oh, I can see zat zer is no point in trying to convince you . . . or anyone, for zat matter.' Maddie's shoulders drooped.

'Sit down, pet,' Hannah said now, and Maddie could have guaranteed what she would say next. Sure enough, as if it would make everything all right, Hannah said, 'Ah'll make us a nice cup of tea and we'll have a talk, eh?'

Feeling limp with the futility of it all, Maddie allowed Hannah to help her up from the floor and lead her to a chair.

After stoking the fire, Hannah pushed the kettle further into the cinders, all the while thinking, Tom *must* get this poor lass ter the doctor, and soon!

Once the tea was brewed Hannah poured out two cups and handed one to Maddie. 'Now, pet, tell me exactly what happened.'

Maddie's cup clattered in the saucer as she reached over to put it down on the table. 'Oh Hannah, I think I am going out of my mind. Things happen to me but always when I am on my own, and it's usually little things, so no one believes me!'

'It's not exactly that we don't believe you, pet, it's just that nobody could have come in while you were upstairs . . . Look.' Hannah got up from the chair and checked the back door. 'All the windows are closed as well, pet. And when ah went out ter the shops, ah locked the front door meself, *and* ah shook it ter make sure,' she said. Then she added very tentatively, 'So do yer think that maybe you *could* have left the tap runnin' . . . accidentally like?'

'Oh, I don't know any more, Hannah. I *was* sure, but now I'm not!' Maddie put her hands to her face. 'Do you think I am mad, Hannah?'

'Noo, pet. Ah don't . . . but ah do think that maybe with all the big changes in your life, like comin' ter live in England, so far from yer family an' all that, and now with yer carryin' another bairn like . . . that yer should pop down ter the doctor and have a little talk with him about all this. He might be able ter give yer something ter calm yer a bit, yer know.' Drawn by the look of desolation in Maddie's big brown eyes, Hannah suddenly said, 'Eee, come here, pet.' She held out her arms. Maddie fell gratefully into them, and sobbed.

By God, ah'm knackered! Tom thought as he flopped down on to a seat on the top floor of the double-decker bus. Working all the hours that God sends, I am.

But he knew he had no choice if he wanted to make enough money to pay the rent on their new home, as

63

well as trying to get enough together to buy a second-hand motorbike.

Then ah'll need ter get a sidecar attached to put Francine in, *and* the new bairn when it arrives. And now that Maddie wants to go home to France to have the bairn, ah'm going to have to find the money for that an' all.

His pride wouldn't allow the French family to pay for it, and that was that! he thought as he bumped around in his usual place of reflection.

'Evenwood!' called the conductress.

He never seemed to manage to get the bus that Maisie was working on these days. Shame, he thought. She's always got something to tell yer that's guaranteed ter make yer laugh. He could do with a bit of a laugh.

His mate George was a lucky chap, to be making a go of it with her. There'd been a bit of a spark between himself and Maisie at one time, but it had been very short-lived.

She'd been the first decent thing that had happened to him after his demobilization and the dreadful upset of having to leave Maddie in France, thinking he would never see her again. He'd got to know Maisie through two chance meetings, one on the bus home, and the other when he'd rescued her from an idiot bloke who'd fancied his chances and had her pinned up outside, against the scout hut wall, during a dance.

He hadn't realized it was Maisie out there in the dark

at first. All he'd heard was some girl in distress while he was waiting for Jessie to turn up, so he'd decked the bloke. Then, recognizing the girl as Maisie the bus conductress, he'd taken her inside to the bar for a consoling drink.

Thank God that fate had played the hand it had, in the shape of Jessie barging into the dance hall, he thought now.

Needless to say, Jessie, in her jealous rage, had got the wrong end of the stick and caused a row, which Maisie had sensibly walked away from. Jessie had eventually stomped off as well, saving him the job of finishing it with her, which was what he'd set out to do that night.

What kind of situation he'd have been in now, if Jessie *hadn't* arrived that night! He might have got together with Maisie, the way things were going. Not on that particular night, but there had been something good between them, and who knows what might have transpired in the future. At that time, of course, never in a million years did he think that there would be any more connection between him and his first real love, Maddie.

After being away fighting in the war for so many years, he'd finally come home, having had to leave his beautiful Maddie behind in France.

He'd been home a few weeks, and he was still trying desperately hard to adapt to the way of life in the village, the way that had once been his way. But so much had changed, and it was hard to see everyday events as normal, or important even, when what he and many others had seen and done had been so dramatic.

He was still plagued by terrifying flashbacks. They struck randomly, usually at night. He would wake up wet with sweat, but at the same time shivering with cold. With the sounds of battle playing loud in his head, he was afraid to allow himself to fall back into sleep, so he would sit up in bed and wrap a blanket tightly around himself. With shaking hands he'd struggle to light a cigarette, while the horrific sight of his mates falling all around him played over and over in his head. The thing that hurt him most was the vision of the torn bodies spread on the ground, in such undignified poses, unrecognizably caked in mud and gore.

He was a different man from the one who'd gone off to war. So young and carefree then. So much so that he hadn't realized at the time just how selfish Jessie, his long-standing girlfriend, had been. Not taking into account that he must have been similar enough for them to get along at one time, he thought she had turned into a monster while he was away. The truth was she'd been like it before he went away; it was he who'd changed, and they were no longer compatible. But she wasn't willing to let him go, having, in her words, 'waited for him all through the war', but he was doggedly determined that she wasn't going to be part of his future.

Since he'd known such love with Maddie in France, he understood now that with Jessie it had never been love; lust maybe, for a while, but *never* love.

Anyway, he was pretty sure that he was nothing more than a habit to her, a habit that her need for security wouldn't allow her to break. And much as he'd tried to help her recognize that fact, it was to no avail. Even though she thought him an ogre and a bastard for cheating on her, he was what she knew and wanted, so one way or another she was going to win him back, and nothing was going to shift her mind from that course.

But Jessie was to be the very least of Tom's problems, for a while anyway, because in an instant everything would change.

From the day that Maddie's brother, Dominic, had arrived in England to tell him of Maddie's pregnancy, nothing would ever be the same again.

Tom was ashamed of himself now, to think that his initial reaction had been to try to dodge his responsibilities. The only way he could excuse his behaviour was to remind himself that he'd just come home to England from the war and wasn't thinking straight. He knew that he was very lucky that, after all the fear and mistreatment that followed, in the end she'd agreed to marry him, and had given up everything she knew to come to live in England.

If only she could settle here without feeling so homesick all the time, everything would be fine and dandy.

He smiled to himself. Yes, he was glad that things had turned out as they had, not only for himself but for George too. He deserved a nice girl like Maisie. It gave Tom a warm glow to know that he was the one who'd introduced the pair of them.

When the bus juddered to a halt, he came down the stairs, two at a time as was his habit, and there, right in front of him, was Jessie. With his head telling him to avoid her at all costs, he found his mouth saying, 'Hello Jessie, how yer doin'?'

Without answering that question, she looked him straight in the eye and remarked, 'Yer look shattered.'

'Aye, I am that,' Tom replied, wondering how the hell he was going to avoid walking home from the bus stop with her.

'Well, yer'd better prepare yerself for more of the same when yer next bairn's born then!' Her smug tone hadn't escaped him. 'Why don't yer pop inter mine and ah'll make yer a cuppa . . . or something stronger?' she offered.

'Ah can't, Jessie, ah have ter get back ter do a bit more decoratin' and stuff, but ta anyway, be seein' yer!' And at that he marched off ahead of her.

Jessie, boiling at this affront, told herself: Right!

Yer've missed yer chance there, mister big man. Ah might just have reconsidered me plans if yer'd deemed ter show me a bit of attention fer once!

Tom got into the house, closed the door behind him and leaned heavily on it. Breathing a deep sigh of relief at having escaped yet again, he wondered, Will the silly bitch *ever* get the message and just leave me alone?

Jessie thundered down the pavement heading for home, determination etched all over her face. In the distance she spotted the unmistakable sight of Nitty Nora, scratching her head and coming straight for her.

'Oh shit!' Nora was the last person Jessie needed right now.

'He—llo, Jessie,' she drawled, while swinging her body as a timid five-year-old might do, rather than the twenty-five-year-old that she was.

'Not now, Nora.' Jessie pushed her to one side and continued walking.

But Jessie was Nora's idol, and there was no way she was going to be shunned. Running alongside Jessie now, she said, in her annoying nasal drawl, 'Ah won't be any bother, Jessie, ah'll just walk quiet-like alongside yer.'

Her smile was an open-mouthed almost toothless grin, which never failed to make Jessie want to vomit. She should be in a home, not runnin' around loose in the streets, Jessie was thinking for the umpteenth time, when Nora suddenly piped up, 'Tom's missus is expectin' agen.' Hearing those words coming from a nutter like her were like a knife to Jessie's heart.

Jessie stopped in her tracks and stared at this unstable excuse for a woman. Taking in the faded grey of her unevenly buttoned-up coat with sleeves much too short for her abnormally long arms, and her unmatching shoes with laces undone and dragging on the ground, she said, 'Stop yer prattlin', will yer, Nora. Yer don't know what yer talkin' about!' She walked on, determined to get rid of this . . . this leech!

'Aw, Jessie, yer know that ah love yer, don't yer, well ah thought yer'd want ter know . . . about Tom like.'

Jessie turned towards her and sneered, 'If ah want ter know anything, ah'll ask yer . . . right?' At this she flounced off leaving Nora standing there, hot, unchecked tears running down her cheeks.

In the next instant Nora was telling herself, One day ah'll do something really special fer Jessie, and she'll be that pleased with me that she'll be my best friend for always. Yes, that's what ah'll do . . . ah will!

Chapter 8

Hannah's House, Evenwood

'Our Rene has a bit of a spring in her step lately, don't you think, Hannah?'

Before Hannah could answer Jack, Jeannie, without looking up from her colouring book, butted in, 'That's because of Rob, I expect!'

'Rob? Who's Rob when he's at home?'

'Oh Grandda . . . don't you know anything? Rob is Ee-an's dad!'

'Ian Mortimer? The southern lad who lived in Evenwood for a while?'

'Yes, Jack, Ian Mortimer's dad.' Hannah managed to get in before Jeannie this time. But on seeing that Jack was put out at being the last to know, she added quickly, 'she hasn't known him for very long, mind.'

'Is that why our Jeannie's over here a bit more often lately?' Jack asked, the penny having dropped.

'Yes, that's why ah'm here, Grandda,' Jeannie gave a prolonged sigh, and carried on colouring.

'Well, *you* don't seem all that bothered about it,' Jack said, looking at Jeannie.

'Ah'm not, Grandda, ah'm pleased . . .'

'By what I understand, it was Jeannie and Ian who engineered the whole thing,' Hannah informed him. 'Our Jeannie thought that her mam got lonely sometimes.'

'And did she?' Jack had seemingly not given any thought to that before. With Rene being surrounded by family and having Jeannie around, he'd assumed that would be enough company for anybody.

'Yes, Jack, to answer your question, I do think she gets lonely . . . Oh, not for people around her but for somebody ter be close to.' Jack looked puzzled, so she glanced at Jeannie, then half whispered, 'Surely you know what ah mean, Jack . . . don't yer?'

When her meaning clicked with him, he exclaimed, 'Well, well, our Rene with a feller, ah had no idea!'

'Well, yer know now, and don't go makin' a big thing of it, it's early days yet,' she warned.

'Ee's lovely, Grandda, ah think yer'll like him.' Jeannie looked up from her colouring as she added excitedly, 'And he's got a car! One of them Morris cars . . . Yer know the ones ah mean, the black ones.'

Hannah laughed. 'Well, most cars do come in other colours, pet!'

'Anyway, his is black, and it's lovely, and he's lovely 'cause he makes me mam laugh.'

'And am ah goin' ter get a chance ter meet this *lovely* chap then?' her granddad grinned.

'Well if ye're lucky, yer'll get a chance ter meet him when he brings me mam ter collect me.' She looked up at the grandfather clock. 'I expect they'll be here in . . .' she hesitated, 'about fifteen minutes.' She looked to her gran for confirmation.

'Yes, that's right, pet, about a quarter of an hour. Now go and fill the kettle and we'll get it on the fire, ready fer when they come in.'

As soon as Jeannie had skipped off to the scullery, Jack said, 'Ah can't believe how well our Jeannie's takin' this. Has she not mentioned her dad at all?'

Hannah thought for a moment. 'No, she hasn't lately, not to my knowledge anyhow.'

'It might hit her later, you know,' and Hannah, surprised at this intuitive remark coming from her husband, patted him on the shoulder. 'Don't fret, love, she'll be all right, ah'm sure.'

He took hold of Hannah's hand. 'Aye, ah'm sure ye're right.' Then looking into her eyes he said on a sigh, 'Things have ter move on, don't they, hinny?'

'Yes, they do, and it's taken a long time, but ah think our Rene has finally accepted that "missin' in action" probably means that, after four years, he won't be comin' back.'

'Aye.' Jack, deep in thought now, lay back in his chair.

Hannah gently nudged him. 'Now don't you be fallin' asleep there, be sharp and get yerself tidied up a bit before they arrive, will yer?'

'All right, all right,' Jack protested. 'I expect he'll have ter leave his car at the top of the street. He'll never get down the back lane with everybody's washin' criss-crossed all the—'

The sound of the door latch lifting, followed by a fair bit of giggling, had stopped Jack mid-sentence. 'What goes on here?' he said, grinning.

'Oh, we just came through all those hanging sheets, Dad, and Rob managed to get himself tangled up in one.' Rene laughed while steering Rob towards her father.

Rob took Jack's proffered hand, and with a shake that was longer than necessary, he said, 'So sorry about that, Jack. I'm Rob, and that wasn't a very good entrance.'

'Ay, never mind all that, come on through, lad!' Jack gently placed a hand on Rob's back.

When Rene saw that Rob, her dad and Jeannie were having no problem in communicating, she followed her mam, who'd beckoned her through to the scullery.

As soon as she entered, her mother grabbed her hand and whispered with some urgency, 'Ah've had a right to-do with Maddie, pet!'

'Oh no, I thought she was settling down better now.

What happened?'

After Hannah had explained about the tap business and a few other things, Rene, without hesitation, said, 'Right, I'll try to get over there at the weekend, see if I can get her to open up a bit to me.'

'Ah've tried, pet. She insists that strange things are happening, and she can't seem to think straight.'

'Our Jeannie scrounged lots of lovely fabric from Rob for her – apparently, she used to make all kinds of clothes back in France ... If sewing is what she was good at, maybe we could get her interested in it again.' Rene was deep in thought at this prospect, when Hannah said, 'It's worth a try, pet. Something's got to be done, that's for sure.'

The two of them set about getting the cups and saucers out of the cupboard, each silently going over the situation in their own mind, when Jeannie came running in. 'Can me and Rob have some bread and drippin' please, Gran?'

'Dripping at this time of day!' Rene enquired none too quietly. 'We'll be having supper when we get home, for goodness' sake.' She pushed past Jeannie and went into the living room, where her dad and Rob suddenly burst into laughter.

'Well, I can see that I don't have to worry about you two getting along,' she said, grinning.

'Ah was just explainin' ter Rob what drippin' was, and me grandda said, "Go and ask yer gran fer some, on bread, and see what yer mam says!" So ah did!' Jeannie sounded unsure as to what it was that she'd done.

'It's all right, pet.' Rene tapped her daughter on the backside. 'It's just your grandda being your grandda,' she said, raising a disapproving eyebrow in his direction.

Her dad looked at her kindly. 'Well, it's not so long ago that you wouldn't have seen the funny side of that, our Rene. Tell yer what . . . ah think this feller here . . .' he placed a hand on Rob's shoulder, 'must be a good influence. He has my approval anyway.'

'Maddie! Maddie! Are you there?' Rene peeped through the letter box.

Jeannie came running round from the back of the house. 'Mam! Mam!' she called. 'Come quick! Maddie's round the back, I think she's fallen over the washing basket!'

'Oh my God!' Rene ran as fast as her legs would carry her, to find Maddie sat on the ground, unable to get herself up.

'Oh Maddie, how on earth did you manage that?' Rene asked in exasperation, as she helped her up.

'Rene! Thank goodness you came! My foot! I could not put pressure on it to get up.' Maddie hobbled along now, hanging on to Rene's arm.

Jeannie went to pick up the pile of fabric samples

from the back of the house, where she'd dropped them at the sight of Maddie on the ground, when suddenly she shouted in disgust, 'No wonder she fell over . . . the bloomin' pavin' slab is stickin' right up!'

Rene got Maddie into the house and sat her down, then pulled up a chair in front of her on which she gently laid Maddie's foot. Next, without even bothering to correct Jeannie on her language, she went straight round to the back of the house to have a look. And there, next to the clothesline, was a paving slab 'sticking right up' as Jeannie had put it, the edge only just protruding through the overgrown grass. Rene bent down to inspect it, and wondered at how loose lumps of soil might have been spread into the surrounding long grass. Must have been an animal digging, she supposed. I'll have a word with Tom later to sort it out, she thought.

When Rene came back into the house, Jeannie was regaling Maddie not only with the story of how she'd come by all this fabric she'd brought her, but how Rob had been taking her mam out for 'proper suppers'.

Seeing Maddie wince at the pain in her ankle as she laughed at Jeannie's tale, Rene came rushing forward, saying, 'Right, that's it, it's off to the doctor for you, my girl, and now!'

No amount of protest from Maddie was going to deter Rene, she could see that, and Rene was thinking, well, this will be the ideal way to get her to talk to the doctor about all this other stuff as well.

'Where's all zis going to end, Rene?' Maddie pleaded as she hobbled towards her.

'I don't know, pet ... I really don't know.' Rene handed her a huge umbrella to use as a stick. 'Here, pet, this will have to do for now. Later on, I'll see if I can borrow a walking stick from one of the older folk around here!'

On seeing Maddie's downtrodden look, Rene searched for a change of subject. 'Hey!' she said a bit sheepishly, 'I've got all sorts of things to tell you.'

'About Rob?' Maddie smiled.

'Yes, about Rob ... but not until we've sorted you out, eh?'

'Oh zat is blackmail, is it not?' Maddie laughed.

As Rene helped her on with her coat, she spontaneously gave Maddie a hug, and their bond deepened.

Chapter 9

Still seething over her brush with Nitty Nora, Jessie got home and slammed the door with such force that her mother came running down the passageway. 'What's all that about? Yer nearly shook the house down, lass!'

Jessie chucked a pile of unironed washing off the armchair and threw herself down hard, ignoring the twang of the well-worn springs.

'Hey, mind what yer doin', lass!'

Jessie took in the sight around her. 'Huh! That's rich comin' from you. Just look at the place, it's a hovel!' She took a breath before repeating, 'A bloody hovel!'

'Well, ah swept up terday.'

'Swept up! The place stinks!'

'Huh! Well, ah don't know who's rattled your cage, but it's no different in 'ere terday than it ever is,' she said, glancing around the room.

'Exactly, and that's why ah have ter get outa here . . . fer good!'

'Ah don't know where yer think ye're goin' ter go, with no money,' her mother answered, confident that she'd be going nowhere.

'Oh, don't you fret about that, Mother, ah'm goin' all right, but not before ah've finished what ah've started . . . and then it'll be ta-ta ter the lot of yer.'

The Blackening Pond

When they reached the dark stretch of road beyond the slag heaps, Jeannie, Molly and second-best friend Amy ground to a halt at the unexpected sight of cows in the field. 'Ah'm sure it's this way,' said Molly. 'Me grandda told uz about it.'

'Well, *my* grandda told me ah was never *ever* ter come here! It's *very* dangerous, and did yer know that *loads* of people have drowned in it?' Jeannie imparted this bit of information with eyes as wide open as they would go.

Amy, who hadn't taken her eyes from the cows, was all for turning back.

'Noo! Come on, we'll edge our way round the field. The cows won't take no notice of us, they're far too busy chompin' the grass . . . Look!' Molly did a good imitation of a cow chewing the cud, in the hope of making her two friends laugh, before pleading, 'We've got ter find it, now that we've come this far.'

With Amy lagging behind, the other two slackened their pace and sniffed at the air.

'Ugh! What's that horrible smell?' said Jeannie.

'It's sulphur or summat,' said Molly in disgust, 'me grandda told uz about that an' all.'

'Well, ah can't breathe properly with all that smell up me nose,' Amy complained. '*And* ah can't see any pond around here. The black pond or whatever colour it is, is probably miles away.'

Jeannie squinted into the distance. 'Ah can see it . . . look! Look down the slope over there!' She pointed excitedly. 'That's it! That's the Blackenin' Pond!'

All three stood staring in awe, at the expanse of murky water, mist lurking above it as if hiding it from prying eyes. Looming through the mist, on the opposite side, was the cone-shaped slag heap that could be seen, even from the village.

Molly nudged Jeannie. 'Come on then, let's go and have a look at it.'

Jeannie glanced at Amy, who looked petrified. 'No, it's all right, ah'll stay here with Amy,' she said, glad of an excuse not to go any further. 'You go if yer like, Molly,' she offered, knowing that Molly was the bravest, *and* the toughest, of the three of them.

Molly looked to the left of the pond, where leafless, black-branched trees stuck up through the mist, in terror-stricken poses. Ignoring the shudder that passed through her body, she raised her head indignantly. 'Well, ah will . . . ah'll go on me own then!'

'But yer musn't go near the edge, mind, 'cause me grandda told uz that it can suck yer in!'

Amy looked at Jeannie now, and thought she seemed worryingly serious as she told Molly this.

'Can it . . .? Can it really suck yer in?' Amy asked now, her imagination working overtime. In her mind she could hear the enormous sucking noise as Molly was devoured by the black, murky water, and she ran off in the opposite direction, shouting over her shoulder, 'Ah'm off home, ah don't want ter be dead before Christmas, with only five weeks ter go!'

Molly, hands on hips, looked at Jeannie in disbelief. 'What did yer go and say that for?'

''Cause it can! It's got summat called silt in it, and if yer tread on it, yer feet go down and down into it, until yer whole body gets sucked under . . . and that's it . . . ye're dead!'

Amy shivered as she stood in the distance now, looking back at her two friends.

'Come on, Molly,' Jeannie implored, 'we should stick together, and we've seen it now anyway! Ah think we should go home.'

'Huh! Well ye're babies, both of yer,' Molly scoffed. But Jeannie guessed that even she was pleased to have an excuse to leave.

'Where on earth have yer been, our Jeannie?' Hannah

sounded so vexed that Jeannie decided to lie, and answered, 'Ah've just been over ter Molly's.'

'Well, ah popped round there, and her mam said yer'd both gone off somewhere . . . So where did yer go then?'

'Just round Amy's.' Jeannie hated lying to her gran.

But Hannah could always tell. 'Right, sit down by me a minute and tell me . . . where did yer go?'

'Aw, Gran, don't be vexed, we only went ter have a quick look at . . . at the Blackenin' Pond.' She looked up at her gran's stricken face, and added rapidly, 'But we didn't go near it . . . honest!'

Hannah felt sick to the stomach, to think that Jeannie would have done such a thing, knowing how her grandda, and everyone else in the family for that matter, had warned her how dangerous it was. Her grandda had even told her about the two boys who'd been paddling just round the edge, and how one had got his feet stuck in the silt, and when the other had tried to pull him out, he'd got stuck himself. In trying to free themselves, they'd both fallen over into deeper water and drowned. To get the message home, he'd even gone so far as to tell her that some people thought the pond was haunted.

Jack had then explained to Jeannie how, after that, the villagers had got together and fenced it off, but it was a long time ago and most of the fencing was down now, due to weather and general erosion. But because nobody went there any more, it had been neglected and pushed from everybody's mind.

Right now, it was to the very fore of Hannah's mind. She was right back to those terrible days when the whole village had mourned with the boys' parents, and it had taken a long time for it not to be talked about any more. And here she was, sick to the stomach, confronting her precious Jeannie about that very thing.

'Gran! Did yer hear uz? Ah didn't go near it!'

'Well, yer might not have done, but ah'm tellin' yer now, if it ever happens again, yer won't be allowed ter come and stay here on a Saturday any more. Yer mam'll have ter find a babysitter in Bishop for yer while she's at work.'

Seeing Jeannie's horrified look at the thought of a *babysitter* was enough to convince Hannah that there would be no repeat performance.

Chapter 10

Marck

'Are you going to marry him?' Simone's curiosity was getting the better of her.

'No, well at least not yet.' Yvette smiled. 'Anyway he hasn't asked me.'

'Oh he will, I'm sure of that. Dominic is crazy about you,' Simone answered knowingly.

The conversation was interrupted by Dominic's entrance into the living room.

'What's all this seriousness about in here between you girls?' He went to Yvette and placed an arm around her shoulder.

'Oh, just girls' talk.' She smiled, gave him a peck on the cheek and said, 'Come, let's go help your *maman* in the kitchen.'

Papa was already home and changing out of his dark blue work overalls, while Maman was setting the table.

'Ah, there you are,' she said, smiling at the three of them.

'Where is Martine?' Dominic asked, surprised not to see her rushing around checking things and draining boiling saucepans.

'She has gone to Madame Molyneux's shop on the corner, to take a phone call from Madeleine.'

'What . . . is Madeleine ill?' asked Simone with a frown.

'No, well at least I hope not. Madame called round to say that Madeleine had phoned to ask if Martine could go to the shop at six thirty, when she would telephone. That is all I know at the moment.' Maman was looking worried, even when she added, 'Probably nothing, just wants to say hello, eh?'

However, when Martine returned it was plain to see by her expression that it wasn't nothing. Martine sat down. 'We are going to have to bring her back here for a while, Maman.' She didn't add that Madeleine had been crying on the telephone. What she did say, was that not only did Madeleine have a sprained ankle, but no one seemed to believe that there were peculiar things going on. And on top of that, she was still suffering morning sickness.

'She wants to have the baby here.' She looked not only at her mother but at the whole family.

'And what does Tom have to say about that?' Maman asked, already knowing the answer.

'Tom is not happy, he can't understand why she would want to make such a long journey. He can't come with her, he has his work to do.'

'I could go and fetch her,' Simone offered.

'You don't speak very much English, Simone, you'd never manage on your own,' said Dominic.

'But *I* do . . . I speak English,' said Yvette. 'I could go with Simone. After all, Madeleine will need all the help she can get, with little Francine to look after *and* her luggage.'

'You would really do that?' Dominic smiled at Yvette.

'Of course . . . if your *maman* and *papa* are in agreement.' Raising her eyebrows, she looked to Dominic's parents, inviting an answer.

Maman hesitated, unsure as to whether this would be a good idea or not. But she couldn't have known then that the decision on who would go to England would soon be taken out of her hands.

Evenwood

Maddie came off the phone, wiped her eyes, and went through to the kitchen to thank Mrs Parkin for allowing her to use the telephone.

'Are yer all right, pet?' Mrs Parkin looked with sympathy at this poor young French lass, who was not only pregnant but hobbling about with a stick.

'You won't mention to Tom or Hannah that I used the telephone, Madame Parkin?'

'No, ah won't, pet, but *you* should, yer know,' she said, adding quickly, 'Ah know that it's none of my business, hinny, but the Dawsons need ter know just how much ye're missin' yer family.'

'But they do so much for me, I don't want them to think that I am not . . . how do you say . . . grateful?'

'They know you are, ah'm sure of that, pet, but this is something different. Ye're homesick, and it makes us sad ter see it.'

'You are so kind, Madame Parkin, I thank you so much. But I feel better now zat I talk wiz my sister. And I will talk to Tom again, but when ze time is right, eh?'

The red skin around her eyes crinkled as she smiled, and for a moment Mrs Parkin felt her heart might break.

'I must go now, *madame*, I left Hannah looking after Francine. She thinks I am at the shop to buy *confiture* . . . er, jam.' Maddie smiled again.

'Ah have some home-made jam here. Yer can say that yer bumped into me in the street, and ah brought yer back here to give yer some jam.'

Maddie hesitated.

'It's strawberry.' Mrs Parkin raised her eyebrows enticingly. She really wanted to do something for this lass.

'Oh . . . *confiture de fraises*.' Her momentary excite-ment made her lapse back into French. 'Yes please, *madame*, zat will be lovely.'

When Maddie arrived home to relieve Hannah of Francine, she felt guilty when she saw how worried Hannah had been about her hobbling up to the shop with her stick.

'Yer should have let me get yer jam, it wouldn't have taken a minute,' Hannah said, unable to understand why she would have wanted to struggle up there herself. 'It's just as well ah called in, mind,' Hannah smiled, 'what with this cravin' that yer've developed for jam lately.'

'I know,' Maddie said kindly. 'I just needed to get out of ze house for a while,' then added, 'anyway ze exercise and fresh air will be good for me . . . no?'

'All right,' Hannah said, not convinced. 'Ah'll pop in to see you tomorrow, pet.'

Glancing at Francine sleeping peacefully in her pushchair, she suggested, 'Now you have a rest like the doctor said you should, lass. By what Rene tells me, you had a bit of a chat with him about the other stuff as well?'

'Yes, Hannah, I did, and ze doctor was very helpful and told me not to hesitate to make anozer appointment if ever I feel anxious. Also, I think that perhaps I will look at what I can make for Francine with some of the material that Jeannie brought for me. The doctor seems to think that it would be helpful if I could involve my mind in something that doesn't give me too much time to think. So maybe while I can't walk too much I can start to sew again, eh?'

Although she forced a smile to reassure Hannah, inside, she knew that it was going to take much, much more than involvement in sewing to ease her mind.

Tom managed to get home earlier than usual, in an effort, at Rene's suggestion, to spend as much time with Maddie as possible while she seemed so down.

Tired and hungry, he walked up the path towards the front door, where from the corner of his eye, he thought he saw a movement in the bushes to the side of the house. That's the second time that's happened, he thought, as he headed round there. After poking around for a while and discovering nothing except a few birds, he mumbled to himself, 'Christ, ah'm so knackered that ah'm seein' things now. Must have just been bloody birds flutterin' around.'

'Hello, love!' he called as he came through the front door.

'Tom! I didn't expect you yet! I am cooking us a stew . . . an *English* stew,' she said proudly.

Tom smiled as he kissed her on the cheek, before sitting down to get his boots off.

'Smells lovely,' he said, feeling even more ravenous as he looked into the saucepan.

'Hannah showed me how to make dumplings, so I will try, eh?'

'Lovely, pet, ah'll have a bath while ye're doin' that. Me whole body's aching after today's shift. And *you* don't want ter be standin' on yer feet fer too long either. How is it today, pet? Yer foot, ah mean.'

'OK, and thank you for putting the paving stone back down level for me, Tom. You must have done that before I was up this morning?'

'Yes, I did it before I went to work so I could get it done in the daylight, 'cause it's nearly dark by the time I get home at five. Roll on the summer, eh, pet. Looked as if some animal had been digging around there, it was all hollow underneath at one end, and the slab had slipped down, making the other side stick up. I had to do it this morning, couldn't let you go round there to throw yourself to the ground again, now could I?' He grinned.

Maddie smiled. 'I went out for some jam earlier, while your *maman* was looking after Francine.'

'Ay, pet! Yer cravin' fer jam must be gettin' quite bad to have hobbled all the way up ter the shops like that!' He pointed to her foot. 'Me mother should have got it for yer!'

'No, she offered to go, Tom, but I needed the fresh air.'

'Fresh air?' he laughed. 'Round here, with all that stuff comin' out of the pit chimney? You'll be lucky.' He slapped her playfully on the backside.

Happy to see that he was in a good mood even though he was tired, Maddie got a spoon out of the drawer to taste the stew. The next moment she was coughing and spluttering, and spitting the mouthful into the sink.

'*Oh mon Dieu!*' she called to Tom. 'I must have put salt in more than once!'

Tom came back into the kitchen. 'Surely not! Here, let me taste it.'

Tom put the spoon to his mouth and, like Maddie, spat it straight into the sink.

'How've yer managed ter do that, pet?'

'I don't know!' she exclaimed. He sounded so disappointed that, once again, Maddie had to fight the tears that threatened to fall.

'I left it when I went to bathe Francine, and must have forgotten and added more salt when I came back.'

As she was saying this, she was acutely aware that there seemed to be something to apologize for almost every day. She was heartily sick of saying, I'm sorry, but here she was again, apologizing. Feeling tired and defeated, she sat down with her back to him, so that he wouldn't see yet more tears.

Tom felt sorry that he'd snapped. Trying to lighten the situation, he pulled her up from the chair and grinned as he held on to her hands. 'Hey! Never mind, pet, we can always have jam and bread, eh?'

Maddie put her head on his chest and sobbed.

Chapter 11

Two weeks later

Maddie recognized the writing on the envelope as soon as she picked it up from the doormat. It seemed so long since she'd heard from Nicole, and she couldn't wait to read what she had to say.

Chere Madeleine,

I hope that everything is good with you? I think of you so often, every day in fact! This is a very quick letter, as I have to go out, and I want to post it at the same time.

I have a couple of things to tell you.

Remember the last time I wrote to you, I told you of Jacques? Well, we have been seeing each other for a while now, and we have been getting very close, if you follow what I mean? And now I

*feel that things are moving in that direction, a
little too quickly for me.*

*I know that it will sound stupid, but I'm
scared and I just feel so ignorant. Probably
sounds ridiculous coming from someone who up
until recently has lived her whole life surrounded
by sex. I wish now that I hadn't closed my
eyes so much to what was going on around
me. And how I wish we weren't living so far
apart, Madeleine, we have so much to catch up
on.*

*The other thing I have to tell you, which is
even more of a worry, is that Maman thinks she
saw her uncle, you know, the horrible slimy one
that I told you about, the one related only by
marriage, thank God?*

*Well, she thinks he is here in Boulogne, looking
for her! And she seems very uneasy about it. She's
since told me things about him, and it's worse,
much worse than I'd thought.*

*I can't tell you all in a letter right now, but
things were so bad for her that she stole money
from him to run away when she was expecting
me.*

He was a bad man, Madeleine!

*I will tell you more when I write next
time.*

In the meantime, if you have any advice on

how you think I should play it with Jacques,
please tell me.
  A bientôt!
  Bons baisers,
  Nicole

Maddie, deep in thought, put the letter down and went to make herself a cup of tea, an English custom that she found herself following whenever she needed to think.

The relationship with Jacques was really important to Nicole. Once she'd discovered her *maman*'s profession, Nicole had never even brought friends home, let alone a boyfriend. Maddie felt very privileged to be Nicole's trusted friend, and she would have to think carefully about her reply. As for the uncle, Nicole had told her a bit about him, in their more serious moments, during the war, and she didn't like the sound of him at all. As far as she could understand, her *maman* had had a nightmare time when he'd been around before, and well . . . she could only imagine how Ginette must be feeling to know that he was close by again now!

On hearing a knock at the door, she bundled up the letter and pushed it into her handbag, out of sight, regardless of the fact that no one in the village could read French anyway.

When she answered the door, it was to find a dishevelled woman staring at her.

Maddie stood in the doorway, not only speechless but transfixed by this woman, who, in reaching up to scratch her head, had let her coat sleeve slip back and unwittingly displayed her wrist. Hanging there for all the world to see was the gold bracelet – Maddie's gold bracelet!

'He . . . lloo!' The woman put her face right up to Maddie's in order to get her attention. But Maddie's shock at the sight of the bracelet was such that she jumped back and slammed the door.

The woman shouted sulkily through the door, 'Ah only came ter see if yer had any old stuff ah might be able ter sell . . . rude woman!'

Really angered now, Maddie yanked the door open. 'Where did you get zat bracelet?'

Adopting an air of childlike defence, the woman turned away from Maddie and slapped her hand over her wrist. 'It's mine!'

Maddie grabbed the woman's arm and pulled her closer. 'Let me see.'

'Ow! Get off! Ye're hurtin' me! It was a present . . . yer French bitch!'

Shaken and hurt at such an outburst, Maddie hung on to the woman's arm and said through gritted teeth, 'I ask you once more . . . where did you get it?'

'Ah told yer it was a present!'

'From who?' Maddie tossed her head in disbelief.

'Secret!' The woman was defiant, and not about to tell Maddie anything.

'You have not heard ze end of zis!' Maddie's urge to slap this woman was so overwhelming that to prevent herself from doing so she turned away quickly and shut the door in her face.

Maddie watched through the window as the ragged woman, still holding tightly on to her wrist, shuffled down the footpath mouthing obscenities to herself.

By the time Tom was due home Maddie had calmed herself well enough to reason that no matter what, there was no way that this woman, whoever she was, could be allowed to keep that bracelet.

When Tom arrived home, they greeted each other, then, after waiting until he'd hung up his coat, in a very calm manner she said, 'Sit down, Tom, zer is something I want to ask you.'

Oh God, he thought, what's happened? Maddie could see by his face just how he was thinking, so she said quietly, 'Who is the woman who talks in a strange way, and wears clothes that don't fit her?'

'Ha! That'll be Nitty Nora. Scratches her head?' He imitated her scratching.

'Why do you ask?'

'She was here today."

'Nitty Nora . . . here? What was she after then?' He frowned.

'She has my bracelet.' Maddie couldn't believe how calm she was when she told him.

'What? Oh, you must be mistaken, pet.'

Annoyed by his sympathetic smile, she said flatly, 'Must I? Just as I'm mistaken about everything else that only I seem to see around here?'

Tom, surprised by the sarcasm he'd detected in Maddie's tone, sat up in his chair. 'You mean you've seen it?'

'I've seen it.'

'She showed you?' Tom's voice had gone up a pitch or two.

'She's wearing it.'

'The cheeky bitch.' Tom jumped up out of the chair. 'Well, she won't be wearin' it much longer . . . Ah'll see yer in a bit.' He gave her a quick peck on the cheek, gently patted Francine on the head, and before she could say any more he was out of the door and gone.

Maddie picked up Francine and held her up high, telling her, 'At last . . . he believes! Your daddy believes me!' And when she laughed, Francine giggled along with her.

Chapter 12

By the time Tom arrived at Nora's house, he'd gone over and over it in his head, must have been a hundred times. What if she was mistaken? After all, how would a lass like Nora get hold of Maddie's bracelet? He knew the bracelet very well, and was sure he would recognize it if it was the right one.

Instead of banging on Nora's front door, as his instinct bade him to do, he made himself knock gently. When there was no answer, he knocked again, but louder this time.

'Wh—at? What d'yer want?' came the familiar drawl of Nora's voice from within.

'Ah just want ter talk to yer for a minute, Nora, open the door, will yer!' Tom's voice had become noticeably more agitated towards the end of the sentence.

'If yer've come ter get me bracelet . . . yer can't have it!'

'Ah just want ter see it, Nora . . . Maddie told uz how nice it is.'

'Liar! She sent yer ter get it, ah'm not daft, yer know! Ah'll chuck it away if yer don't leave uz alone, mind!'

Worried that she might throw it on the fire or do something equally stupid, Tom had to think quickly.

'No, no, Nora, there's no need fer that. How about, if yer show uz it, and if ah like it when ah see it, ah buy it off yer. I expect yer could do with a few pennies . . . couldn't yer?'

There was a moment's silence. 'Half a crown then?'

'OK, two and six, and it's mine if ah like it, eh?' Tom smiled to himself, he could have put a bet on her saying half a crown. It was a fortune to her, and where money was concerned she almost always thought in half-crowns.

The door opened slightly, and Nora, still without showing her face, pushed her wrist through the gap.

Tom recognized the bracelet as Maddie's as soon as he laid eyes on it.

'Where did yer get it, pet?' He tried to be calm and pleasant as he spoke through the gap in the door.

'It was a present. Ah told yer French wife that but she didn't believe uz.'

'Well, how nice that somebody gave yer a present like that. Who was it from then, pet?'

'Ah'm only meant ter be lookin' after it for a while, and ah've got ter tell nobody, else ah'll be in big trouble . . . So do yer want it or not?' she said, remaining invisible to Tom.

Tom sorted some change from his pocket, and pressed a half-crown coin into her outstretched hand. When he saw her fingers enfold the coin, he gently removed the bracelet from her wrist. She quickly pulled her arm in and slammed the door shut.

Not satisfied with her answers, Tom pushed the letter box open and asked again, 'Please, Nora pet! Tell me who the *very* kind person was who gave yer this lovely bracelet.'

'Nooo! Go away, else ah'll get me ears boxed. Ah'm not allowed ter tell anybody, ah told yer that already. It's secret!'

'Was it Jessie?'

There was no answer at first, then in a sudden panic, Nora shouted, 'Ah never said that! Ah never said that!'

Tom banged his fist on the door in frustration, before turning and leaving. There was no doubt in his mind now that it was Jessie who'd somehow managed to steal the bracelet and had got that poor demented lass to mind it for her, till the coast was clear.

Tom deliberated on his way home, Do I tell Maddie that Jessie was behind this, or do I just let her think that Nitty Nora took it?

Maddie rushed to the door when she saw Tom approaching. And Tom, having thought better of mentioning Jessie's name at all, looked up, to see her standing there in the doorway.

With a huge grin, he walked up the footpath dangling the bracelet enticingly in front of him.

'Oh Tom! You don't know what zis means to me!' She flung her arms around him.

'Ah do, pet, and that's why ah've made sure that Nitty Nora won't be botherin' you any more.'

'You didn't hurt her?' Maddie, looking horrified, pulled away.

'Wasn't necessary . . . there's other ways, pet. Let's just leave it at that, shall we.'

He hugged her to him to make an end of the matter.

In the meantime Nora unfurled her grip on the half-crown and stared at it where it lay in the palm of her hand, wondering what had made her do such a thing as to hand over the bracelet. Suddenly she was scared of what Jessie's reaction might be. Her first impulse was to run away, but even she knew that would be stupid; after all, where would she go? She was aware that she had no other friends, so instead she grabbed her coat and ran as fast as her legs would carry her, all the way to Jessie's house. The back door was open.

Jessie, feeling a tap on her shoulder, dropped the armful of clothes that she was carrying and turned to see Nora standing there, blubbering about something as usual.

'You bloody idiot! Are yer tryin' ter give uz a heart attack or what?'

'S-sorry, Jessie.' She could hardly speak.

Experiencing an unusual and brief moment of sympathy, Jessie said, 'Oh sit down, Nora, fer heaven's sake. Who's upset yer now?'

Nora threw herself down on top of the pile of clothes on the armchair.

'Not there, stupid!' She yanked Nora from the chair. 'Ah've just ironed those.'

Nora, even more upset now, wailed, 'Ah can't do anything right. All ah want ter do is make yer pleased with uz, and all ah do is make yer vexed.'

'Shut yer blubberin', Nora, and tell uz what's up! And hurry up will yer, ah need ter get this packin' done, and hidden, before me mother gets back from nosing around the neighbour's house and admiring her new . . .' she put on a derogatory and fake posh voice, *'three-piece suite, huh*!'

Seeing Nora's gobsmacked expression, and realizing that in her frustration she'd said far too much, Jessie added quickly, 'Ah meant ah want ter get these things packed away . . . ter make more room in me wardrobe like!'

'Oh . . . ah was really worried there for a minute, ah thought yer meant packin' ter go away like!'

'And where would ah go then, yer daft thing?' It was when she made herself pat Nora's hand that she noticed her bare wrist. She grabbed her other arm and roughly pulled up the coat sleeve. 'Where is it?'

Norah couldn't speak.

'The bracelet, where is it?' Jessie glared at her, waiting for an answer.

Nora was terrified, and before she had time to put her confused mind straight, she blurted out, 'Ah lost it!'

Jessie, in disbelief, gave a little laugh. 'That's funny, even for you, Nora. Now, where is it?' She was leaning over Nora menacingly.

Too afraid to change what she'd said, Nora cowered, and with her arm defensively over her head, she repeated, 'Ah've lost it.'

'*What!* Do you know how much that was worth? It was gonna fetch at least twenty quid! *Twenty quid!*'

When Nora heard that, somewhere in her jumbled mind she tried to work out how much less half a crown was than twenty quid.

Jessie's next thunderous words penetrated straight into her befuddled brain, and she understood exactly what she was saying.

'Ah was goin' ter use that money fer me fare outa here, yer dimwit!'

Nora jumped up, and holding her hands tight to her ears against the shouting, she said, 'Yer've given uz a headache.'

'Ah'll give yer more than a headache if yer don't find the bloody thing. Now *get out*! And don't come back till yer've found it!' Jessie opened the door, and shoved Nora unceremoniously down the steps.

As the evening approached, Nora became more and more depressed. Jessie had made her feel very unhappy. If she'd been bright enough to put a word to her feelings, it would have been 'disillusioned'. All she knew was that no matter what she did for her, Jessie always seemed to be vexed with her, and she felt tired and useless, and sometimes of late she'd even shocked herself by her own thoughts. Maybe she didn't want Jessie as her friend any more. Maybe then the pain would go away.

But, really, deep down, she knew that this time it must be all her own fault. She'd sold the bracelet to Tom, to get rid of him because he scared her. For that brief moment she'd given no thought to Jessie. No wonder Jessie was vexed with her. All she'd asked her to do was to keep the bracelet safe, because it was insurance for her. Nora hadn't understood the exact meaning of that, but she had sensed that it was very important. Jessie would never trust her with anything again. She must think of a way to get twenty quid . . . Was that the same as twenty pounds, or was it twenty guineas that was more than twenty quid, she wondered briefly. 'Oh, ah can't think, it's all too confusin',' she muttered. She had a hand pressed to each side of her head, willing the confusion to go away.

She knew that if she did get the money, that would

mean Jessie would be pleased with her, but then she would go away and she wouldn't ever see her again. But if she didn't get either the money or the bracelet back, she wouldn't be allowed to see Jessie ever again anyway. 'Oh, what to do?' She wrapped her arms around her body and began to rock back and forth.

When she'd been a baby, she'd stuck her thumb in her mouth for comfort. Yes . . . that's what she'd do until she felt calm enough to think. So there she sat, alone in her sparsely furnished house, rocking back and forth, sucking furiously on her thumb.

'He's really screwed her up,' said Jack as he climbed out of the tin bath, where it sat proud, in its usual position, in front of the living-room fire.

'Mind where ye're splashin' that water, Jack!' Hannah crouched to mop her wet rug. 'And as for our Tom screwin' Jessie up, ah think she was on that route long before Tom was seein' her. There's always been something about Jessie . . . Oh, ah know I always welcomed her into this house. But she always seemed ready ter blow, even then.'

'Aye well, maybe ye're right. Ah think our Tom's had a lucky escape, as hard as it is for him now, what with a French lass who wants ter go home and a second bairn on the way. All that's nowt, compared ter how it might have been with Jessie, 'cause by all accounts she has *blown*, as you put it.'

'Mind you, ah think it's all front with Jessie,' Hannah said. 'She's like a little girl under all that bravado. But that said, she's a right handful fer anybody, never mind her frail old mother!'

'Frail! Her? Why, she's no more frail than you or me. She's a sponger, and a lazy old b—'

'Jack! That's enough,' Hannah said quietly, disapproving of the description he was about to use.

'Gran! Gran!'

'Here she comes.' Jack smiled at Hannah in a resigned way.

'Yes, Jeannie?'

'Yer'll never guess what!'

'What?'

'Ah've just seen Nitty Nora walkin' down the street . . . well, shufflin' down the street, *and* she was suckin' her thumb!' Jeannie's eyes were wide.

'That woman should be somewhere she can be looked after properly.' Jack addressed this to both Hannah and Jeannie. 'But she kicked up such a song and dance last time somebody tried ter talk to her about it that apart from the odd visit from the social, they've left her to it. Huh! Probably thinkin' that us lot in the village will keep an eye on her.'

'Well, ah s'ppose we do . . . sort of, anyway,' Hannah answered.

'Oh Gran,' Jeannie said, seeing Hannah push the flat iron on to the fire grate to heat. 'Ah was just thinkin' of doin' some toast on the fire. Ah had that much practice when Great-grandda Elliott was stayin' here that ah can do it perfect now. *And* without droppin' it into the fire.'

'Go on then,' said Jack, 'and yer can do me a slice while ye're at it.'

'You'll not eat yer tea, either of yer, if yer start on toast at this time of day.'

Jeannie looked at the grandfather clock. 'There's an hour and a . . . well, a bit more yet,' said Jeannie, not sure how long the bit more was.

'An hour and three-quarters before yer mam gets back.' Hannah smiled.

'So can we, Gran? Just one *teeny* slice each?' she squeaked.

Hannah looked from Jack to Jeannie. 'Well, it looks as if ah'm outnumbered here. Just one, mind,' Hannah warned as she grabbed a tea towel and bent to take the flat iron from the grate.

A rumble in the back yard stopped them all in their tracks.

When the door opened and in walked Tom, grinning from ear to ear, all three looked up in wonder. He wasn't due back for at least another hour.

'Come and have a look at this,' he said, summoning them to the back yard.

'A motorbike!' Jeannie rushed over to it. 'Can ah sit on it, Tom? Is it yours?'

Jack could see at a glance that it wasn't up to much.

Apart from the fact that the tyres were worn, the paintwork was in need of a fair bit of attention, and that was before looking into the mechanics of the thing. But he'd have to be diplomatic, he decided.

'Where did yer get it?' Jack asked, his face not betraying a flicker of horror at the object leaning up against the wall.

'It's not mine yet, but ah brought it home for you ter look it over for me, Dad.' He looked at Jack. 'Well, yer know a bit more than me about bikes.'

'From where ah'm standin', lad, ah can see a fair bit of rust on it, but ah'll have a look at the mechanics anyway.'

'It'll need ter be strong enough ter attach a sidecar, of course,' Tom said, looking at it with more of a critical eye now, and wondering if in his initial excitement he might have been a bit rash.

Jack crouched down beside the bike. 'Ah don't need ter tell yer that it's an ex-army bike.' He tapped his finger on his chin. 'Hmm, BSA W20. See these bolt holes here in the side?' He pointed.

Tom leaned over to look.

'It's where a sidecar has been fixed, probably for carryin' stuff from one camp to another.' Jack couldn't help feeling intrigued now, wondering just what this bike might have been involved in during the war. He stood up behind the bike and looked along its length, then pulled Tom alongside him. 'If you look at the bike from above, yer can see that the wheels aren't properly lined up. By, it's had some rough treatment, this bike.'

The look on his dad's face was enough to tell Tom that he'd made a mistake.

Jack shrugged. 'There's too much needs doin' fer me ter help yer fix it, ah'm afraid, and ah've got to say, Tom, that ah'm surprised yer didn't notice any of this yerself. After all, yer spent long enough on one of these things during the war.'

Tom felt a rush of embarrassment. 'Mebbe ah was too hasty . . . Aw, Dad, yer know what ah'm like!'

'Aye, ah do that, lad. Summat else'll turn up, you'll see.' Jack placed his hand on Tom's shoulder and looked down at the bike with disdain. 'Well, if ye're thinkin' of gettin' a bike ter take that lass of yours ter France, *and* addin' a sidecar fer the bairns, ye're goin' ter have ter get something that's a sight more dependable than this, our Tom.'

'Ah know ye're right, Dad. It's just that this was goin' cheap, and it looked good on the surface . . . well, ter me like, and the engine seemed ter have some poke in it an' all. Then when the feller at the garage told uz ah can pay it off a bit at a time, each month . . . Well, ah guess ah was in too much of a hurry, wantin' ter surprise Maddie. She's had such a hard time of it lately.' Tom looked deflated.

'Well, lad, it's up ter you what yer do, but yer'll have an even harder time if that thing breaks down on the way ter France . . . why, it's at least two days' journey from here, and that's if ye're travellin' day and most of the night!'

Hannah, recognizing her son's disappointment, smiled at him. 'Yer dad's right, you know . . . Just bide yer time and something'll turn up, you'll see.'

Chapter 13

Boulogne

As she walked down the street, there was a knot of nerves in Nicole's stomach. Her instincts were telling her that this could be *the night*. It was this thought that made her slow her pace momentarily, but the urge to be with him was stronger, and she couldn't wait to see him.

In the forefront of her mind were the words of advice offered by Madeleine, in the letter she'd received only that day.

> *If you are not sure, Nicole, you must wait a while*
> *longer. After all, look what happened to me, it*
> *only took just one time! If Jacques really cares for*
> *you, surely he will understand? That's if he*
> *knows just what it is that he needs to understand,*
> *of course.*
>
> *Maybe it would take the pressure off a little if*

you explained something of your background to him? I'm sure that you will know when the time is right. And if events lead you naturally in that direction, then I have a feeling that there will be no time to think!

So, my dearest friend, all I can say is, go with what your heart tells you, not me or anyone else.

Nicole's pen had been poised to reply immediately, but Jacques had called to ask her if she would meet him at his house. And although she walked briskly and confidently towards the street where he lived, confident was the last thing that she was feeling. She'd been conditioned by her former life, and what it had done was to make her dubious of men. But something within her deeper self told her to give this one a chance. Unlike any of the boys she'd met during her school years, Jacques had an air of dependability about him, quite apart from the fact that in Nicole's eyes he was very handsome. She smiled to herself at the thought, as she carefully weaved her way through the rubble of the war-shattered derelict street adjoining his own.

When eventually she looked up, it was to see the house right there in front of her, and although she'd been there before, something told her that this time it was going to be different. If that was because she was ready for it to be different or if it was just intuition, she wasn't sure.

She took a deep breath, and, hesitating slightly, she lifted her hand to knock on the door. As he opened it, Jacques looked so happy, and almost relieved, Nicole thought, to see her. After ushering her in with some urgency, he said enthusiastically, 'I didn't think you would come.'

She felt a pang of guilt as she thought how close she'd been to doing just that.

He took her coat from her and hung it over the back of a chair.

Her eyebrows were raised as she asked, 'Why would you think that?'

'I felt that I was putting pressure on you, the last time we were together, about something that you weren't ready for.' He pulled her gently towards him. She looked up and into the depths of his sparkling hazel eyes, and his melting smile, as always, caught her off guard.

And as had happened so often in the past, the words that came from Nicole in response weren't exactly what she had meant. 'Oh, it's nothing, Jacques.'

But it *was* something, it was very much something to her, so why had she said that?

It would have been so easy, in that moment while their eyes were locked, for Nicole to fall into his embrace, but with a suddenness that caught Jacques by surprise, she playfully flicked a wayward strand of his hair that hung over his right eye, and swung round, saying as lightly as she could, 'It's just . . . It's just that I know what should be happening with us, and I'm ashamed to say that I'm afraid . . .'

'Shush, shush . . . don't say it. What you are talking about, it's not a case of it *should* be happening, my darling. It will happen when we are ready, both of us, I'm sure of that.' He smiled. 'I do understand, you know.'

'Do you? Do you really, Jacques?' She sat on the wide sill, in the window, her legs pulled up to her chest and her chin resting on them. 'I don't think you do . . . How can you? You don't know my history, you only know me as you see me now.'

'Well tell me, my dear Nicole, make me understand,' he said, pulling up a chair and placing it next to her.

She looked at this patient man and smiled. 'I warn you, you may not like what you hear.'

'I like *you*, don't I?' he answered with a grin. 'So try me . . . see if you can shock me, eh?'

'It's a chance I have to take, but you may well be shocked enough not to want anything more to do with me.'

'Just tell me, Nicole,' he said, looking straight into her eyes and gently taking her hand.

They stared at each other for a moment, and taking in the frown on his forehead, Nicole said suddenly, 'Well, I'm sure you must have guessed that you are my first proper boyfriend . . . and you must also wonder why, after all these weeks, we have never even kissed, well, not properly, anyway . . .'

Nicole held up her hand to stop him as he was about to speak. She had to tell him this right now, and with no interruptions, or she never would.

Jacques stayed silent while Nicole told him of how, at the age of ten, she'd discovered just what it was that her *maman* did for a living. It had come about one day when she and her *maman* were walking hand in hand down the street, heading for her school. Someone walking towards them had spat out the word 'Whore'. And although Ginette had carried on walking with her head held high, Nicole had not dared to ask her what the word meant, because she could tell, instinctively, that it wasn't good.

So without wasting a minute, as soon as she had said goodbye to her *maman* at the school gate, she rushed into the library room, and there, in a ragged-edged dictionary, she found the word. She could hardly breathe . . . It had been as though her heart had stopped for a couple of beats. Trembling, she had slammed the book shut and run from the room. From that day on, she'd never taken any friends home or formed any close friendships, fearing that people would judge her *maman*, whom she loved dearly.

Nicole looked into Jacques's eyes, willing him to understand, and Jacques, unable to speak immediately, squeezed her hand tightly and swallowed hard, to clear the lump he could feel forming in his throat.

The warmth of his understanding had reached Nicole, and she felt able to continue more confidently now, telling him how she'd been unable to get that word out of her head. With no one to talk to about it, and because she couldn't bear for anyone to think ill of her *maman*, she'd become a bit of a recluse. Until, that is, her dear friend, Madeleine, had come into her life.

She went on to explain how she and Madeleine had become so close, boosting each other's spirits through the wretched years of the war, and how for the first time she'd felt that she'd found someone she could talk to, who wouldn't judge.

Still gripping her hand, Jacques smiled, encouraging her to go on.

Nicole tried to explain to him how those growing-up years had affected her, even though she'd never seen or heard anything untoward; her *maman* had made sure of that. But nevertheless she had been aware of the goings-on in the house, especially during the early years of the war, when the three girls had still been working for her mother.

She stopped for a moment and looked at Jacques, who still said nothing, and she wondered what he was thinking.

'Many of the clients were married men, or men who were in a relationship already.' She said this with an almost resigned shrug of her shoulders. Then as an afterthought, she added, 'From what Maman has told me since, most of them were ordinary, some even quite nice, businessmen, lonely people and suchlike. Maman would have been very choosy about her clients, I'm sure of that.'

'May I speak now?' Jacques asked at last.

'But of course!' Nicole tried to hide the awkwardness she was feeling at that moment.

If Jacques was surprised by what he'd been hearing, he certainly didn't show it. 'I just want you to know that I consider it a great compliment that you have trusted me enough to tell me of this, *chérie*. I can see in your face how distressing it is for you.' Then with his arms outstretched, palms upwards, he added, 'You mustn't be ashamed about something over which you had no control.'

Seeing her sitting there with her head lowered, he stood in front of her, and, taking a firm hold on her shoulders, he turned her towards him and looked down into her face. 'There is nothing new in this, you know, *ma chéri* . . . in this line of work, I mean. And the fact that it's your *maman* that we are discussing, well . . . I can see how difficult it has been for you over the years. But look at you . . .' He placed her at arm's length, looking into her questioning eyes. 'Such a beautiful girl!'

With a flap of his hand, he dismissed those words as

being too flippant. 'I am talking about inside. You have a beautiful nature, *ma petite*, and I can only congratulate your *maman* on doing such a marvellous job. Bringing you up on her own while she was trying to deal with what must have been a very difficult situation, well . . . you must be very proud of her, non?'

'Oh yes, of course I am, I never forget how much love she's given me. And her time . . . more time than she could probably afford over the years, let alone making sure that I never went without anything.' Looking intensely into Jacques's eyes now, she said, 'It's not just anyone who would understand these things the way you do, Jacques. I know that from the way some of my teachers behaved towards me. It makes me realize that I am so lucky to have you in my life.'

But even as she was saying this to Jacques, quietly seeping through the warmth that she was feeling towards him was the thought that every step closer they came to each other was another step closer to the moment she was so afraid of. Sex, to her, had always been something forbidden, something that men paid for. And because of it she was scared, scared of losing him.

Jacques stood up. Holding both of Nicole's hands now, without a word, he pulled her up from the sill and held her close.

She looked up into his face, and with his thumb he gently wiped the tears from her cheeks.

'That's not all, Jacques,' she said. There was a sad

finality in her words, and he watched the neat creases form on her forehead as she frowned. His eyebrows raised in question, he looked at her in anticipation of what might be to come.

'It's Maman's uncle . . . but by marriage only, you understand!' She put great emphasis on this last bit of information. 'The man my mother ran away from when she was expecting me. Well, he is here . . . here in Boulogne. Maman saw him in the town, and she thinks he is looking for us.'

'Why would he be looking for you after all this time?' Jacques was puzzled.

'Probably because my mother had to steal money from him.' She searched his face for a reaction, but there was none. 'That is how she was able to get away.'

As he felt her tension, Jacques was pensive for a moment, and gently he squeezed her shoulder. 'Try to relax, *chérie*. I will make us some coffee, yes?'

'That would be lovely, thank you.'

As Jacques filled the coffee grinder, Nicole stopped talking, wondering if Jacques had heard enough. But when he turned to her to ask, 'So what happened?' she continued, 'Well, Maman, once she was settled, felt an obligation to send a little money from time to time, to his wife, Tante Louisette. Partly, I think, because she'd stolen the money. Louisette is Maman's mother's sister and she had been kind to Maman, but weak . . . so weak, and dominated by her husband.' She pulled a face, scowling, as she felt obliged to mention his name, which came out in a whisper. '*Gaston* . . . Anyway, Louisette must have accidentally let something slip, or left some information lying around, because he seems to have found out that Maman lives in Boulogne. That's what we think, and now Maman is convinced that he's coming after her to make her pay. Knowing him as she does, she's afraid that it may not only be money that he's after.'

From the other side of the road, he saw her. Thinking she hadn't seen him, he grinned arrogantly as he crossed the road and headed towards the café where Ginette sat in a window seat, staring into her coffee cup.

She hadn't needed to see him, she could sense his presence as he approached her table. Without looking up, she asked, 'Why are you following me?'

'Why do you think?' His face sobered, and the menacing grin faded. 'You owe me.'

Ginette looked up now and growled across the table, 'I owe you nothing! Have you any idea how my life has been all these years?'

'Oh, I know only too well what you've been doing all these years . . .' he looked her up and down, 'and pretty good you must have been at it, judging by the clothes. After all it was me who taught you, wasn't it?' His grin returned.

Feeling sick as the memory of what she'd spent all

these years trying to forget ebbed and flowed through her head, she spat, 'I will give you what I took from you . . . with interest, then I want you to go away and leave us alone.'

'Well, that's a start, but it's not as simple as that, my dear Ginette.' He pulled out a chair and, with a sickening smirk, sat down facing her.

Ginette's stomach was in knots.

'Still the stunner,' he winked, taking in every inch of her trembling body.

Hidden down by her side, her fists were clenched as the urge to slap the smug expression from his face was quickly becoming all-consuming.

How could this happen after all this time, and just when Nicole and she were starting a new phase of their lives? She was still to meet Jacques but she knew that he must be very special to Nicole; she couldn't remember ever seeing her daughter so happy. And as for herself, it had taken the pain and distress that they'd suffered at the hands of those stupid, misguided vigilantes in Boulogne to make her realize that Nicole had been right all along: it was time to give up everything to do with her previous life.

After all, it wasn't as if they would be dreadfully poor. Ginette had been very careful with her earnings, having told herself early on that there was no way she would spend her working life doing this job without something to show for it in the end. During the war years, her business had been booming, due not only to the fact that she'd had three girls working for her but because she'd continued to run a clean, discreet and elegant house.

But once the decision had been made to close the business, she'd been so relieved as one by one she'd rid herself of her past clients. In her mind's eye she'd finally been able to see, for herself and Nicole, the kind of life that she'd so often dreamed of.

There had been no nastiness from any of her clientele. Some of them had even, over the years, considered themselves to be her friends.

Since then, she had spent much of her time getting to know her daughter all over again. Not only had they taken a holiday together, but to Nicole's delight, her *maman* had even looked into buying a small business where she could indulge her passion for antiques.

She guessed that this passion must have been passed down to her from her parents, who had loved beautiful old furniture.

How different her life would have been had her *maman* and *papa* not rushed back from an auction one day, worrying that they were late to collect her from school. It wasn't everyone who had a road vehicle, but Maman and Papa had a van. She remembered how, as a child, she'd always wished that it was a car, but, she supposed, they couldn't have run their business without a van.

Her parents hadn't arrived to collect her from school that day, nor would they ever come again. Instead she'd been taken home by one of her teachers, who'd looked very serious as she sat her down to tell her of her parents' accident. That was the day her life changed for ever.

She'd wanted to live with her teacher, but it was explained to her that it was the responsibility of her *maman*'s sister to take care of her now. She hardly knew Tante Louisette, much less her husband, Gaston. She'd been immediately uncomfortable in Gaston's presence, and she'd found herself unable to refer to him as 'uncle'.

Tante Louisette had done her best to console her for the loss of her parents during that first year, and life had been just about bearable. Then came her fourteenth birthday, from when every day had turned into a nightmare.

It started when she needed to leave the dining table, to go to the kitchen for salt. He sat in his usual place at the head of the oblong table, in front of the door into the kitchen, which meant that to get to the kitchen, it was necessary to pass his chair. The size of the dining room meant that there wasn't enough space to pass the end of the table easily. And he hadn't even looked up as he placed his hand between her legs as she squeezed by. She'd slapped at his hand and rushed on into the kitchen. Had her aunt seen? She didn't know. How to behave when she returned to the room? She didn't know. She could hardly breathe as she lingered in the kitchen, salt in hand. She remembered how her aunt had called to ask if she was having trouble finding the salt.

'No, no, I have it here,' she'd replied, and had rushed back to the dining room and on to her chair, careful not to glance in Gaston's direction. She didn't tell her aunt on that day or any of the other days when the furtive touching took place. But when, on the day she turned sixteen, he climbed into bed alongside her while she was sleeping, she knew she'd have to take control. No more, she decided, would she put up with the filth and degradation in that house.

Heaven knows how she would have coped, if it hadn't been for the friendship of Jean Paul. He'd been her friend all through school, and she had wanted to tell him about Gaston so many times, but couldn't find a way to do so. She knew that he cared for her, but her embarrassment was such that she knew she could never tell him. Anyway, what could he do?

After the sordid introduction she'd had to the world of sex, from the vile Gaston, she hadn't been prepared for the tenderness Jean Paul had expressed the first time they slept together. It was with him that she'd had her first taste of love. Two months after that, when she discovered she was pregnant, she knew she could live in her aunt's house no longer. Her one consolation was the knowledge that Jean Paul was definitely the father. He was the only one to have entered her. The 'pig', as she thought of Gaston, had always spent himself over or beside her. In the dead of night she'd taken Gaston's money, and, with hope in her heart and fear in her head, without even telling Jean Paul, she'd left, never to return.

The cough, accompanied by the smell of Gitanes, reached her over the table, bringing her abruptly back to the present.

Ginette glared at the creature across the table from her, and her stomach churned as the scent of him reminded her of the closeness of his body. The body that she'd endured for so many years. How stupid was she? She'd asked herself that question time and time again. Why hadn't she confided in someone? All she could come up with was that she was ashamed, afraid, terrified even, with no means or know-how to get away from what would be the resulting chaos. He was respected in the village. And she'd known that no one was likely to believe her, except maybe Jean Paul. And because of her fear, his actions and her lack of action, the whole course of her life had been dictated from there on. She knew now that there was no way she could allow his return to ruin the rest of her life, or that of her daughter.

She'd kill him first.

Chapter 14

How they ended up in the bedroom, Nicole didn't quite know.

Jacques had gently wiped the tears from her eyes. The kisses had been slow at first, tentative even, the kind of kisses aimed at mending an anxious heart, but somewhere in the process, the kisses had turned into something more. She found herself falling deeper and deeper, until her senses of sound and reason just melted away, and she let go of them gladly, until they floated off to somewhere far in the distance.

And now, entwined in Jacques's arms, she found herself lying on the bed. The window was open, allowing the scent of sea air to fill the room, and her body, with the kind of freedom that the sea always seemed to evoke in her, and she was ready, ready to give herself totally to this passion.

Lying side by side, they stopped kissing for the briefest of moments, and the question in Jacques's eyes was erased immediately by Nicole's answering caresses. Showing no sign of the doubt or fear that she'd expressed no more than half an hour before, she stood up, and without taking her eyes from his, she slowly began to unbutton the front of her dress.

Taking his lead from her, Jacques quickly removed his shirt. Afraid to take his eyes from the vision in front of him, he tossed it aside.

Standing by the bed, Nicole allowed her dress to fall to the floor, and the audible intake of breath from Jacques made her shiver.

Thinking she was cold, he pulled her down beside him, and they slid under the covers together.

This caring act brought a warm glow to her body, making her feel protected and secure in his arms, and she knew this was going to be unlike any of the horrors that she'd imagined. But even so, just for the briefest of moments, she suddenly felt timid about her nakedness, pulled up the sheet and held it with both hands tightly under her chin.

Jacques, still in the throes of passion, had picked up on Nicole's momentary shyness. Gently he pulled the sheet down, whispering, 'No, Nicole, leave it . . . You are beautiful, so beautiful . . . I have thought of this moment so many times, please don't take it from me now.'

Within seconds, and with no time to think, she was gasping, as his mouth covered her breasts with adoring kisses. Rolling from one side of the bed to the other, his hands and teasing fingers covered all the previously unawakened parts of her body, the parts that had been so well hidden, along with any sexual feelings that had dared to show themselves.

The electricity generated by each gesture and caress took her by surprise, and drew her further and further from anything she had ever known. She returned his kisses with equal passion, until, without any thought or plan, her hands moved slowly, caressingly, down the length of his back, resting only momentarily on his buttocks, before coming slowly round to his groin, where her hands sought that part of his body which had been pressed so tightly against her. And even though she had never even seen, let alone held, a man's most 'prized trophy', as she'd heard Maman's working girls call it, she was far too deep in the moment to feel any shock or fear, and she needed no instruction as she guided him into her.

Ginette jumped out of the taxi, rushed to the front door of her house and fumbled with the keys. She unlocked the door, let herself in, slammed the door behind her and stood there, her back pressed hard against the cold metal of the doorknob and one gloved hand held tightly to her mouth. She desperately hoped that he hadn't seen which of only five houses left standing in the street she had entered.

His last menacing words had made her storm out of

the café. '*I will find you*,' he'd whispered, then leaning further in, 'After all, it can't be that difficult, I will just ask any man in Boulogne.' And with a sickening smirk he'd delivered his final blow: 'Maybe they will know your daughter too, eh?'

As if struck by a thunderbolt, Ginette, who hadn't realized that he knew of the existence of Nicole, had jumped to her feet and left.

To harass her was one thing, but to threaten her daughter was quite another. How in hell did he know about Nicole? she wondered. She would never have shown it in front of him, but she was terror-stricken. Stay calm, stay calm, she told herself as she ran up the stairs, through the old reception area into the living quarters and through to the kitchen, to the window at the front of the house. Peering through a crack in the shutters, she could see it, the other taxi, just sitting there, engine still running.

Oh mon Dieu, I hope Nicole doesn't come home now . . . Does he know her? Will he recognize her? she wondered. After all, if she did turn up, she could be any girl. But would he have seen Nicole with her before? He'd obviously been watching her, otherwise how would he have found her in the café? Panic was setting in at the very thought.

She paced back and forth, questions buzzing around her head like an angry wasp. If she went outside now, he would see where they lived. She rushed through to the reception area and picked up the phone, then suddenly realized she had no way of contacting her daughter. All she knew was that she had arranged to meet Jacques somewhere. She replaced the receiver, peeled off her gloves and grabbed a pile of papers from the top of the desk. Somewhere among them was a list of numbers that she'd seen Nicole with recently. There wouldn't be many numbers on the list as Nicole didn't know many people who owned a telephone, and she'd no idea if Jacques would be one of them.

Ginette was deeply regretting not having pushed to find out a bit more about Jacques. But she had seen that for the first time her daughter was actually smitten with someone, and had decided to let her speak about him when she was ready. Because of that, she didn't even know a simple thing like whether he had a telephone.

Finding nothing in the pile of papers, she now rummaged recklessly through the drawers of the desk, all the time berating herself for her ignorance. In the end, frantic and frustrated, she threw herself down on to the desk chair in despair. Just then the phone rang so loudly by her head that she shot up, knocking the receiver off its stand.

Grappling to pick it up, she screeched, 'Hello!'

'Maman! What on earth is the matter? You sound as if you are in a tunnel!' came the voice.

'Oh Nicole!' Ginette, limp with relief, sank back into the chair.

'Maman!'

'Listen to me, Nicole, *do not* come home.'

A moment's silence passed.

'He's here, isn't he?' Nicole already knew the answer.

'Yes. He's outside, in a taxi. He followed me, and now he is waiting to find out where we live. He didn't see which house I entered.'

'Oh Maman!' Nicole sounded scared. 'There are so few houses left in the street, it won't be difficult. Is he violent?'

Hearing the tremble in Nicole's voice, Ginette avoided answering that question.

'I am going to sit it out, and you must stay away. After all, the taxi driver can't stay there indefinitely, can he?' she said lightly, in an effort to disguise the fear in her own voice. Realistically, she had no idea how long Gaston would wait, but even if he did go away, he now knew which street they lived in, and it wouldn't be long before he discovered which was their house. After all, she wasn't exactly unknown in the area.

'Are you still with Jacques?' Ginette asked, changing the course of Nicole's question.

'Yes, Maman. I was bringing him to meet you, that's why I telephoned.'

Ginette managed a smile. 'There will be time enough for that, *ma fille*, when we find our way out of this.'

'I will talk with Jacques, see if we can think of something.'

'No! You *must not* come back . . . you understand, Nicole?'

'I understand, Maman.'

She wasn't sure that Nicole really did understand. She wouldn't put it past that bastard out there to kidnap Nicole for revenge, and she wouldn't even let her mind go to what that could lead to with a man like him.

'Good girl. Is there a number where I can reach you?' Ginette fought to keep her voice steady.

Nicole gave her mother the telephone number for Jacques, telling her that they would wait there until she contacted them.

Jacques had picked up on the content of the conversation and said immediately, 'I must go to help your mother, Nicole.'

'But how?' Nicole's arms were outstretched in desperation, all the delicious warmth of their lovemaking diminished now by this devastating turn of events.

'We must find some way to distract him and lead him away from the house, to give your *maman* time to get out. Then we can bring her here.'

'And after that, Jacques? What then? We can't stay here for ever!'

Chapter 15

Within half an hour Jacques was running down the street, asking himself how the hell he was going to handle this situation. It had been hard to convince Nicole that she shouldn't come with him, but he needed her to stay where she was, in order to telephone her mother to ask her to get a few things together, along with whatever Nicole herself might need for at least a few days. Somehow, in the meantime, he had to try to trick this bloke, Gaston Dugas, to get him away from Ginette's house, so that she could escape and take a taxi back to his place, where they would have time to think what to do next. He had no plan of action, and no idea what he might be getting himself into. All he knew was that he loved Nicole, yes, loved her – he allowed himself a brief smile at that realization – and he would now do whatever it took to free them from danger.

Following the frantic call from Nicole, Ginette had yanked her valise from the top of the wardrobe and thrown in it whatever she thought might be necessary. As she was sorting through Nicole's wardrobe, she was stopped by a knock at the door.

She ran to the window. It was getting dark, and although she was unable to see the front door through the crack in the shutters, she realized that the taxi was gone! Breathing a sigh of relief, she ran down the stairs, stopping at the door to ask, 'Who is it?'

'Quick!' The answer sounded muffled.

She didn't recognize the voice. 'Who is it?' she asked again.

The next sound was like an animal in pain, then the muffled, gasping voice came again. 'Jacques . . . Quick! Open . . . the door.'

There were sounds outside, scuffling shoes on the step, then a bang on the door so loud that it shook in her hand as she opened it. She was almost pushed over as two men came tumbling in, the younger man on top of the unmistakable figure of Gaston Dugas.

Jacques grabbed a handful of Dugas's hair, pulling his head up until his eyes were level with Ginette's. Chillingly he smiled, allowing a repugnant cocktail of garlic, coffee and sweat to waft into Ginette's nostrils. With a crunching sound Dugas was dropped to the floor, where his limbs jerked in an uncontrolled spasm.

Terrified, and struck motionless for a moment, Ginette stood with a hand pressed to each side of her head. What to do? Dugas's torso lay twisted and motionless. Jacques was leaning over to check him out when suddenly, with a sharp, well-aimed backward move, Dugas's right elbow struck Jacques in the base of the neck, rendering him senseless. It was when he collapsed over Dugas's prone body that Ginette was spurred into action.

She ran up the stairs, grabbed a heavy crystal vase from the dresser and was back down in a flash, by which time a recovered Dugas was on his knees above Jacques, punching wildly at his face and upper body. Before she knew what was happening, Ginette had lifted the vase and bashed Dugas over the head with all her strength. The ensuing silence was even more frightening than the scuffle had been.

Crouched unsteadily beside Dugas, Jacques looked up at Ginette, who sat on the bottom stair holding on to the vase with both hands. Dazed, she looked at the handsome, anxious and bruised man in front of her. 'I think you must be Jacques,' she said with some irony.

'Never in a million years did I envisage meeting you this way, *madame*, but yes, I am Jacques.' He looked down at the figure lying on the floor. 'I caught up with him just as he thumped on your door, and knowing that I must stop him before you opened the door, I jumped on him.' He shrugged his shoulders, conveying to her that in that instant there was nothing else he could have done. 'I prayed that I hadn't got the wrong man, but from the very sketchy description that Nicole had given me, I thought it had to be him. After all, she had never met him either, so she could only tell me what you had told her in the past . . . So, what do we do now?'

There was no movement from Dugas, but he was breathing.

They both stood looking at him, until, as if a light had suddenly come on in her head, Ginette looked towards a door at the far end of the passage. 'The cellar.' She nodded towards the door. 'If we can drag him there, we could lock him in until we get away.'

Without hesitation, Jacques nodded. 'He's very heavy. Will you be able to take the weight of his legs, if I try to drag him?'

'We will manage if it kills us,' Ginette said, determined that this was what they would do. 'But we must hurry, before he comes round.'

Ginette ran upstairs to where she kept the cellar key while Jacques remained in the passageway, staring down in disgust at this excuse for a man. Even though he was against violence of any kind, he felt no remorse. He deserves everything he gets, he thought. He'd learned enough about him from Nicole to visualize his worthless life of cruelty and selfishness.

Somehow, in the narrow passageway, together they pulled and shoved the heavy lump towards the now open cellar door.

At the top of the steps, Jacques looked down into the darkness where the foundations of the house formed the walls that were to contain the body of this despicable man. Wedging his foot under the limp form, he lifted it with such force that Dugas rolled easily down the steps. With a slight groan, he landed at the bottom. Ginette and Jacques looked at each other in silence.

'Can you find something to bind his hands, and something to gag him?'

Without a second thought Ginette took to the stairs again, and ran straight through the old reception area to one of the three bedrooms that weren't used any more. She yanked open a cabinet drawer, where she had no trouble in finding a length of rope. After all, enough of it had been used in this room in days gone by, she thought wryly. And for clients of a more unusual taste, the tools of the trade had been kept in a little side cupboard, where she found some tape that would be strong enough to gag a lion. Duct tape. She remembered. She had a vision of the English soldier who'd kindly brought the tape round to effect a temporary repair of a leaking pipe under the kitchen sink. It hadn't been long before her working girls had found other uses for it.

Surprised at the speed with which she'd found these items and thrown them down the cellar stairs to him, Jacques got to work immediately, telling her to telephone for a taxi.

'Yes, of course, I didn't think.' Wasting no time, Ginette went straight back up to the reception area, called for a taxi and finished collecting what she thought Nicole might need. By the time she was downstairs with the two suitcases, Jacques had bound and gagged Dugas, stopping only when an unwelcome feeling of pity had fleetingly edged its way in, and he'd laid Dugas's head on some folded sacking he'd found in the cellar. This he considered to be much more than the man deserved.

After locking the cellar door, Ginette and Jacques glanced at each other.

'Go on.' Jacques gestured towards the door at the top of the stairs, while attempting a reassuring smile. 'Go and lock the door to your apartment.'

Ginette, in a daze, pulled the hefty door to the apartment closed, locked it and placed the key safely in her handbag. The cellar key she handed to Jacques. Once outside, they concealed it under a cumbersome stone that he had managed to heave out from a pile of rubble to the side of the house.

The dismal-looking stones were all that remained of most of the houses in what was once a beautiful tree-lined street, where the occupants hadn't been so lucky during the bombing of Boulogne. It never ceased to amaze Ginette that their building, along with the four others clinging to it, were the only ones to survive in the rubble-strewn wasteland.

They had just reached the gate when the taxi drew up alongside them. Jacques lifted the cases into the boot of the Citroën while Ginette climbed in, and it wasn't until Jacques had given the address that they were able to sit back and draw breath. They looked at each other, in silence at first, neither able to believe what they'd just done.

'I will call the *gendarmes* tomorrow,' Jacques whispered.

'Tomorrow? He may be dead!' Ginette whispered back in alarm. Not that she was in the least bit concerned for the monster in the cellar, but if he died then they really would be in trouble.

Realizing that their animated whispering was drawing attention from the taxi driver, they remained uncomfortably silent for the remainder of the twenty-minute journey, each deep in their own thoughts.

Jacques was thanking God that he'd trained so vigorously, in order to come up to the standard expected in his job of helping coach the local football team. Without that, and possibly his younger years, he doubted if he could have overpowered the older man. Although fat, Dugas had not been easy; there'd been in him the kind of strength only derived from sheer determination and bloody-mindedness. But Jacques's body had been fuelled with adrenalin all day, since the moment Nicole had entered his house, in fact, and it had been building up throughout the dramatic events.

Their lovemaking, far from depleting him, had fired him up, and by the time he'd arrived on Ginette's doorstep his strength had been at its peak.

Ginette, on the other hand, was sitting there frightened out of her wits at what had just taken place. It was like some kind of terror-fuelled hallucination. All the sick-making experiences of her early teenage years, which she'd thought had finally been squeezed from her memories, were now tumbling back into her head, fast and vividly – so much so that she could still feel Gaston's hot clammy hands touring the intimate parts of her body.

Nothing, and no one since, not even in the years of trading her body, had revolted her in the same way. She remembered the helplessness of being unable to call out to her aunt, who, unaware of the ongoing assaults, was snoring deeply in the next room.

'Ugh!' The word had jumped out involuntarily, and startled Jacques from his own thoughts.

'Are you OK, Ginette?'

'Yes, yes, I am OK. Sorry.' She forced a smile.

'I think you are not OK . . .' He looked out of the taxi window. 'We are almost there now.'

'At your house?' Ginette asked, taking in the area, which looked more industrial than residential.

'I will explain,' he said quietly.

The taxi pulled up at the top end of a road in which Ginette could see nothing that she would describe as a house, only what appeared to be a row of factory buildings. Puzzled, she climbed out of the car and waited uncertainly on the footpath while Jacques retrieved the cases from the boot and paid the driver.

Seeing Ginette's worried look, he said, 'I thought it better not to be dropped off at my house, as the *gendarmes* will soon be looking for you. And we could not risk the taxi driver giving them my address and leading them straight to you.'

'*Oh mon Dieu!*' She put a hand to her head. 'I had not thought of that. So how far is it from here to your house?' she asked, looking down despairingly at the cases.

'Half an hour, by car.'

'But we have no car!' Ginette said. She sat on a case, resting her shoulder on the dusty wall to her right and feeling stupid at having stated the obvious.

'That is why we are here, Ginette. I have a friend who runs the car body shop, look, over there.' He pointed hopefully. 'He will let me borrow one, I know he will . . . I just hope that he is there today. I only thought of this as I was about to give the taxi driver my address . . .' He looked at her intently. 'You must wait here.'

'Here! On my own?'

He could see that Ginette was showing signs of the shock of what had gone before.

'I will be very quick. If you wait here with the cases, I can run . . . You trust me, eh?'

'Of course I trust you, Jacques, I'm just cold . . . and afraid.' She pulled her coat tightly around her trembling frame.

Jacques placed a reassuring hand on her shoulder. 'Five minutes, I'll be back in five minutes.'

'Go, just go, Jacques,' she said shivering.

Jacques ran off, turning only briefly to hold up five fingers, affirming his promise to Ginette.

Nicole stood at the front door of Jacques's house, her frown of puzzlement at the unknown car pulling up outside changing to relief as she saw her mother and Jacques getting out of it. Ginette ran straight into Nicole's arms. '*Oh ma fille, ma fille*,' she said, desperately running her hands over Nicole's hair, unable to bear the thought of what could have happened. If Nicole hadn't phoned but had just made her way home as usual, she might have been apprehended by that monstrous man and never have arrived!

With their arms around each other, they waited while Jacques took the second case from the boot of the car.

'Nicole.' He leaned forward and kissed her briefly on the mouth.

'Your face, Jacques!' She cupped his face in her hand. '*Oh mon Dieu!* What happened? And the car?'

'I must return the car in the next hour or so. So come, *ma chérie*, let's get your *maman* inside and make her a coffee, preferably with something very strong in it, and we will tell you what has happened.'

Chapter 16

Evenwood

It was late in the afternoon and the social worker had come and gone, leaving Nora even more agitated than usual.

She had understood only too well the talk of sending her to a place where she would be looked after properly, and she didn't like it, not one bit. The house she was in was the only home she had ever known, she had been born there and nobody was going to get her out of it. Not if she could help it.

Before her mother had died a couple of years ago, she'd said to Nora, 'It's all yours now, lass. You just make sure you keep in with the villagers and they'll see yer all right. Yer won't never need ter live anywhere else.' And since then she'd managed to live, for the first year, on the bit of money that her mam had left her, then it was all gone, and somehow she'd managed to scrimp and cadge her way through the second year. But it was becoming harder and harder.

People were getting fed up with her badgering them for this and that all the time. Jessie would give her a few pennies now and then, sometimes even a sixpence, but only if she did as she was bidden, which usually included a bit of shopping. Nora didn't mind this too much, as every now and then the shopkeeper would give her some ham offcuts and other stuff that nobody else wanted. But the rationing went on and on, and things were so tight that there wasn't much that other folk didn't want. Unless she went at just the right moment, often other folk had gone off with the bits and pieces she might have had.

The social woman had said somebody had telephoned them to say she didn't seem to be well. That was a lie, she was perfectly all right thank you very much, and she was going nowhere. She'd get Jessie on to it, that's what she would do. Jessie would sort them out!

Decision made, she yanked her coat on, buttoned it up in her usual cack-handed way and, thumb firmly in her mouth, trudged down the street to Jessie's. After tripping over her undone shoelaces several times, she knocked on Jessie's door.

There was something about the tone of Jessie's voice as she answered the door that made Nora hold fire before she asked anything of her.

Leaving the door open for her to enter or not, Jessie marched down the passageway ahead of her.

Entering the living room, Nora noticed some of Jessie's things hanging out of the suitcase that Jessie had just attempted unsuccessfully to kick out of sight behind the armchair.

'What you up to then?' Nora asked quite coherently for once, in spite of her despair.

'Nothing for you ter worry about . . . What yer doin' here anyway when ah told yer not ter come back until yer got the bracelet?'

'Ah still haven't got the bracelet, Jess, but ah'll get yer the money before ah go, and if ah can't get the money ah'll get yer something even better . . . ah will, Jess!'

'Ha! And pigs might fly. Can yer find uz a husband and a bairn then, miss clever dick? Oh and while ye're at it, a house ter live in with me husband and me bairn would be good.' Nora, recognizing the sarcasm in Jessie's words even though she wouldn't have been able to put a name to it, just stood there, looking helpless and painfully sad, saying nothing.

'And what d'yer mean before yer go . . . go where like?' Jessie smirked at the very thought.

'They comin' ter get uz, said ah'm not capable of lookin' after meself any more. Ah want yer ter sort them out for uz, Jess.'

'Don't know what yer expect me ter do about it.'

Totally indifferent to Nora's plight, Jessie didn't even bother to look at her as she continued folding her clothes. She had much more important things on her mind, and none of this would matter once she was out of this place.

Nora was perturbed. There she was, telling Jessie something very important, telling her that she might be taken away, and Jessie just stood there folding clothes! In a desperate effort to get her full attention, Nora bent forward until her face was under Jessie's. 'Pleeeese . . . will yer sort it for uz, Jess?'

Jessie's hand came out none too gently and pushed her away. 'Get off, will yer, with yer rancid breath and everything. Yer *need* lookin' after, and *ah* can't . . . won't do it, so there yer are. Ye're on yer own!'

Nora just stood there for a moment, her bottom lip trembling. As hurtful as this treatment from Jessie was, it was what she knew and understood, and nothing would make her think of Jessie other than as her best friend. Unusually for Nora, she didn't kick up or have a tantrum this time. She knew in her own mind that it was just one of Jessie's bad moods, and it would be better to talk to her later.

So she walked out of the house, knowing that she was going to do *something*. She didn't know what yet, but it would be something that would make Jessie be her best friend for ever.

*

At Maddie's house, she and Rene looked at each other and laughed. Rene had been filling her in on her escapades with Rob. And although they laughed, Maddie knew that this relationship was developing into something serious, and she was really happy for her sister-in-law.

Likewise Rene was feeling happier about Maddie. She seemed to have settled down a bit more over these last few weeks, and hadn't even complained for a while of anything peculiar happening around the house.

Tom had been actively looking for a motorbike, and that had helped lift Maddie's spirits too. Rene could understand how it would make her feel that much closer to France if they had the means to travel, although she couldn't think how they were going to afford it. As far as she could see, any concern about the money they would need for the journey seemed secondary to Maddie. It would be a case of where there's a will there's a way, she suspected.

'Shall I put ze kettle on again, Rene? Have you time?' Maddie asked hopefully.

Rene smiled at how Maddie had picked up this very English custom of making a cup of tea whenever anyone called round. 'Go on then, just a quick one. I must go and fetch Jeannie from Mam's in a minute.'

'Yes, Hannah loves to have Jeannie to visit, doesn't she, and Hannah is so good wiz Francine too. She has been a big help to me during zis pregnancy, especially when my ankle was so painful,' Maddie said as she busied herself making the tea.

Rene glanced around the room. Although there weren't many ornaments or pictures yet, the light-coloured walls gave a feeling of freshness and space, and now that they had carpet on the floor it felt so much more homely. 'You've got it so lovely in here now, Maddie, you must be very pleased with it.'

'Yes, well, it's been a difficult time for Tom as you know, Rene, trying to do up ze house after his work, and me pregnant, wiz a bad foot, and even worse, wiz me missing home so much. Poor Tom, poor Hannah, poor you and everyone! I don't know how you have put up wiz me. I don't know how *I* have put up wiz me even!' On impulse she walked over to Rene and hugged her.

'Thank you for being my friend, Rene. It can't be easy sometimes.'

'Hey, come on, you'll have me in tears in a minute, and I mustn't spoil my make-up before I see Rob, now must I? We understand, you know, we really do, and it's as good for me to have you as a friend as the other way round. After all, who could I tell all these secrets to, if not you?'

They both laughed again, and continued chatting happily as they sipped their tea. When Rene got up to leave, they said their goodbyes with a kiss on both cheeks, a French custom that Rene had willingly adopted, finding it so much more civilized than a quick 'Ta-ra, lass!' which was the norm around the village. She'd even taken to doing it with Rob, which he loved. Anything for an extra kiss, he'd said.

Next morning, the post arrived before Tom left for work. Maddie was looking a bit pale.

'What is it, pet?' Tom asked, automatically leaning over her to look at the letter, even though he wouldn't understand the French words in it.

Biting on her bottom lip, Maddie scanned the letter again. 'It's from Nicole. She and her *maman* are in some kind of trouble, and she wants me to call the telephone number that she has given me as soon as I can.'

Her worried look prompted Tom to say, 'Well, you must go over to Mrs Parkin's to use her phone, she won't mind. I think she's got a soft spot for you.' He smiled. 'Tell Nicole that if we can help with whatever it is, we will, of course.'

'Thank you, Tom.' She looked up and smiled back. 'I think it must be something very serious for her to ask me to telephone.'

Nicole had been sketchy in her note, saying that she could explain much better on the phone.

Tom gathered his work gear together and said thoughtfully, 'Don't worry about takin' Francine with yer, pet. I'll drop her off at Mam's on me way ter work, and you can collect her after the phone call, eh?'

Maddie stood on tiptoes, her kiss tender on Tom's cheek as she answered playfully, 'Thank you, M'sieur Tom, you are so gallant.' Then she added more seriously, 'But will she mind, at this time in the morning?'

'Mam? Mind? Are yer jokin'? Why she'll be in her element, won't she, lass!' He addressed this to Francine, who was busily trying to pull off the hat which Tom had just put on her.

As Maddie shrugged herself into her coat, she couldn't help but think that Tom was seeing this from a man's eye view. Nevertheless, she couldn't really take Francine with her if she was to concentrate on speaking with Nicole, especially when she had no idea what the conversation would be about.

'Am I to take some toys with me?' Tom asked.

'The doll she is holding will be enough, I won't be very long anyway. Will you tell your *maman* that for me, Tom?' Maddie quickly kissed a now whimpering Francine, telling her sympathetically, 'I won't be long, *chérie*.' Then reaching up to kiss Tom, she said, 'She will be OK as soon as I've gone.'

'I know. Well, it is a bit early for this kind of upheaval, ah s'ppose. Just go quickly, pet, and I'll pacify her'. He looked down at Francine and pulled a gruesome face, which in an instant made the drooping corners of the little girl's mouth to turn upwards into a gaping toothless smile.

*

In the cosy living room at Mrs Parkin's house, Maddie was trying to hand over some money to pay for the phone call but Mrs Parkin would have none of it.

'Anyway,' she said kindly, 'you haven't made the call yet, so we don't know how much it would be. Now you just get on and telephone your friend, pet, and we'll worry about that later, eh? Ah'll give yer a bit of privacy, ah'll just be in the kitchen finishin' me spam sandwiches. Ah like a bit of spam in the mornin's, yer know.' She disappeared into the kitchen.

'Oh I am so sorry, Madame Parkin, I did not want to interrupt your breakfast.'

'Nay worries about that, pet, you just get yer call made. Ah hope it's not bad news.'

Maddie's heart was thumping when she spoke to the operator. Then, before she knew what was happening, she heard, '*Allô?*' It was a man's voice.

'*Allô*, may I speak to Nicole please?'

'Madeleine?' came the eager question.

'Yes . . . is that Jacques?'

'Oh thank God! Hello, Madeleine, and yes, it's Jacques. One minute please, I'll get Nicole.' Maddie smiled at Nicole's squeal of delight when she heard him tell her who was on the phone.

Nicole explained what had taken place, and how she and her *maman* had been staying at Jacques's house until the furore had died down. Dugas had been found, after an anonymous phone call.

Jacques had let a whole day and a morning go by before he'd gone to use a public phone to let the *gendarmes* know that they would find a man in the cellar at the address he gave them. Then he had promptly left the phone booth, before they had the opportunity to ask who he was, who the man in the cellar was or who lived at that address.

With no idea of the condition of Dugas, or even if he was alive, it had been decided that if Madeleine could accommodate Nicole and Ginette in England for a while, he would go immediately to organize their cross-Channel tickets. Jacques himself would stay in France to try to find out what had happened to Dugas and, most importantly, if he was alive.

Madeleine didn't even have to think before she answered, 'Yes, yes of course, you must come, you must get as far away as possible, as it will be no time before the *gendarmes* discover who lives at that address. That's if that pig Dugas hasn't told them already! Make the arrangements, and you can phone me on this number with the details.'

Suddenly changing her language to English, Madeleine called through to the kitchen, asking, 'Is it OK I give your number to my friend, Madame Parkin?'

Having picked up that this was some kind of crisis, her hostess came back into the living room full of concern. 'Of course, pet,' she said, 'I wouldn't have it any other way.'

*

'They've what?' Astounded at the news, Tom paced around their living room. 'Are they likely to be traced by the police then?'

'No, I don't think so . . . From what Nicole told me, most of the scuffle between Jacques and Dugas took place inside the house, and there are no houses opposite, they were all demolished during the bombing. The only person who is likely to remember Dugas is the taxi driver who took him there. But he would have left before Jacques attacked Dugas, so they hope that no one saw anything.'

Tom reached up and took two mugs down from the shelf, then stood by her, staring at the letter which she'd picked up again.

'Well, we must help them as best we can, pet, but don't forget that we have a young bairn in the house now, not to mention another on the way.' He gently ran his hand over her stomach. 'So ah'm sorry if ah sound a bit hard, but ah've got to look after me family now, haven't I? You do understand, don't you?'

'Of course I do, Tom, but I also know that Nicole and her *maman* would never put any of us in danger.'

'Not intentionally.' Tom said this more to himself than to Maddie, as he turned away to reach the tea caddy from the cupboard. With his mind miles away he moved automatically as he put three teaspoonfuls of tea into the tin teapot and poured the boiling water over it. Still deep in thought, he stirred the tea vigorously.

Within a few minutes, they were sipping quietly when they heard a gentle knock at the door. Tom raised his hand to stop Maddie from getting up. Draining his mug as he rose, he called, 'Who is it?'

'It's Mrs Parkin,' came the quiet voice from behind the door. Maddie jumped up now, and was alongside Tom when he opened the door, saying, 'Come in, come in, Mrs Parkin. What brings you out at this time of night?'

The older woman looked straight at Maddie. 'Yer've to come back with me now, pet, and yer friend is going to ring yer in ten minutes, by what I could understand. Her English is not as good as yours.'

While Maddie ran off to get her coat, Tom looked at this kind lady, who was tugging her coat round her to keep warm, and said apologetically, 'Right to-do this is, Mrs Parkin! Sorry yer had ter come out on this bitter night.'

'Well, ah wouldn't do it for just anybody, Tom, but ah really feel for that wife of yours, bein' so far from home and all that, it's the least ah can do.'

Maddie came through from the back, half in and half out of her coat. 'If I'm a little while, you won't forget to check on Francine, will you, Tom?'

'Am ah likely to forget about her?' he said with a laugh, getting hold of her evasive coat sleeve. 'Come here, let me get you into that coat properly, it's bloody freezin' out there.'

Although Maddie laughed, she was feeling really anxious. She linked Mrs Parkin's arm and together they walked up the street to her house to await the phone call.

Chapter 17

Bishop Auckland

The sharp intake of breath from behind made Rene turn round from the soapsud-filled sink where she was carefully washing her favourite sweater. She didn't move immediately, but smiled at Rob where he stood in the doorway, with a look on his face which she could only describe as appreciative.

Without a word, Rob made a move towards her. Grabbing at her soap-covered hand, he pulled her away from the kitchen sink and into his arms, where he held her close, his eyes never leaving hers, as he steered her into the passageway and along to her bedroom. Neither uttered a word. Rene's mind had been totally on the sweater she'd been washing, but she didn't pull away, knowing that if they didn't do *something* about this desire that had been building up between them over the weeks, they might explode.

Anxiety and nervousness of spoiling their friendship had stopped them so far. And they'd repeatedly avoided any situation that might have led up to this point.

But now composure had gone out of the window and Rob had decided to ignore the risk. Able to think of nothing else, he'd thrown down the newspaper he'd been half reading and seized the initiative. As he kissed her now, not in the tender way he had done the first time but with such determination and strength that her heart began to thump, each began to devour the other with a passion to surpass anything that had gone before.

They fell to the bed, where each caress, each touch, each tingling sensation ripped through their bodies, fusing them together, until, to Rob's mind, they mimicked a long-forgotten sculpture he'd seen in a gallery somewhere as a child. His mother, seeing how captivated he was by it, had covered his eyes and hastily pulled him away. But now there was no one to cover his eyes, and as he looked down on this ravishing lady he marvelled at how lucky he was to have found such a woman, and in such an unexpected way. Who would have thought that two children could have brought such perfect love and companionship to two lonely people?

When at last she pulled away from him, she gasped, and Rob, feeling the hot tears plopping on to his chest, asked, 'What is it? Why are you crying, my pet?'

'Oh I have no idea. It's stupid because I'm happy, really happy.'

'Remind me not to make you sad then, won't you?' He grinned, and pulled her tightly towards him.

After a few moments' silence, he released her slightly and asked with some concern, 'Are you worried that your husband may not be . . .' He didn't want to upset her by saying the word, so changing tack he asked, 'Are you worried that he may come back?'

'I don't know . . . are you?'

'Well, I can't say that it's never crossed my mind.'

'It's been so long now,' Rene sighed. 'If he did come back, I'm sure he would be different . . . I am different. The war has changed us all.'

'I think we're getting a bit philosophical now, pet. Look, if it happens we will cross that bridge then, but for now, let's have a glass of something special, shall we? After all, this moment will never come again, and I want to remember everything exactly as it is now . . . always.'

'Now who's being philosophical?' Rene laughed, throwing a pillow at him as she swung her legs over the side of the bed. But before she could get up, he'd grabbed her and was once more on top of her.

'Oh no you don't,' he said, grinning. 'You will have to pay a penalty for that. But we'll go slowly this time.'

The sound of her laughter was suddenly muffled, as once more his mouth was over hers and no more words were spoken.

*

Hannah paused for a moment. 'Oh, ah don't know, Jeannie, about yer takin' Francine out in the pushchair. She's quite happy, she's been scribbling on that bit of paper for hours. Let's leave it fer another time, eh?'

'Aww, well ah just wanted ter show her off ter me friends, Gran, 'cause they're all about on a Saturday like.'

'Ah know, pet,' Hannah said with some sympathy, 'but she's still very young, and so are you ter have that kind of responsibility.'

'But me teacher says ah'm very responsible *and* grown up for me age!'

'Look, yer can get yer friends ter come here. Not all at once, mind.'

'OK, ah s'ppose that's better than nowt.'

'Ah think yer mean better than *nothing*, don't you, our Jeannie?'

'By . . . ye're soundin' just like me mam, Gran!'

'Well, she's worked hard ter get yer ter speak nicely, pet . . . and ah want yer ter talk better than me . . . better than all of us. And it won't be long before little Francine starts talkin' and ah'd like ter think that you will set an example to her an' all.'

'Just like Ee-an's s'pposed ter be doin' with me?'

'Yes, pet, just like that . . . How is Ian anyway? Ah haven't seen him in a while.'

'He's OK. He's at school quite a bit, and he has a lot of homework at the weekends, but he still comes round fer his tea like! Mostly on a Sunday, when me mam and Rob can get together an' all.'

Hannah took this remark as an opportunity to ask, 'Do yer like Rob, pet?'

'Oh yes . . . ah love him even, he's kind,' Jeannie answered without any hesitation.

Although Hannah knew in her heart of hearts that there was no chance of it happening, something Rene had said lately had made her wonder just how confusing it would be for them all if Jeannie's dad ever did come back. Rene had read about a man who'd turned up after he'd been missing for near enough four years. He'd apparently had terrible leg injuries and been unable to walk for months. The French family who'd taken him in had been at great risk, as in the meantime the Germans had rounded up many of the local Resistance fighters, making it impossible for him to get any messages back to England.

Knowing how close Rene had become to Rob, Hannah feared for her. There'd been no mistaking her horror at what she'd read.

Chapter 18

'You give the wrong impression, that's your trouble, going out all over the place with yer skirt clingin' ter yer arse fer dear life. And heels on yer shoes that yer can hardly walk in. Huh, what kind of a man do yer think that's goin' ter attract?' Jessie pulled away as her mother leaned towards her. 'Well, ah'll tell yer . . . you'll attract men just like yer da. Why, sometimes yer act no better than the trollop he ran off with, and good riddance ter the pair of them!'

'Well, yer'll be sayin' good riddance ter me an' all soon, 'cause ah'm off the minute ah've collected me wages at the end of the week. Ah'm leavin' this god-forsaken hovel, and ah'm *never* comin' back.' Jessie's obvious delight in saying this got right up Maude's nose.

'Don't you dare talk ter me like that, ye're acting no better than a slut!' she yelled, as she burned herself trying to light the butt of a cigarette from the embers of the fire.

'Ha! From where I stand there's only one slut around here—' Jessie's words were brought to an abrupt halt by a resounding slap across her face.

'Ah've been called a lot of things in me lifetime that might or might not be true, but ah've *never* been a slut . . .' Maude glanced sheepishly around the living room, 'not the kind you're talking about anyhow. There was only ever yer da in me life . . . more fool me.'

Shocked, but more amazed than anything, at this outburst from her mother, Jesse stood with her hand to her smarting face. Never, ever, had her mother lashed out at her, no matter what she'd said or how she'd behaved. The thought briefly crossed her mind that maybe if she had, Jessie might have had more respect for her and things might have been different between them.

What was she thinking? Of course things wouldn't have been different. There was a time when Jessie would never have believed that a man running off with a younger woman, scrubber or not, would turn his wife into what her mother had become. Her bitterness had made her into a mean-spirited, slovenly, chain-smoking troublemaker.

But she had to concede that, for the first time ever, she had some idea of what being let down by a man might do to a woman. For that, she need look no further than herself. If she was honest, what had *she* become since Tom had gone from her? Well, there was no way she was going to turn out like her mother, over a mere man!

Plenty more fish in the sea, and she was going fishing.

Wanting no further confrontation with her mother, she flung her shoes off, swung round and ran up to her room, all the while thinking resentfully, It's probably my own fault that she's turned out this way. If I'd paid her more attention when my excuse for a father ran off, then maybe . . . Oh, I don't want to think. Feeling a headache coming on, she put her hands to her head. She'd never felt pity before and she'd no idea how to deal with it. It was too late, it was all just too late, she decided.

An hour or so later, when she returned downstairs, Maude was standing in the hall, looking reasonably tidy, with her coat on. This was unusual enough in itself. 'I'm off out,' she said calmly. 'Don't know what time ah'll be back.'

Jessie stared at her mother for a moment. Then, with a flicker of a smile, she said something her mother had said to her time and again over the years.

'Well, yer might find the door locked when yer get back.'

Maude replied in as flat a tone as she could muster, 'Please yerself! Lock it if yer like!' Then, with a satisfied smirk, she gently slipped her hand to her pocket, where the tiny bump created by the spare key gave her all the reassurance she needed, and without another word she left the house.

As soon as her mother closed the door behind her, Jessie sat down, trying to get her head around what had just happened. Staring into space, she became aware that there was something between them, she wasn't sure what, but it was there, and at the realization, when the words came out they did so very slowly. 'Well . . . ah'll . . . be . . . buggered.'

'Well, if yer ask me, ah think Jessie's goin' to head off out of here as soon as she gets the chance.' Jack was drying his hands on the towel in the kitchen.

'It'll be for the best if she does,' Hannah replied, as she dragged the pan containing the browning joint of beef out of the oven.

'Eee, the smell of roasting meat never fails ter get me juices goin', lass. Yer certainly know how ter keep a man happy,' said Jack, tapping Hannah on the backside as he passed.

'We'll have less of that an' all,' Hannah jested, 'else yer'll get no Yorkshire pud—'

Hannah stopped mid-sentence as the back door was flung open and Jeannie, flushed and breathless, rushed in. 'Ah've got the emergency eggs fer the Yorkshires, Gran, and ah never broke even *one* on me way back!'

'Ah can't believe that, the way yer've just rushed in. A whirlwind couldn't have caused more of a commotion!'

'Oh Granddad, you do exaggerate,' Jeannie sighed. Then, nudging Hannah, she said, 'Hey, Gran, shall ah show yer how Mrs Hobbs counts the eggs, just by movin' her lips with no sound comin' out?' Without waiting for an answer, Jeannie very slowly and with exaggerated carefulness picked up an egg from the basket and silently mouthed, *one*. Then she placed the same egg in a bowl, counted it again and mouthed, *one* again. Then back to the basket she repeated the process, this time mouthing, *two* . . . and again *two*, as she placed it in the bowl, then *three* . . . *three*. She repeated this mimicry until she'd removed all six eggs from the basket to the bowl.

By this time Jack was spluttering with laughter and Hannah was drying her eyes with the hem of her pinny.

'And she handles them like they were *gold*!' Jeannie added as if it were the most ridiculous thing in the world.

'Aye, and then you carry them home swingin' the basket about, as if it had nowt but feathers in it!' Jack said, still grinning from ear to ear.

Hannah and Jack were still grinning about Jeannie's mimicry of Mrs Hobbs when Rene arrived half an hour later, panic written all over her face.

'What is it, pet?' Hannah rushed to her side.

'Where's Jeannie?' she whispered.

'Yer've just missed her. She's popped out to see Amy and Molly but she'll be back for her roast beef and Yorkshires shortly. Why?'

'I had a phone call from the Air Ministry, to say that in view of the airman who'd been presumed dead . . . you know, the one I told you that I'd read about, well, they've decided to take a closer look at all the farmhouses nearby. Another two Spitfires came down in the same area as the man who's . . . come back from the dead, so to speak. Apparently there were two more missing, and they think one of them might have been . . .' She couldn't bring herself to say his name. 'Oh God! I don't know whether to be hopeful and happy, or terrified . . . Johnny could still be alive, Mam!' Rene looked at her mother in desperation.

'Oh pet!' Her mam went to put her arms round her daughter. 'What a situation to be in. No one's grieved longer or harder than you have for Johnny, and just when yer were getting round ter makin' a new life fer you and the bairn, this happens. All ah can think is that if he *is* still alive, the chances are he doesn't know who he is, otherwise he'd have come back, wouldn't he?'

'Oh, I don't know *what* to think, Mam.' Rene broke away and paced round the living room. 'And there's Rob! What on earth will I do about Rob? What a mess . . .'

'Come on, love, sit down a minute.' Now it was Jack trying to console her. 'Until we know what's what, there's no point in getting yerself all wound up.'

'Do I tell Jeannie or what?' Rene spread her arms, palms upward, in frustration and worry.

'No, there's no need for that just yet. Let's wait and see, eh?' Hannah said, pushing the kettle further into the fire.

Not knowing what to do with himself, Jack had got

the teacups out of the pantry and was measuring the tea into the pot. 'Tell me exactly what they said, pet, this Air Ministry or whatever they call themselves?'

Rene took a deep breath. 'The man . . . a very nice man, said that they'd got some information from the man who's come back, somebody Tucker . . . "Tuck" his nickname is . . . Anyway, they'd interviewed him and he'd told them that he remembered two other Spitfires going down. One he said had blown up on impact, but the other, a few minutes later, had seemed, as far as he could tell from up above, to skid through a ploughed field. He'd not seen the outcome before he'd been hit himself. After several days he'd come round in a French farmhouse, with no recollection of who he was. For over a year he'd helped on the farm. He wondered if one of the other two might still be alive. He was pretty sure that the first one would have been a goner!' Rene took another deep breath. 'He figured nobody could have survived that explosion. And Mam, apparently Johnny was on that same mission!'

Listening to this incredible story, Hannah flopped down on to the couch. Jack, left to pour the tea, said in disbelief, 'Well, yer'd think they'd make sure that one of them had survived, and more ter the point, *which* one, before putting you through all this! Tactless, that's what it is.'

'Aww, Dad, ah suppose whichever way they do it, they know it's going to be a huge shock for the family.'

All three sat in silence, each turning over the enormity of what this could mean. Then Rene, who hardly ever swore, suddenly said, '*And* on top of all that I went to see bloody Jessie yesterday, to try to mend some bridges, and she was an absolute bitch! She made it quite plain that she wants nothing more to do with me. And she said she was leaving the village soon. Wished me a nice life with my "too big for his boots" man, even though she's never met him. So all in all I'm totally pissed off!'

If Rene's news hadn't been so serious, Hannah and Jack would have laughed their heads off at her language, but as it was, they just glanced at each other and gulped at their tea.

Jessie's mother didn't know where she was going when she left the house. All Maude knew was that she had to do something to stop her daughter from leaving. Quite apart from anything else, how on earth was she expected to find money for the rent once Jessie had gone? These thoughts were going through her mind as she trudged along the street, when without warning an idea came into her head. 'But she'll hate uz more than ever,' she muttered, 'if ah do that.' Then, answering herself, 'Why, she couldn't hate uz any more than she does now, could she?' Decision made, she continued down the road.

Arriving at Hannah's door, she hesitated a second before knocking loudly.

When Hannah opened the door, you could have knocked her down with a feather. Never, never in a million years would she have expected to see Jessie's mother stood on the doorstep.

'What's happened?' Hannah asked, full of concern. Jack was at work and she was alone in the house.

'Can ah come in a minute?' Jessie's mother was already halfway through the door.

'Sit down, sit down.' Hannah indicated a chair by the table.

Maude glanced around the immaculate living room and sat down, resting one hand on the table and holding her head with the other.

'It's our Jessie, she's leavin' the village,' she said, despair and resentment oozing out of every word.

'Oh, ah'm sorry ter hear that.' Hannah made out that she didn't already know.

'Well, ah ask yer, what am ah s'pposed ter do?' Her arms were outstretched in a gesture of hopelessness. 'Ah'll have ter go in a home 'cause ah'll have no means of support like.' Dejected and demoralized, she sat there, head down. Hannah couldn't help but think, uncharitably: Well at least she'd be encouraged ter keep herself clean in a home. But instead, she said, 'Oh noo! It'll not come to that, ah'm sure . . . Maybe Jess will have a change of heart when she's had time ter think and she'll realize how badly it will affect yer if she goes, eh?'

Even as Hannah was speaking, she couldn't help but

wonder why on earth Maude had come to her to talk about this. She'd have to ask.

'Was there something that yer thought ah might be able ter help yer with?' Dreading the answer, she waited.

'Well, ah thought, if your Rene could give our Jessie a job, in 'er shop like, then she would think she'd come up a bit in the world and she would stay.'

Hannah sat back on the couch. She'd never expected to be asked such a thing, or to be put on the spot like this.

'Well, ah've got ter say yer've put me in a bit of a fix there . . . Our Rene and your Jess don't even get on. How could they work together? And even if they weren't at loggerheads, ah think our Rene is fully staffed.'

They stared at each other for a moment. Maude's lips formed a straight tight line, and before she could say anything Hannah said, 'Look, ah'm really, really sorry about what's happened, but Rene can't sack somebody just ter make way fer your Jessie, now can she?' Hannah had added this last bit more lightly, but Jessie's mother was having none of it.

'If yer just give uz Rene's shop phone number, ah'll make sure that that French lass of your Tom's has a better time of it.'

Hannah, shocked and puzzled at what she'd just implied, snapped back, 'What do yer mean, make sure Maddie has a better time of it?'

'Exactly what ah said,' was the curt response.

'You'll have ter do better than that!' Incensed now, Hannah added sharply, 'Don't you try ter blackmail me with yer threats, 'cause two can play at that game! Ah'm sure yer don't want our Tom calling round yours, now do yer?' She gave this woman a look, telling her that Tom would be a force to be reckoned with.

'Huh, Tom bloody Dawson, 'ee doesn't frighten me.' Maude's voice was full of bravado.

'Just go, will yer.' Hannah couldn't continue this childish exchange any longer.

'Well, ah'm sorry ter have bothered yer, ah'm sure. Ah'll have ter go ter Bishop and inter the shop ter see the *manageress* meself then.' She made sure that Rene's title was given the sarcasm she felt it deserved. Looking Hannah straight in the eyes for a second, she added threateningly, 'Remember what ah said!' And with that she was gone, leaving the back door wide open.

'*Well!*' Hannah exclaimed to herself. 'Not so much as a thank you, or a kiss my backside!'

'Is that you talkin' ter yerself again, wifey?' Jack peeped round the door to where Hannah sat motionless on the couch.

'Oh Jack! Ah didn't expect yer back from work yet!' Hannah went to get up.

'Noo, stay where yer are, hinny, there's obviously summat on yer mind. Come on, spill it then,' he said, the twinkle in his eyes emphasized by the black coal dust covering the rest of his face.

By the time she'd related what had just happened, Jack was already on his feet, saying, 'Right, ah'm not havin' that, it's tantamount ter blackmail, man! Ah'm off round there ter see her.'

'Jack! Jack, no!' she called after him, but he was up the road and out of sight before she'd come out of the back yard.

Chapter 19

Bishop Auckland

Unable to sleep, Rene had tossed and turned for most of the night.

In her nightmare, she'd seen Johnny in the distance, immaculate in his Air Force uniform, his arms held out towards her – but she couldn't move, not while Rob was holding on to her arm so fiercely.

It was no good, she wasn't going to sleep now. She swung her legs over the side of the bed, pushed her feet into her slippers and pulled on her dressing gown.

She couldn't help but dwell on what might be about to happen. But neither could she allow herself to think that it might be true. The possibility that Johnny could still be still alive was beyond belief.

Feeling deeply troubled as to why, in her dream, she hadn't tried harder to get to Johnny, she wandered into the kitchen, where in a trance-like state she put the kettle on and lit a cigarette. As she paced around the room waiting for the kettle to boil, without warning her legs began to give way beneath her. Afraid she was about to faint, she grabbed the edge of the table for support.

'Phew!' She shook her head in an effort to clear it. Probably because I haven't smoked for such a long time, she thought. Cigarette in the middle of the night, not good, she chastised herself.

But half an hour later, when she had to run to the toilet, feeling not for the first time recently that she was about to vomit, her mind began to work in another direction altogether.

Evenwood

Jessie brushed past her mother as she came into the living room, carrying an armful of newly washed clothes. They were neatly folded but not ironed. Feeling her mother's eyes on her, she placed the clothes carefully in her suitcase, while her mother sat in the armchair quietly watching.

There had been a calm in the house since their last bust-up. Both knew that they'd overstepped the mark with their insults, and rather than apologize, they'd dealt with it by becoming resentfully civil towards each other.

'So ye're definitely goin' then?'

'Yes, Mother, I am. Surely ah don't need ter explain why ah have ter get away?'

'Well ah never thought ah'd say it, but it's goin' ter be quiet around here without listenin' ter yer complainin' about summat or t'other.'

'And when have you ever *listened* ter my complaints?' Jessie said, but without malice this time. She almost smiled, but unable to bring herself to smile in a genuine way at her mother, she just said, 'Look, Mam, we'll both be better off away from each other. We can't live in the same house any more, and neither can ah live in the same village as *him*.'

'Yer mean as *her*, don't yer?'

'Ah mean all three of them, soon ter be four. There's only so much ah can take, yer know.'

'Yer've still got friends here surely?' Maude was clutching at straws now.

'No, ah haven't!' she exploded, then feigning a posh voice she added, 'Rene's gone on to grander things, she doesn't want to hang around with the likes of me, now you know.'

'What about yer friends at work then?' her mother persisted.

Jessie didn't really have any friends at work. Tiring of this discussion, she answered, 'Well, what about them?'

Maude, for once taking the hint that any further chat would be painful, said finally, 'Well, make sure yer don't just disappear. Let uz know which day ye're goin', will yer?'

'You'll be the first ter know, Mother,' she said, before adding coldly and somewhat mysteriously, 'And *them* . . . they'll know an' all.'

Maude had decided not to say anything to Jessie about her visit to the Dawsons' house. She would get a bus to Bishop tomorrow morning, and by the time she got back, the thing would be done: Jessie would have a job in Rene's shop. That would surely change her mind about going away, and it would be better than that thankless job she had in that bloody telephone exchange, just sitting there on her arse gasbagging all day. And if she played it right, she'd get more than the pittance they paid. Maude rubbed her hands together at the thought.

Bang! Bang! Bang! She shot out of the chair at the commotion outside the front door.

''Ang on! 'Ang on, will yer,' she called to whichever impatient git was out there. She'd give them a piece of her mind, she would, frightening the life out of her like that.

She yanked the door open and Jack almost fell over her, so heavily was he leaning on it.

As he straightened himself up in the passageway, he grabbed her arm and pulled her towards the living room. 'Get yer arse in here, you!'

The racket brought Jessie running down the stairs.

'What the *hell* is going on in here?' She stopped abruptly when she saw Jack standing in the middle of the room, his coal-blackened face only serving to emphasize the fierceness of his anger. She'd never seen him in this house before. Or so mad, come to that.

'What's this about, Mother?'

'Yer might well ask,' Jack yelled.

His penetrating glare chilled Maude to the core.

Jack had never hit a woman in his life, but by God, if ever he wanted to, it was now.

Instead, forcing himself to exercise some control, he pointed first at Maude then circled his finger until it rested on Jessie. With an eerie calm, he said, 'Ah'm on ter you, so yer'd better watch yer step . . . the pair of yer.'

His glare held them both motionless for a moment. He turned and walked out of the front door.

'Well! You've got some explainin' ter do, Mother.' With arms folded, Jessie stood in front of her mother, waiting.

Knowing that there was no point in trying to lie her way through it, Maude related what she'd done, making it sound as unselfish as she could. Jessie, not remotely taken in by her supposed reasons, interrupted sharply, 'And you actually thought I'd be willin' ter go ter work for that upstart? And yer actually told Hannah that you'd make sure that that French piece had an easier time of it, if Rene gave me a job?' Jessie's voice had risen dramatically.

'Well, ah couldn't stand her lookin' down her nose at uz, so ah had ter say summat ter make her sit up and listen!'

'And just what made you think that yer could help that French lass out then, eh Ma? And more ter the point, what makes yer think she needs helpin' out?'

'Aw come on, Jess, ah know that yer've been up ter summat. Ah could have got yer to stop whatever it is ye're up to, in return fer the job.'

Jessie leaned right in towards her mother now, and snarled through gritted teeth, 'You know nothing! So just keep *this* out of it,' and she tapped twice on the side of her nose.

At that, Jessie turned abruptly away, yanking her coat and handbag from the hook behind the door, while Maude puffed on her cigarette. 'What are yer doin' now?' she asked shakily.

With a scowl, Jessie turned to her and said, 'Right now, Mother, if I stay here a minute longer, ah'm goin' ter do something ah might regret. Ah'm off!'

Chapter 20

Bishop Auckland

Rene looked lovingly at Rob, who was perusing the newspaper, and thought, yet again: How much longer can I put it off? I have to tell him, but how?

'Look!' he said, putting his paper down on the table and pointing at her cup. 'You've let your coffee get cold, I'll pour you some fresh.'

As he rose to pick up her cup, Rene reached over the table and gently placed her hand over his. 'No, Rob, leave it a minute. Sit back down, will you.'

'Oh, do I need to be worried?' he said, concerned at the seriousness of Rene's tone.

'I don't know how to say this, Rob, other than to come straight out with it.'

Rob gripped her hand. 'What? What is it, pet?'

Seeing the genuine concern and distress in his eyes, Rene burst into floods of tears. Hardly able to speak, she stuttered, 'I . . . I'm preg . . . pregnant.'

With a leap, Rob was out of the chair, pulling Rene up from hers and into his arms. 'Are you quite sure?' His voice had suddenly increased a pitch or two.

Surprised by his exuberance, Rene replied, 'As sure as I can be . . . Are you pleased then?'

'Pleased! I'm over the moon, aren't you?' He swung her round.

'Steady, Rob, if you don't want me to throw up all over you.'

'Sorry, pet.' Rob placed her gently back on the floor.

'The thing is, Rob, we're in no position to have a baby . . . What do we tell Jeannie and Ian? And even worse, what if Johnny *is* still out there somewhere?'

'As far as the children are concerned, they're surprisingly adaptable. Once they get used to the idea, I think they will be thrilled to bits, if not rather embarrassed.' He smiled.

'And Johnny?' she prompted him.

'Well, pet, all I can say is that we'll have to cross that bridge if and when we get to it.'

The bridge was to be crossed much sooner than they knew.

'I've come to talk to you about a very delicate matter, Mrs Miller.' The uniformed man at the door looked kind enough, but Rene's heart was thumping wildly. He had no need to tell her what it was about . . . she knew.

'Come in, Mr . . . ?

'Oh sorry, it's Officer Jeffries, British Military.' He held out his hand.

'It's OK, I know where you're from.' She stood to one side to allow him to pass. Closing her eyes moment-arily, she pushed the door to, turned back to face him and as pleasantly as she could she said, 'Come this way.' She walked ahead, leading him through the shop and up the stairs to her flat.

'Please sit down.' She gestured towards a chair at the table rather than an armchair. Pulling out a chair for herself, she perched nervously on the edge and waited.

'Sorry we couldn't go into more detail on the phone, Mrs Miller, but you understand, the authorities thought it might be easier for you if someone came to talk to you in person.'

Why is he wittering on? she wondered, but what she said was, 'Please, just tell me.'

'OK . . . It's your husband, Johnny—'

'He's alive.' Her interruption had come out in a whisper. It was amazing, she thought, how after all the years of hoping, of loneliness and of longing, she actually felt nothing more at this moment than the tingles permeating her numb body. She'd imagined so many times how it would be, if ever Johnny did come back. She'd always seen it as a beautiful dream, where everyone lived happily ever after. But this? This was a nightmare.

Neither spoke for at least a full minute.

It was Officer Jeffries who broke the silence. 'Can I make you a cup of tea ... or something stronger, maybe?'

'No, no, I'll do it, sorry.' Rene desperately needed to do *something*! Anything, so she didn't have to think.

Sensing the bewilderment slowly inching its way into her world, Officer Jeffries said, 'I'm so sorry, Mrs Miller, I can see what a shock this is for you. I'm at a bit of a loss as to what to say myself. Kathy, the lady who was supposed to come with me, is away sick. She would have been much more of a comfort than me on my own.'

Rene looked over to him and smiled. 'I'll be OK in a minute. As soon as I get my head straightened out. It's strange because, after your call, I was sort of expecting it. But having it confirmed like this makes it all so real. It's ridiculous, I should be rejoicing; after all, it's not as though you've come to tell me he's dead!'

'I would think that the shock could be just as great as if he had died. I have only once before been called upon to inform a family that their loved one, presumed dead, wasn't dead after all, and I can tell you, they were as much at sixes and sevens as you are.'

Rene finished filling the kettle and placed it on the hob. She took a cup from the cabinet and promptly dropped it. Her hands shaking, she stood there in silence. Officer Jeffries rushed over to her. 'Here, let me see to it. You sit yourself down.' He led her back to her chair at the table.

By way of thanks, she pointed. 'The tea is in the caddy on the second shelf there.'

Two cups of tea were poured, the second laced with more than a drop of cooking sherry, the only alcohol he could find. 'Shame it's not brandy, but get it down yer,' he said lightly. 'This ongoing rationing's got something to answer for, eh? Anyway, I must tell you it's our base that has been in touch with Johnny, not me personally. The information we have now is that the squadron were flying over the colossal sand dunes of Berck-sur-Mer . . .' Seeing her puzzled look he explained, 'Er, northern France, Pas-de-Calais. Fire was coming from all directions, he was hit and his engine failed. He got down to about two hundred feet, went into a spin and by some miracle dropped right way up into a ploughed field. Last thing he remembers is skidding through hedges, legs trapped between his seat and the cockpit wall. It's more than likely he would have taken a bash on the head. Lots of trees in the area, you know. Could have been hit by something as simple as a branch.' Jeffries stopped here for a moment, waiting for some comment from Mrs Miller. When there was none, he continued. 'We knew he'd gone down, but with all the firing and commotion it was impossible for anyone to see where, or what exactly happened. Two of them went down at around the same time. One pilot stood no chance, plane exploded before landing.' He went quiet for a moment.

Rene said gently, 'His is the family who should be comforted, not me. What have I got to be devastated about?' She suddenly felt very guilty.

'His family have been informed.' He pondered for a moment. 'It's all so difficult . . . telling the relatives, I mean . . . even more so after all this time has gone by. The mission was only meant to take an hour and a half.'

'Yes. I can't imagine . . . It must be hell.' She went quiet. 'So, what I can't understand is why no one tried to find out if anyone survived the two crashes at the time?'

'It was impossible . . . There'd been a terrific mix-up over the Channel, you see.'

Surprised that Officer Jeffries seemed about to give her a detailed account, Rene sat very still and waited.

'The Germans were attacking a convoy of ships, our ships. Johnny's squadron had been sent up to defend them. The report that came in said it was impossible to tell which were our planes and which were German. Machine-gun fire, bombs, smoke . . . I'm sure you can imagine.' Officer Jeffries looked at her intently.

Rene swallowed hard. 'Yes, but only from the news-reels I've seen at the pictures.'

He continued, 'There was another fight going on a few thousand feet above their heads. Flying Officer Miller . . . er, Johnny, remembers, before he came down, that he hit a Messerschmitt . . . He watched it going down, completely out of control, then saw the pilot bail out by parachute, down, down he went, somewhere close to the French coast. The last thing he remembers was the terrific column of water as the plane smashed into the sea, for at that very moment Johnny was hit himself.'

'Just like him,' Rene said with some affection. 'He probably lost concentration, wondering what had happened to the pilot who bailed out. For that split second, he would have seen him as a man, a human being, not just the enemy, and now he's paid for it . . . God! This bloody war.'

'I know, I know. Trouble was that there was no trace of anything in the area afterwards. Turns out that the farmer who pulled Johnny out of the wreckage had the plane broken up and hidden deep in the woods . . . out of sight of the Germans on the ground, you see. The family would have been slaughtered if a British airman had been discovered hidden in the house. I think by now Johnny will be feeling a very close connection to this family who risked so much to save him. I expect he will be very fond of them, possibly just as fond as he once was of his own family . . .'

'Oh!' Rene hadn't even thought of this.

'Just felt I should warn you, that's all,' Officer Jeffries said kindly.

'Yes, thank you. How selfish of me not to have even considered that possibility.'

'Well, we can't be expected to know what it was really like out there. The French had to live alongside the detested Germans, not daring to put a foot out of place but determined to go about their daily business. They had their living to earn. Trouble was, many of the French were connected to the Resistance, one way or another, and the Germans were aware of that fact . . . For all we know, some of the family who saved Johnny may have been members.' He shrugged.

'So . . . what's the procedure now?' she asked tentatively. 'In circumstances like this, I mean?' Inspired by thoughts of the bravery of this family, Rene decided that she must stop fretting and get to grips with the situation.

'Well, if you both, that's you *and* Johnny, want to follow this up, we can arrange for you to meet at our RAF base down at Hornchurch, just outside London. You would need to get yourself there, of course.'

'Yes . . . yes, I understand. And yes, I would want to follow this up . . . I couldn't live with myself if I didn't. For Jeannie's sake as well as my own, I must see him.' Before she'd finished saying this, her stomach was in knots.

'OK.' He rummaged in his pocket and pulled out a

card with a name and contact number on it. As he handed it to her he said, 'It won't be me that you see when you get there. My job is done, so to speak. But you will be well looked after, they're a good crowd down there, so don't worry.'

Rene took the card and led the officer back down the stairs and through the shop. Stopping at the front door, they shook hands. 'Good luck,' he said. 'I hope it all turns out the way you want it to.'

As he climbed into his car, Rene raised her hand, waved and smiled a silent goodbye to the new life she had tried to make for herself and Jeannie.

Hornchurch, two weeks later

In an effort to control her trembling body, Rene walked rapidly towards him, taking in his whole appearance at a glance. She was suddenly flooded with sympathy for this man before her, who bore no resemblance to the man she'd married twelve years earlier.

His overcoat he'd obviously been given, too large, hung precariously around his now tiny frame, making him look unkempt, although she did notice the shadow of a crease down the front of his grey trousers. Even with his slight stoop, and her in high heels, he was still at least four inches taller than her.

Her eyes brimming with tears, she reached up and

kissed him on the cheek. It felt strange, wrong even. This once dapper young man whom she'd loved so much, and grieved for, for so long, was a stranger to her.

'Hello, Johnny,' she said with a casualness that belied this momentous meeting.

She thought about how, when the official from the Air Ministry had contacted her to ask if she wanted to see Johnny, her legs had turned to jelly. But how could she not take this opportunity to find out if it really was him? Just like the other airman, he had been found living and working on a farm in northern France.

And now here he was in front of her, and she could feel no glimmer of the love and desire she had once felt for him.

As for Johnny, he looked confused as he studied her closely. 'Oh God, how am I supposed to talk to you, Rene? I don't really know you. All I really know about my past is what I've been told.'

Rene took hold of his hand and looked into his eyes. 'Do you remember *anything*? Anything at all?'

'Bits, but not really joined-together bits, if that makes sense.'

'Yes, it makes sense, Johnny.' She felt so sad for him that she wanted to fling her arms around him and tell him that everything would be OK.

But she knew that it wouldn't be OK, not as far as he and she were concerned.

Seating himself at the table, where Martha, a kind

lady who worked in the office, had placed two mugs of tea and a saucer of biscuits, Johnny pulled a photograph from his wallet. As he proffered it to Rene he said, 'This is the family who have looked after me, ever since they found me and my Spitfire in their ploughed field.' He smiled, and for the first time Rene saw a semblance of the man she once knew.

'Do you remember that you have a daughter?' she ventured, as she in turn handed him a photograph and watched as his eyes filled up. He sat for quite a while, just staring at the photograph.

Rene, desperate to break the embarrassing silence, was about to speak, when suddenly he spoke up. 'Jeannie,' he said, dropping the photograph to the floor.

As they bent together to pick it up, Rene pressed the picture into his hand. 'Keep it,' she said quietly.

Johnny smiled briefly, and placed the picture carefully in his pocket.

When at first the strange sound came from his open mouth, Rene thought he was about to laugh. But this was no laugh: it was the distressing sound of a broken man, howling like an injured animal.

Shocked at this sudden outburst, Rene was uncertain how to react at first. Then, when the inarticulate sounds turned into gasping sobs, she jumped up and flung her arms around him. When he tightened his arms around her, her own tears fell and his terror seeped through, saturating her own body. 'Shush, shush,' she soothed, as best she could.

The door opened, and with concern and question in her expression Martha from the next room looked in, but Rene held up her hand to let her know that she could cope. The other woman quietly closed the door, leaving them to a situation that she had most probably come across before.

Slowly, slowly, the sobs subsided, until there was just a sporadic gasp. Feeling mortified now, Johnny looked at Rene, the horror of what had just happened etched on his face.

'Oh God! I'm so sorry, Rene, it's a long time since I've done that. Used to happen all the time at first, you know. But if I'd had any idea it might happen today, I wouldn't have come and put you through that embarrassment.'

'Please don't feel awkward, Johnny. I'm not embarrassed, I'm sad. Sad for what you've been through, sad that we find ourselves in this position, and sad that all this time I didn't know that you were alive. I hoped . . . oh *God*, how I hoped! But as time went on I had to come to terms with the fact that you would never come back. I grieved for you, Johnny . . . and how. And now here you are, alive, and I don't know how to be.'

Seeing how Johnny's hands trembled, Rene leaned over and took both of them firmly in hers.

Johnny looked into her pleading eyes. 'Neither one of

us knows how to be, Rene . . . but take another look!' He leaned towards the table and held out the photograph he had brought, showing himself with the group of people on the French farm. 'I am happy there, Rene, see for yourself.'

Rene took the photo and looked again at the French family, who were so obviously now *his* family. What jumped out at her this time, much more plainly than before, was that in the line-up of mainly older people, Johnny's arm was draped around an attractive young woman who was leaning in towards him. She wondered briefly if he had chosen this photograph especially, to tell her something.

'What a lovely-looking family,' Rene said, adding carefully, 'and I can see that you are all very close. You must have been through a lot together, and it's good to see that you had someone near to your own age too.'

Johnny looked awkward and shifted in his seat.

'Oh Johnny . . . Johnny, it's OK! It really is!' She took hold of his hands again, to confirm how genuinely she meant every word.

'You're very kind, Rene, and I can see what must have attracted me to you all those years ago. But I have a different life now, and I'm not sure that I could . . . or that I would want to change that now.'

'Johnny, I don't want or expect you to change anything. You must go back to your life in France, and the lovely lady in the picture.' She smiled knowingly.

'Colette, she's called Colette.' He relaxed a little as he told her this, enough for Rene to say, 'That's a lovely name . . . I too have a new life, Johnny, and also a close friend. His name is Rob.'

'That's wonderful, really wonderful . . .' He slapped his knee with surprising enthusiasm, although Rene suspected it was probably out of relief. 'Maybe we could all meet some time . . .' He suddenly stopped. 'Oh, how insensitive of me, you would probably prefer a clean break. Sorry, I'm not thinking straight!'

'No . . . no Johnny, I'm pleased that you asked me that. It would be much too final to say goodbye now, here in this strange little room.' She looked around at the dingy office, furnished only with the table and the chairs they sat in, then turned back to him with a smile. 'Anyway, what about Jeannie? She will want to see you, I'm sure . . . well, once she gets over the shock, of course.'

At the mention of his daughter, the old Johnny seemed to emerge. The stress that this meeting must have caused him appeared to be easing, and he looked quite different fom how he'd looked an hour or so ago, when they'd first met.

Rene wondered if he thought the same about her, as she also was feeling easier in his presence. But not easy enough to tell him about her pregnancy, no . . . this wasn't the right time, she decided. Nor was she going to tell Jeannie, just yet, that her dad was alive and living in

France. No, she would bide her time. It would be enough for Jeannie to come to terms with the fact that she was going to have a little brother or sister.

But she *would* tell Jeannie about her dad, when the time was right – and then she couldn't see why they shouldn't all meet up. So, as if confirming it to herself, she reiterated what she'd just said. 'Yes, Johnny, I would love that, and once I've told Jeannie, I'm sure she would too. But it may take time . . . you understand, don't you?'

'Of course I do, but try not to leave it *too* long.' He smiled. 'It would be nice to see my daughter while she's still a little girl.'

'I don't think that Jeannie has ever been a little girl,' Rene said affectionately. 'Eleven, and she's far too old for her own good, that one!'

During the next hour they had a pleasant if slightly disjointed conversation about what had happened over the last few years. He told Rene how frustrated he'd been at not being able to talk to his rescuers, not only because of the language barrier. If he didn't know who he was, what did he have to talk about?

'I could hear them all downstairs, talking fast, very fast – well, it sounded more like jabbering to me – when all I could do, in those early days, was lie in bed, wondering where I was, who I was and what they could be talking about. I might as well have been on the moon! But . . .' he said suddenly, 'I was so lucky that some members of the family were able to speak a few words of English. And because of that, with a lot of help . . . from Colette in particular, I can now conduct a reasonable conversation in French. Technicalities excluded, of course.' Rene could see the pride in his eyes, as he laughed lightly.

'Of course!' Rene couldn't fail to be impressed, as she laughed gently with him.

'How about you?' he asked now. 'What have you been up to?'

Although he had no recollection at all that Rene was involved in fashion, he listened intently, and with interest, as she described how she'd risen to the position of manageress, with living accommodation for herself and Jeannie above the shop.

'That would explain your stylish sense of dress,' he said. 'Being in the fashion trade, I mean.'

Rene felt a slight reddening of her cheeks at the compliment.

He looked down at his own clothes and grinned. 'I'm afraid I dress as a farmer. All my clothes were originally hand-me-downs from Colette's brother – she has two brothers,' he offered. 'But now, even if I buy an item of clothing, I have to think practical, which doesn't lend itself to fashion, as you can see.' He shrugged his shoulders, palms outstretched, and it was at that moment that Rene saw, really saw, that he had become a Frenchman.

They talked amiably for a while, but as the conversation went on Rene found it increasingly difficult not to include Rob's name in almost every sentence. This meeting should be all about me and Johnny, she told herself, and thinking that Johnny was probably experiencing the same with regard to Colette, she started to look for ways to end the meeting. There was a gentle knock on the door and Martha entered. This time she offered them a sandwich and a pot of strong tea.

Trying not to look too relieved by the interruption, both of them accepted eagerly. The eating process helped to diffuse the intensity of the conversation a little and they continued to talk, each making an effort to skirt around the two main people in their lives. He talked about the farm, and how he'd taken to farm life 'as a duck to water'.

Rene talked about the town of Bishop Auckland, about Tom, and how he was now married to a French girl, with a daughter of his own. She went on to mention other family members, her mam and dad, and what they were up to, all the time looking and hoping for a glimmer of recognition from Johnny. But it was only at the mention of Tom's name that she detected a warming in his eyes.

'Strange,' he said, 'both of us ending up with a French girl . . .' But he said nothing more on the subject. The second of recognition had been snuffed out.

'What do we do now then?' His question was sudden.

'I haven't let myself think that far ahead, Johnny,' she answered, knowing that he wasn't referring to right now but to their future.

'I know that this sounds awful, but can you give me some time to get my head around all this?' she asked. 'If you want to divorce, I won't stand in your way. It's just that I don't want Jeannie to think that I've abandoned her daddy.'

'To tell you the truth I was hoping you'd say that. We'll be fine as we are for a while longer, I'm sure, and if the time comes when either of us wants to marry again, maybe we can discuss it?' He raised his eyebrows in question.

'That's settled then.' She smiled and took hold of his hand. 'I can't tell you, Johnny, how happy I am that you're alive, and that you are happy.'

He gripped her hand and smiled back.

Seeing that he was too full up to say anything, Rene quickly put in, 'I will write a few things down for you before I leave. Names of family members, for instance. Their ages, what they do, etc. Maybe it will help you remember. I just feel that I need to do something to help you to know who you are.' She stopped for a moment before adding, 'Or were.'

'I think that's a great idea.' He nodded. 'I'll study it on my way home.'

Rene couldn't quell the peculiar feeling in the pit of

her stomach when she heard him refer to the farm in France as home. She took a pen and paper from her handbag and wrote down the names and details as promised, while he quietly sipped at his tea. After handing him the piece of paper, she pulled him towards her and hugged him tightly. 'Be lucky,' she said.

'You too, Rene.' Gripping both of her hands in his now, he looked into her eyes. 'I'm so very sorry.' Rene knew that he was feeling some kind of connection; something similar had happened to her as she'd hugged him not a second before.

The brief conversation after that seemed to steer itself easily and naturally to a close.

Johnny, who was sailing from Dover to France the following morning, was momentarily comforted by the November sun on his back as he headed towards the black car where the companion he'd travelled with was waiting.

Rene walked towards the underground station. She would take the tube into London, where she had arranged to meet Rob.

After a few paces she couldn't resist glancing over her shoulder, and there was Johnny, standing next to the car, watching. With a final smile, he raised his hand, climbed into the vehicle and was gone from sight.

Rene settled herself down on the train for the short journey into London. As tired as she was, she was looking forward to meeting Rob there, but at the same time her mind was muddled.

After dropping Rene off at the station that morning, Rob had spent the day sightseeing in London, but not without a troubled mind. His concern was not only for Rene and how she must be feeling about this encounter, but if he was honest with himself, his thoughts were playing havoc in other directions. What if her feelings for her husband were rekindled? The thought kept on popping into his head at the most inopportune moments. Maybe this meeting would bring alive all the old emotions, along with everything that went before? After chastising himself for being selfish, he'd immediately wonder whether selfishness could be bad when you loved someone so much. Rob shook his head. He'd thought he would never find a love to match that which he'd had for his dear wife, Isabelle. And now here he was, terrified that he might lose this wonderful woman, the woman who'd turned his life around almost from the moment they'd met. And it was all thanks to their amazingly perceptive children.

For a moment Rob wanted to laugh at the ridiculousness of his concerns. Rene wasn't that fickle, he knew that in his heart of hearts. If anything, she was likely to be confused, and deeply saddened, by the whole affair. He was expecting that, and that was why he'd chosen for them to spend the night in what he'd described to her, as a 'posh' hotel. He hoped that it would help to relax her after an extremely unusual day, before they took to the road the following morning for their journey back to Bishop Auckland.

Chapter 21

Evenwood

Rene had been and gone, and Hannah, too restless to sit still on the couch, got to her feet and paced around her living room. It was all a bit too much to take in. Not only had Rene seen Johnny but she was pregnant, and she and Rob were really happy about it, by all accounts! How Jeannie was going to take the news, Hannah couldn't imagine.

Hannah had lived through some tough times with Rene, especially when she'd first heard that Johnny was missing in action, a kinder way of saying 'dead' as far as Hannah was concerned. Even so, she had always tried to be optimistic, at least in front of Rene. And then they'd discovered that he was still alive after all, and now Rene was talking about divorce! How things had changed, and what Jack would have to say about it all didn't bear thinking about. But then he would remember, like all of them, she supposed, just how happy Rob had made Rene over these last months . . . Oh, it was all such a mess. And then there was that poor lass Maddie, desperate to get home to France, and Tom workin' all the hours that God sent, to afford a motor-bike and sidecar, so he could get her there more frequently.

Jeannie had taken to answering back and being a bit deceitful just lately. She could do with more discipline in her life, that's for sure, Hannah thought. Not like before though, when Rene was on at her all the time, about etiquette and all that stuff. But it had gone the other way now, since Rob had been around, taking Rene here, there and everywhere and sweeping her off her feet. Well, he'd swept her off her feet all right, because here she was now, expectin' his bairn, and her husband come back to life!

'Hannah! Hannah!' Jack broke in on her thoughts as he came in through the back door, black as soot, while the rainwater made white rivulets through the coal dust matted on his cheeks.

'Oh Jack!' Hannah leapt up from the chair. 'Look at the mess on the floor. Stay by the door till yer get yer boots off, will yer.'

'It's pissin' down out there, man.' Jack dragged his work coat off, and hung it to drip on the back-door hook. Hannah rushed to put some old newspapers under it and sat him on the stool next to the door, where, during the kerfuffle of helping him to pull his boots off, casually as you like, the words just tumbled out of her mouth. 'Our Rene's pregnant.'

Jack sat looking at her in stunned silence.

'Yes . . . you heard right, and there's more.'

'More?'

'Johnny's still alive.'

Jack couldn't get straight in his head which bit of news had created the biggest shock; one seemed to be cancelling the other out. Picking up on the second bit of information, he exclaimed, 'Johnny's alive! Eee, that's grand news!' He looked at Hannah again. 'Isn't it?'

'Well, work it out fer yerself. Of course it's grand news for Johnny, but what about our Jeannie? And just when she's got used ter havin' Rob around.'

'Where's our Jeannie now then?'

'She's at Maddie's. Rene's gone round there to fetch her back, armed with an umbrella and a raincoat for her.'

Unknown to Hannah, Jeannie, wrapped in the raincoat, had been sent back ahead of her mother, who wanted a word with Maddie about something private, she'd said. Well, after what Jeannie had just heard her gran and granddad talking about, it wasn't private any more.

They'd been making such a racket, rattling about with the pans of water that had been heating on the fire, then tipping the hot water into the cold to get it nice and warm for granddad so he could wash the coal dust off himself. They'd carried on talking and hadn't heard her come in. She'd been just about to open the door from the scullery into the living room when she'd been stopped in her tracks. Hearing the name Johnny, she'd stood there wide-eyed. Johnny was her dad's name, she didn't know any other Johnnies, so she had listened through the crack in the closed door.

By what she'd understood, her dad was still alive, and living in France with another family. She felt her tummy lurch. She had to slap her hand over her mouth and swallow hard to stop herself from being sick, right there in the scullery. *How could he?* The tears were running over the hand slapped to her face. How could he want to live with another family, when they'd waited so long for him? What about her? And what about her mam?

But it was the next thing she heard that had made her slide down the wall to the floor. They were talking about a baby, her mam's baby! She just sat there, for what seemed like ages. She must be dreaming; people were fat when they were having a bairn and Mam definitely wasn't fat!

She was so vexed with her gran and granddad that she didn't want to talk to them. She didn't want to talk to her mam when she got back either. Huh! Bet that was why she wanted rid of me over at Maddie's, Jeannie thought. Probably telling her all about it. Probably everybody knows except me! She wanted to cry some more but however tightly she squeezed her eyes no more tears would come. Shaking, she peered through the crack in the door again. She could see Granddad with his back to her splashing about in the half-filled tin bath, and no sign of Gran. She guessed that she must have popped upstairs to get some aired towels from the cupboard up there.

The fire was crackling away noisily, having been stoked up to keep Granddad warm, and as she looked through the gap in the door, there, just to her left, she caught sight of the magic cupboard . . . Granddad's magic cupboard. She knew that the medicine was kept there, the medicine just for grown-ups that seemed to make everybody feel better when they'd been sad and worried. Well, she thought, ah'm sad and worried, and if it works for them maybe it'll work for me. After all, ah'm nearly grown up, everybody says so.

She managed to push the door open enough to squeeze through, until she was able to reach the cupboard door. Without the need to put both feet into the room, she crouched down and pulled at it.

On her hands and knees now, she reached behind their 'posh' glasses into the back of the cupboard, grabbed the medicine bottle, pushed the door to and gently reversed back into the scullery.

Once in there, she sat on the floor and peered again through the crack in the living-room door. Granddad was still washing himself, but not singing as he usually did. She lifted the bottle and looked at this magic brown stuff. It was half full . . . Should be enough to do the trick, she thought.

This is goin' to make everything that ah've just heard go away. It's lies . . . all lies!

Chapter 22

Struggling to close her umbrella, Rene came stumbling into her parents' house.

'Grief! It's absolutely pouring down out there!'

'Well, that's better phrased than yer dad put it when he came in,' Hannah commented, looking beyond her for Jeannie.

'Bet Jeannie was soaked when she got in too,' Rene said as she struggled out of her dripping coat.

'Jeannie? Ah thought she was with you?' Hannah was still looking beyond her.

'No, I sent her back in advance so I could have a private word with Maddie.' She glanced at her dad, then looked at her mother. Eyebrows raised, she whispered, 'You know what I mean?'

'Yes, and yer dad does too, so there's no need ter whisper . . . Where's our Jeannie then?'

'She probably saw that her grandda was in the bath

and sneaked out of the way, straight up the stairs. I'll go get her,' Rene said.

'Ah was upstairs when yer da was in the bath, and ah didn't hear her.' Hannah was sounding a bit panicky now, so Rene ran up the stairs, calling out, 'Jeannie? Jeannie!'

Rene ran back down the stairs, alarmed herself now. 'It's getting dark outside, where could she be?'

'Maybe she's in the lav?' Hannah grabbed the newspaper to cover her head and rushed out into the back yard. But the toilet door was ajar, with no sign of Jeannie.

Rene looked at her mother. Part of her wanted to laugh at the ridiculousness of the situation, but the other part wanted to run out into the street, yelling her daughter's name. 'She promised she'd come straight back, and that was well over an hour ago!'

'Yer know what she's been like of late, Rene, a bit defiant like.'

If Rene hadn't been so worried she'd have picked her mam up on that declaration, but it would have to wait. Instead, she grabbed her coat and umbrella. 'I'm going out to look for her. I can't go into this right now, Mam.' She looked directly at Hannah, the hurt she felt at the remark apparent on her face.

Her dad, frowning at Hannah, also grabbed his overcoat from its peg just along from his still dripping work coat, and yanked it on as they rushed out of the door.

Hannah stayed behind in case Jeannie turned up. She was just closing the back door behind them when she heard a hiccough. Startled, she looked towards the coal house. Then she heard a movement, and spotted a glimmer of light seeping from under the coal-house door. Even more startling, the light was moving around! She rushed back into the house to get a torch. 'Oh good Lord! There's somebody in the coal hole!' she muttered. She rushed into the scullery, and opened the cupboard door where the torch was usually kept. With no sign of it, she opened all the other cupboard doors. Still unable to find it, she grabbed the first thing to hand.

With the hefty saucepan poised above her head in readiness to bash the intruder, she yanked the coal-hole door open. There lying at her feet, her face as black as the coal itself, was Jeannie, out for the count, torch in one hand and almost empty whisky bottle in the other.

'Oh . . . good . . . Lord!' Those three words kept tumbling from her mouth. 'What on earth? Oh good Lord!' Hannah couldn't comprehend that this obviously drunken young girl was her granddaughter.

In a quandary as to what to do, she tried to pull Jeannie out into the yard, where the puddles were almost ankle deep in places. In desperation Hannah looked around her. Catching sight of the wheelbarrow up against the wall, she dropped Jeannie on to the concrete, brought the barrow over and tipped it on to its side, next to where Jeannie lay on her back with something resembling a smirk on her face.

Hannah tugged and pulled until Jeannie was half in the barrow, then with an almighty heave she managed to get the thing upright. Jeannie was now face down in the barrow, with her arms hanging out on each side. Hannah was wheeling it towards the house when the back gate burst open and Rob, head down against the rain, came rushing in, almost falling over the wheelbarrow in his haste to get into the dry. 'What on earth's going on here?' he said, looking at the scene in disbelief.

'Oh, thank God you're here, Rob. Did you see Rene and Jack in the village?'

'No, I've just come to pick her and Jeannie up to take them home as planned.'

Rob stared down at Jeannie, recognizable only by the yellow ribbon dangling precariously from the flattened wet ringlet on the back of her head. 'Has she had an accident?' he asked, taking hold of the barrow handles.

'No, she's drunk!' Hannah said it in such an odd way that Rob laughed.

Seeing that Hannah hadn't even raised a smile, he pushed the barrow through the back door and bent down to sniff the child's breath. 'This isn't possible,' he muttered.

Hannah explained very briefly what she thought might have happened, and was just telling him how

Rene and Jack were out looking for her when Jeannie began to stir. In an obvious state of confusion, she lifted herself on to her elbows in the barrow and looked around her, then tried to turn herself over to climb out. As Rob and Hannah rushed to steady her, she shrugged free of Rob and held on to Hannah.

Brushing aside his hurt at the rejection, Rob said, 'I'll leave you to get her out of those wet clothes, Hannah, while I go to look for Rene and Jack.'

As soon as Rob was out of the house, Jeannie rushed to the kitchen and hung over the sink, retching noisily several times, but nothing came out.

'We need ter have a good talk, young lady,' Hannah warned in no uncertain terms as she dragged Jeannie towards the bath. 'But for now, get in that water that yer granddad's just got out of.'

'Ugh! The water's all dirty and ah've still got me underclothes on!' Jeannie protested. The look of disgust on her face would have been comical at any other time.

'Get in that bath while it's still warm, my girl, or ah'll throw yer in!' Hannah was in no mood for shilly-shallying.

'Huh! Ye're goin' ter be horrible to uz now that me mam's havin' a *new* bairn. Well, see if ah care. Ah can always go and live with me dad in France!'

With Hannah left standing there open-mouthed, Jeannie rushed back to the kitchen sink, where this time she was able to do the business.

Hannah, dazed with shock at what Jeannie had just said, slowly sat down on a chair by the table. So that's what all this is about, she thought in dismay. She must have come back without us hearing her, and she's heard every word ah was telling Jack. Oh poor bairn, she must be devastated. Hannah's sympathy was beginning to cancel out her initial horror over what had happened, and she asked, in a more subdued tone, 'Why did yer get the whisky, pet?'

'Because it's medicine, and it always makes the grown-ups feel better. But it didn't make me feel better, and it tastes *horrible*, but when ah got used to it ah kept havin' a bit more 'cause ah still wasn't feelin' better, and ah didn't know how much yer needed ter take ter make it work. Then the next thing ah knew ah was upside down, in the wheelbarrer!' Her eyes were wide.

Hannah didn't know whether to laugh or cry. She was clutching the edge of her pinny to wipe her eyes when Rene, Jack and Rob came in, making a right commotion with all their questions.

Hannah put her hand up to stop them. 'We need ter talk,' she said, 'all of us.'

'Not in front of Jeannie, Mam!' Rene was uneasy at her mam's forceful attitude.

'Yes, in front of Jeannie,' Hannah said without hesitation. 'Jeannie knows what's goin' on, she heard me tellin' yer dad and she was so upset that she got the "medicine" out of the cupboard and hid herself in the coal hole to take it. She only wanted to make herself feel better, like the grown-ups.'

'Oh God, Jeannie! What on earth were you thinking of, to do such a thing?' Rene could see the paleness of her daughter's face, even through the blotches of coal dust. 'Come here, pet.' Rene got her out of the bath and wound a towel around her. Pulling her daughter up on to the couch next to her, Rene took the soaped flannel from Rob and gently washed away the remaining patches of coal dust. Hugging Jeannie close, she said, 'I wanted to talk to you about these things, pet, but I hadn't had the chance yet, and I thought it might be too much for you to take in all at once.'

'But what about me dad? What's goin' ter happen ter him?' The despair in Jeannie's big brown eyes as they looked into hers made Rene gasp at her own stupidity in not giving her daughter at least some inkling of what was afoot. And so, while Jack replenished Jeannie's glass of water, Rene explained the whole situation as best she could. When she told her that her dad had made a life with a new family, Jeannie's only question was, 'Does he not remember me then?'

'Well, yes, I think he does, because when I showed him a photograph of you he said your name. So that's good, isn't it?' Rene smiled at her daughter.

'And will we be able ter see him sometimes?'

'Yes, we talked about that as well, and he would like us to go over to France to meet his family.'

Rene glanced at Rob now, and added, 'And your dad knows about Rob. He would like to meet him, and Ian too of course, so we can all go together. What do you think?'

At this Jeannie turned her head towards Rob and smiled self-consciously.

'Now, miss, I think we'd better get you home and to bed. This has been quite a day, and I have a feeling you're going to have a bit of a headache in the morning,' Rene said with a sympathetic smile.

'Ah've got one now, and it's killin' uz. Can ah stay here tonight? It *is* Sunday tomorrow, so no school.'

Rene looked at her mam, who nodded in response. 'Of course she can, ah'll go and make the bed up.'

'Thanks, Gran.' Jeannie smiled.

Chapter 23

'Look, Tom!' Maddie held up her letter from France. 'Dominic is getting married! My little brozer, I can't believe it. But I'm so happy for him, Yvette is a lovely girl.'

Tom looked at the letter. 'That's fantastic news, pet, but you forget I can't read French.' He handed the letter back. 'What else do they say?'

'Well, Simone has taken her exams for the pharmacy, and she thinks she has done quite well. She awaits ze results now. And Martine – my dear sister Martine, who helped me through ze war – has found someone at last! I think she is in love, by ze way she writes . . . see?' She held the letter up to him again. 'Oh, I forget . . .' she said absentmindedly.

As she went on to translate the letter for him, she could see that Tom's mind was elsewhere. She knew that he was worrying about Rene and the predicament she found herself in now. He was also struggling to grasp the fact that Johnny was still alive, and had made his life somewhere else.

Maddie knew that Tom had felt the loss of Johnny as much as anyone else. After all, they'd been such good friends before both had gone off to war. But much worse than all that, she knew how he wished now that he hadn't called in at Rene's flat in Bishop, on his way home that fateful night last week.

All he'd planned on doing was to have a talk with Jeannie, regarding her recent escapade with the alcohol in the coal house, and her new-found, rebellious attitude.

He'd told Maddie how, when he arrived at the shop, Rene was still cashing up at the till downstairs. She'd welcomed him with open arms, relieved to think that a bit of Tom's influence might get through to Jeannie.

'She's upstairs with Ian. I'll only be about ten minutes here, so you go on up,' Rene had said.

Tom had taken the stairs two at a time, as was his way, but when he arrived at the kitchen door, there they were . . . Ian and Jeannie with their arms around each other and kissing full on the lips, totally oblivious to Tom's presence. When they stopped for a moment, Jeannie took Ian by the hand and led him through to the living room, where they fell giggling on to the settee.

'Oh shit!' Tom ran his hand through his hair. How best to handle this situation? He had no idea. To get Rene up there would cause mayhem, and to walk in on them would be embarrassing all around. This was the last thing he'd expected. His mind was in overdrive. Bloody hell, it's not five minutes since they were content to be playin' marbles together! he thought as he peered round the corner.

They seemed to have simmered down a bit, and were only talking and messing about now, in the way that children do. Probably just experimenting, he told himself. But they'd obviously developed ideas above what you would expect from bairns of their ages. Hell, he reminded himself, they're only eleven and thirteen!

Worried that if he didn't interrupt now, they might start their shenanigans again, Tom seized the opportunity, coughed and strode into the room.

'Now then, you two, what are you up to?' he asked in as casual a way as he could muster.

'Tom!' Jeannie jumped up from the couch. 'Ah didn't know you were comin' over!'

'Well, ah thought we might have a bit of a chat, lass, 'cause ah don't see yer very often these days. What with bein' at work all day, then soon as ah've had me tea ah'm off doin' bits and pieces ter the house.' Tom glanced at Ian, who was looking decidedly flushed. 'Now, lad,' Tom said in a stern voice that made Jeannie look up sharply, 'ah was wonderin' if we might have a word on our own, Jeannie?' Jeannie looked from Tom to Ian. Ian, not knowing what to say, just shrugged in response.

'Do yer mind, Ee-an?' she asked, trying to smile while feeling furious with Tom for showing her up in front of Ian. 'Ah'll be seein' yer tomorrow anyway, eh?' she said with a lightness that she certainly didn't feel.

'Ah've got me homework to do anyhow,' Ian replied, looking puzzled at suddenly being turfed out.

As Ian went down the stairs, Tom pulled up a chair, and with no time to waste, knowing that Rene would be up any minute, he said, 'Now look, Jeannie, this isn't why ah came ter see yer, but ah've got ter mention it . . . Ah saw you and Ian in the kitchen when ah came up the stairs.'

Jeannie jumped up from her seat, all pink, defensive and defiant. 'We weren't doin' anything wrong. We just practising, what's wrong with that?'

'Oh Jeannie pet, where do ah start? Ye're so young, all that stuff will come naturally enough in a few years' time no doubt, but in the meantime, there's other stuff yer should be *practisin*' . . . like yer—'

'What, like me homework and stuff? Boring! Ah like Ee-an, and he likes me, so there!' Red in the face now and obviously embarrassed, Jeannie suddenly ran off, bumping straight into her mother at the top of the stairs.

Rene, unable to catch her distraught daughter and not knowing whether to run after her or to find out what was going on from Tom, hovered uncertainly at the top of the stairs.

Tom came running blindly towards the stairs, and before he knew what was happening he felt the collision. He desperately tried to grab her but Rene was past catching, and she tumbled down the top four stairs to the first landing where she lay motionless.

'No . . . noooh!' howled Tom. He was crouching beside his sister, repeating over and over, 'Rene, Rene . . . come on, Rene!' Downstairs, he heard what sounded like one of the fitting-room curtains being pulled open, and the next minute Jeannie had raced out of her hiding place and was by his side on the landing. With unchecked tears streaming down her pale cheeks, she cried, 'Oh Mam! *Mam!* Wake up!' She reached over, as if about to shake her mother. Tom grabbed her arm. 'No, no, don't touch her. Sit by her while I run downstairs to the phone.'

'Hurry up, won't you!' Jeannie looked up at him through her tear-filled eyes.

Listening to Tom almost shouting the address down the phone, followed by, 'What? No, now! We need somebody now! She's pregnant!' Jeannie put her head on her mam's tummy, and sobbed, 'I'm sorry, mam, I'm really, really sorry for bein' such a bad girl.'

Tom came up behind her and pulled her gently away from her mam. 'Here, come here,' he said, pulling her towards him. 'You're not a bad girl, pet, just lost your way a bit, not your fault.'

'But it is my fault, if ah hadn't been doin' *that thing*

you wouldn't have been vexed with me and ah wouldn't have run away, makin' you run after me and then knockin' me mam down the stairs!' Jeannie put her arms tightly around Tom's neck. 'Is she gonna die? Me mam . . . ? Is she gonna die?'

'Not if ah can help it, pet. No, she isn't. The ambulance'll be here in a bit, then we'll get her fixed up, eh?' He struggled through his own fear to console her.

But his assurances hadn't really put her mind at rest, any more than his own.

Rene looked very still now. Tom leaned in until his cheek was over her face, and listened.

'What you doin', our Tom?' Jeannie gasped, trying to pull him away.

'It's all right, pet, ah was just checkin' her breathing.'

'Is she not breathin' then?' Jeannie's voice had risen to a screech.

'Yes, course she's breathin', pet.'

He pulled her closer to him. The only sound now was Jeannie's intermittent sobbing.

'Come on, stop yer blubbering now, pet,' Tom was saying gently, when he heard a loud knock at the door and jumped up from where they'd been huddled on the stairs. 'It's here! Stay with your mam,' he called over his shoulder as he ran down the stairs to let the ambulance men in.

Jeannie could hear Tom explaining to the men as they

ran through the shop. 'Looks as if she hit her head when she fell.'

Within seconds, two men were crouched at Rene's side.

'Don't let her die! Please don't let her die!' Jeannie sobbed.

Tom could see that Jeannie was verging on the hysterical, and rushed to pick her up from the floor. With some difficulty, he led her to the sitting-room couch, where he sat with her, while the medical people lifted Rene on to a stretcher, got her down the stairs and carried her into the ambulance.

Left alone now, the two of them looked at each other. Tom said, 'Right, pet, ah'm going ter get the bus and go ter the hospital—'

'Ah'm comin' too,' Jeannie interrupted.

'No, pet, it's no place for you, not right now any road. Not till we see what's happening.' He put his hand up when she was about to interrupt again.

'So . . . ah'll phone Mrs Parkin and get her ter tell yer gran and granddad what's happened, and yer gran'll more than likely come over ter sit with yer . . .'

'What about Rob?' Jeannie piped up, in a moment of calm. 'He'll need ter know, won't he.'

'Oh aye . . . ye're right, he will. I expect his phone number's here somewhere. Ah'll call him from downstairs.'

'It's in me mam's handbag.' She pointed at the bag where it sat on the floor by Rene's chair. 'Yer'd better take it to her in the hospital 'cause she's lost without it. Her lipstick and stuff's in there,' she said in all seriousness, her own form of common sense momentarily superseding her distress.

Less than an hour later, Tom was arriving at the hospital, with a terrified Rob close behind, and Hannah was at Rene's flat, trying her utmost to hide her distress from a fretting Jeannie.

Maddie put the letter down, and taking in the rigidity of Tom's body as he sat in the armchair opposite, she asked gently, 'Are you thinking about Rene, *chéri*?'

'Yes, it all seems a bit hellish to me. Surely they should have been able to do *something* to save the baby?'

Without speaking, Maddie got up and placed a hand on his shoulder.

Tom remained lost in his thoughts. He lit a cigarette and inhaled deeply, allowing his head to fall back while he watched the smoke billow up to the ceiling.

Maddie herself had cried and cried when they got the news from the hospital. She was so sad for Rene. All the plans they'd made of how Rene's baby and her own would be of a similar age, and how they would play together, all gone, in a moment of tragedy . . .

Tom interrupted her thoughts. 'And then there's Johnny out there in France, not remembering anything about his past life. Strikes me as very odd, that does.'

Tom sounded so incredulous and upset that Maddie quickly put in, 'Maybe it's better that he doesn't, as things have turned out. After all, can you imagine how it would be for Rene and Rob? Especially now that they have lost the baby.' After a moment's thought, Maddie continued, 'Rene is going to need a lot of support when she comes out of hospital, and we must do everything we can to help.'

For the first time, Tom had a glimmer of hope that Maddie was imagining a future life in Evenwood. He turned to her now, saying, 'Aww, pet, does this mean that you might settle down better here in England then?'

'Well, I still must go home for the birth of our baby, Tom.' She looked up at him, concerned that he might try to change her mind. Then she added, 'But Rene will be unable to work for a while, and zer is time for me to help to make things easier for her before I go, *and* when I come back, of course!'

'If ah know anything about our Rene, before we know it she'll be back at work. She's not one for hanging around too long feelin' sorry for herself, and no doubt me mam'll be on hand too if she's needed.'

'Yes, I think you are right. Rene needs to work, but she is going to feel very sad for quite a while, I think.'

That thought, and the knowledge that Rene would need Hannah's services, made Maddie realize just how heavily she herself relied on Hannah, not only for looking after Francine but for companionship too.

'Poor Hannah must be beside herself with grief,' Maddie said now. 'I will go to see her in the morning.'

Tom got up from his chair, threw his cigarette butt into the fire and pulled her towards him. 'Don't look so worried, pet, me mam and dad are dealin' with it in their own way. They've got Jeannie there while Rene's in hospital, so she'll keep them occupied. And after all, pet, they've had all kinds of things ter deal with over the years, and they always get through . . . together like. Just as we will, eh?' He smiled down on her, and as always her heart skipped a beat.

Chapter 24

Bishop Auckland

Jeannie was past consoling. She sat on one side of her mother's bed while Rob sat on the other, occasionally pulling faces at her in an effort to make her smile. But she just got up and went to the kitchen.

'Don't try too hard, my love.' Rene squeezed Rob's hand. 'She blames herself for this, and no amount of reassurance will convince her otherwise at the moment.'

'You are being so good, so brave about all this, Rene,' he said, holding tightly on to her hand.

'I have my moments, but I am still here and I'm thankful for that. I wouldn't want to leave you.' She smiled.

'Oh Rene, don't, love . . .' As he said this, he used the heel of his hand to brush away the wetness on his cheek. 'I wouldn't want Jeannie to see me cry.'

The pain in his eyes was plain to see, so full of unshed tears, just waiting there for the words that would make them fall. And he was afraid that if he started, he would never stop.

'Tell you what!' Rene said suddenly. 'Let's have a nice cup of cocoa, shall we? They didn't have any cocoa in the hospital. Shame, because it always makes me feel warm and comforted inside . . . Maybe it will work on all of us?'

Unable to speak, Rob got up swiftly from his chair and rushed to the kitchen, where he found Jeannie sobbing into a damp tea towel. 'Can I share that with you, pet?' he said gently.

She looked up at his tear-filled eyes and said, 'Oh Rob! What have ah done? Ah know that you're hurtin' too, and you've always been so kind ter me and me mam, and yer don't deserve it.' When she flung her arms around his waist, he could feel her tears mingling with his own as they ran down his shirt, until eventually the soaked cotton clung to his skin.

'Come on, love,' Rob said, gently loosening Jeannie's hold around his waist. 'How about you get the tin of cocoa out of the cupboard and I'll put some milk on to heat. We'll make us all a nice drink, shall we?'

Attempting a smile, Jeannie looked up at him. 'OK. Me mam likes chocolate, so that might make her feel better, eh?'

'I'm sure it will . . . for now anyway. But you need to

be prepared for your mam to feel a bit sad, every now and then, for quite a while.'

'But she will be all right one day, won't she?' she asked, willing him to say what she wanted to hear.

'We'll make sure she is, won't we.' Rob gave her a quick hug. 'Right, come on now, let's get this drink sorted.'

Later that day, Rob and Ian were at home talking about an impending visit to a boarding school they'd been interested in for some time. Rob had decided not to mention it to Jeannie, or Rene for that matter. He figured that they had enough to cope with right now. He didn't want Jeannie getting it into her head that it was because of her that Ian was being sent away, even if there was an element of truth in it. He knew she would never believe that Ian actually wanted to go to this particular school, where according to him the sports facilities were second to none.

Ian had discussed it with his dad long before Tom had seen him and Jeannie kissing. In fact, it had been his dad who was against it.

Rob had attended a boarding school himself as a boy and he'd had a hard time of it, so he felt he had good reason to be apprehensive. Bullying had been rife. He remembered how the very boys who'd been bullied had eventually turned into bullies themselves. And as for some of the other stuff that went on, well, he couldn't even allow his mind to go there. But all that had been a long time ago. Things could be different now, he told himself. He hadn't gone into any of the details of his own schooldays with Ian but had skirted around the edges, in an effort to prepare him for what he might find, especially when it was highly likely that, as a southerner, he would be in the minority.

'I can look after myself, Dad,' was all the response he'd had to that particular conversation.

Ian could go as a day-boy, Rob had been informed, when he'd finally agreed to make an appointment to meet the head of the school.

On that first visit he'd discovered that most of the sport, particularly football, which was where Ian's interests lay, took place after the day's lessons. The school was thirty miles away, so it would make much more sense for Ian to board.

In addition, Rob had learned that Ian and Jeannie had rapidly, and right under their noses, moved on very far from marbles. He'd had to admit to himself that the children were growing up fast, and with Rene and him both working it would be almost impossible to keep an eye on them. This had played a big part in his decision. He'd come to the conclusion that it would be the best thing for all concerned if Ian and Jeannie were to be parted for a while.

Experimental stage it might be, he told himself, but all kinds of things could happen while they were both developing. Now that he and Rene had been alerted, they had realized just how physically obvious it was that Jeannie was growing up.

With Ian, although it was less noticeable to the eye, more than likely there were hidden thoughts working overtime in that handsome little head of his. That's if he's anything like I was at that age, Rob thought, smiling to himself at the recollection. In fact, the more he considered it the more absurd it seemed that neither he or Rene had ever had any misgivings about the two young ones spending so much time together. Yes, no doubt about it, Rob had convinced himself, it was definitely too dangerous for them to be left alone together for long periods of time at this impressionable stage of their lives.

Ian was in the process of discussing with his dad just how he was going to tell Jeannie, when there was a knock at the door.

'Here she is!' his dad said. 'It's up to you how you tell her, Ian, but take it steady, eh?'

Ian went to answer the door while Rob made himself scarce, heading out to his greenhouse.

'Hello, Ee-an!' Jeannie greeted him cheerfully. She didn't barge past him, as was usual, but stood at the door. 'Me mam seems a bit better this afternoon. She even laughed at summat ah said, and now she's gone off ter sleep, so ah've just popped out ter see yer for a minute, and ter bring this.' She held up his deflated football. 'Yer left in such a hurry the other day, and ah thought yer might be needin' it.'

'Ta, it'll need blowing up by the look of it.' He returned her smile. 'I'm pleased that your mam's feeling a bit brighter. Come on in.' He stood to one side to allow Jeannie to pass.

Ian pushed the door closed and took a deep breath. 'Sit down, Jeannie,' he said, sounding like a man twice his age.

Jeannie gave him a look, raised her eyebrows and flopped down into an armchair.

'Jeannie,' he started, 'you know how much I like football?'

'Yes, course ah do,' she answered quickly. 'That's why ah brought yer ball round, silly.'

'Yes, well, thanks for that . . . It's just that there is no football at the school I'm at, and not much of any other sports, come to that. Leaping around, supposedly exercising, and learning to dance with the girls is about as good as it gets.'

'So . . . yer can play football over the rec, can't yer? Most other lads do.'

'Yes I can, but I want to be trained properly . . . you know?'

'Isn't there somebody somewhere that can train yer?'

'Yes there is, but it's at a school about thirty miles from here.'

'Well, that's no good.' She laughed. 'How would yer get there anyhow?'

'I'd have to stay there.' He looked up at her.

'What! Sleep there, yer mean?'

'Yes, it's what's called a boarding school.'

'I know what a boarding school is, ah'm eleven, soon ter be twelve! And ah'm not stupid,' Jeannie answered, full of indignation.

'Sorry, I know . . . It's just that it would be such a good opportunity for me. You must see that?' He looked directly at her, willing her to see his side of things.

'Huh! Well, by what ah've heard about boarding schools, ah'd give them a wide berth if ah was you.'

'It's different for you, Jeannie. You're a girl. You can probably get all you need from the school you're at.'

'Huh! Can I now? How would you know? You're only a boy!' she retorted, getting up from the chair. 'What ye're really tryin' ter say is that yer want ter get as far away from me as possible. Well, you do just that! See if ah care!' At that she stomped off and was out of the front door in a flash.

'That went well then?' Rob had come in to make himself a cup of tea and had heard the tail end of the conversation.

'She'll come round, I expect. It's just that she's got so much going on at the moment,' Ian replied with a sensitivity his dad hadn't realized he possessed.

These children never ceased to surprise him. 'That's a very sensible attitude, Ian. I take it that you still want to go to this school then?'

'Yes, Dad, I do, more than ever now.'

Chapter 25

Evenwood

Jeannie sat down heavily on a chair by the side of her gran's dressing table, her head resting on her hand as she stared at herself in the mirror.

Its two hinged, swinging mirrors, one at each side, which, at a young age, she'd discovered you could line up in such a way that you could see hundreds of yourself, held no interest for her today. Right now, she didn't even want to see *one* reflection of herself. For today was the day that Ian was going to boarding school.

It had been six weeks since her mam had fallen down the stairs, and five weeks ago this very day that Ian had told her he was leaving her. Well ... she thought, he didn't actually use those words but he might as well have done.

As she stared deeply into the mirror and beyond, the reflection there wasn't of herself, but of Ian. She could see him in the distance running across the recreation ground towards her, his face fresh and full of positivity at what he was doing. He was kicking a ball, hard and fast, and when he suddenly kicked it in her direction she managed to kick it back with such force that he was flabbergasted. She could still see his expression now, as she squinted even more deeply into the mirror, and he was laughing so much that he grabbed her arm and she came toppling down beside him in the damp newly mown grass of the rec.

They lay there giggling for quite a long while, and then when Ian finally pulled himself up, he did some-thing that made her gasp aloud: he leaned over and kissed her, not on her mouth but very close to her mouth. Misunderstanding her gasp, he looked worried and jumped up quickly, at the same time yanking her to her feet, but she lost her balance and toppled towards him, her face right next to his, and she kissed him, not next to his mouth but right on it! She had no idea what had made her do it. But that had been the start.

She could see it all now, as plain as day. Ian had just stared at her, for ever, it felt like, saying nothing, and it had seemed to her at the time that she'd taken leave of her senses. She'd been so mortified that she'd just laughed and given him a shove, before running off into the distance.

That feeling of embarrassment was still rife in her. And as she continued to look into the mirror, she could feel the heat of that moment rising up through her body and into her face. She'd felt that same heat almost every time she'd seen Ian, since that day a few months back.

She didn't know why she should feel like that because the next time they saw each other Ian had obviously got over the initial shock. He'd got a taste for this kissing lark, and he'd been keen to have a go whenever the opportunity presented itself. The right or wrong of it had passed Jeannie by. She only knew that she felt so good and grown up when they did it that she didn't mind one bit!

Jeannie was going over all this in her head, and mentally telling her reflection in the mirror, Don't be so daft, he loves this kissin' lark as much as you do.

Unknown to her, Maddie, unsure whether or not she should disturb Jeannie's thoughts, had been standing in the dark recess by the bedroom doorway. On hearing a sound behind her, Jeannie jumped and turned round. 'Oh it's you, Maddie, ah didn't see yer there.' She sounded flat.

Maddie walked towards her, asking gently, 'May I talk wiz you, *ma chérie*?'

Jeannie turned soberly back to the mirror, and without even glancing at Maddie she answered uncertainly, 'If you like.'

Maddie smiled, and as Jeannie moved uneasily along the stool to one end, Maddie took it as an invitation and sat down next to her at the dressing table. Not looking directly at her but looking at her reflection instead, Maddie said, 'I think you are hurting very much at the moment, Jeannie . . . no?'

'Ah don't know,' said Jeannie. Then just as Maddie was about to speak again, Jeannie shook her head. 'Ah only know that my best friend in the whole world has gone away, and ah can't bear it.'

Still looking at Jeannie in the mirror, Maddie pulled her close. Lifting Jeannie's hair from her eyes, she said, 'Just look at you, so pretty, and wiz so much to look forward to in ze future. Ian *will* be back, and he will still be your friend. He is thirteen, nearly fourteen, so he will probably only be at school for a few more years, and he will be coming back sometimes for the weekend.'

Jeannie was feeling very young. She wanted to cry, but she mustn't cry here, she told herself, she must wait till she got home. But she mustn't cry there either 'cause what about her poor mam, having to see her upset when she was still so upset herself about the baby?

Sensing that Jeannie was close to tears, Maddie chose to ignore it and continued, 'After all, you have your whole life to live, and many more boys to meet, *certainement*. But not yet, eh?' She lifted Jeannie's hair from her eyes again and they both smiled into the mirror.

'Has somebody told yer about this kissin' stuff?' Jeannie suddenly sounded suspicious.

'I do know about zat, but I am much more concerned

about how you are feeling at ze moment, Jeannie.'

'Ah wasn't bein' a bad girl, yer know, Maddie.'

'You are not a bad girl, Jeannie, you are growing up, zat is all, and finding out about life, as we all have to do.'

'Is our Tom really vexed with uz?'

'No, you mustn't think zat. He hadn't realized how grown up you are, but he knows now and zat can only be a good thing . . . no?'

'A good thing? Ah s'ppose . . . yes.'

Still looking into the mirror, each smiled at the other. Then Jeannie, her bottom lip trembling, hugged Maddie, whispered, 'Love you,' jumped down from the dressing-table stool and fled.

Hannah looked up as Maddie came down the stairs. 'Thank you for coming over to do that, Maddie. I thought that you might have better words to give her than I have. Ah'm not very good with affairs of the heart, ah'm afraid, and ah can't believe that ah'm referrin' to our Jeannie when ah'm sayin' that! She's only a bairn and she seems ter be heartbroken over a lad! We never knew owt about stuff like that when ah was a bairn! Eee, ah don't know what the world's comin' to.' Hannah looked tired.

'I will put ze kettle on, Hannah, and we will have tea . . . no?'

Hannah raised a smile at the very endearing way that Maddie so often ended a statement with the question, 'no?'

'Yes, let's do that, pet, and maybe yer can fill me in with what's goin' on. Ah seem ter lose track a bit these days, hinny. Anyhow, Jeannie seemed brighter when she came downstairs. She's gone over to see Molly, so that's a good sign.'

'And you, Hannah? How are you? You may not have ze words for affairs of ze heart but you have everything else. You just seem to go on and on, helping *tout le monde*, even through your own suffering.' Maddie's arms were outstretched, gesturing the breadth of Hannah's generosity.

'Oh, go on with yer!' Hannah smiled timidly and flapped her hand, indicating that it was nothing to her to help where she could.

As she sat down Maddie's eyes strayed to the hearth, where a bowl of bread dough stood with a crisp tea towel hanging loosely over the top. As Hannah had once explained to her, it was not only to keep the mixture free from sparks jumping out of the fire but also to assist with the rising of the yeast. With an ecstatic expression on her face, Maddie allowed the smell of the previous batch of baking bread to envelop her, and she was reminded of home. 'I think I could die happy with that aroma around me. You're a saint, Hannah, you really are!' she said in all seriousness.

'Well, you don't need ter be dyin' just now,' Hannah joked, 'yer haven't had yer tea yet!'

'Oh Hannah, you are funny, nothing deters you from

keeping everything normal. Coming here always lifts my mood and everyone else's, I'm sure. How do you do it?'

'Well, ah s'ppose ah just manage ter put me mind to other things, pet. For me it's bakin'.' She stopped to think for a moment. 'The feel of the dough in yer hands, now that's an experience in itself . . . and yer can always bash the hell out of it, if yer need to.' She smiled. 'That makes yer feel better for a start . . . Then there's the smell of it as it rises in the oven, and your spirits rise with it. It always works for me anyhow . . . Even you, Maddie, yer face lit up when yer came down the stairs.'

Hannah didn't need to prove her point. Maddie was already saying, 'And the best part of all is eating it.'

Hannah grinned, and said, 'Why don't you wait a while, and when it's cooled a bit we can sample it together. And ah've got some lovely home-made strawberry jam from Mrs Parkin, we'll spread a dollop of that on it an' all, eh?'

As Maddie nodded her head vigorously, Hannah continued, 'And ter answer yer original question, before ah went off on a tangent about me bakin,' ah'm fine, pet. Especially now that our Rene's getting better, and talkin' about goin' back to work already. Ah'm happy about that. All this other stuff will, no doubt, pass one way or another . . . it always does.'

'I learn a lot from you, Hannah. I admire very much

how you cope, and one day I hope to be ze same. Well, similar, eh?' she smiled.

When Hannah returned the smile, saying, 'Just keep yer pecker up through thick and thin, pet, and bash the dough good and hard when yer need to, because yer never know what might be round the corner,' Maddie could have had no idea just what *was* looming round the corner.

Chapter 26

Evenwood

Tom looked at the clock, put his mug down and rose abruptly from the table. 'Come on, pet,' he called up the stairs, 'we've got to go if we're to be on time to collect Nicole and Ginette from the station!'

Maddie came running down the stairs and stood in front of him with her arms outstretched to display the coat in its entirety. 'Well, what do you think?'

'Beautiful, and you made it all by yourself?' he asked, admiring the perfect contrast of her dark hair and how it fell around the collar of the red plaid coat.

'I did!' She sounded excited. 'And it didn't cost me a penny, it's all from the lovely material that Jeannie brought me from Rob's factory. There was even enough for pockets. Look!' She pushed her hands into the patch pockets, and as she stood there, looking so pleased with herself, it was all Tom could do to stop himself from dragging her upstairs to show her just how beautiful he thought she really was.

'OK, modelling over, let's go.' Laughing, he took her hand. And as she checked herself in the mirror by the door, he pulled her away, saying, 'Come on, pet, anyone would think you weren't in a hurry to meet our friends.'

Warmed by Tom's phrase '*our friends*', she smiled, lagging slightly behind him and taking two or three steps to his every one, as they strode hand in hand along the footpath towards the bus stop. Catching her breath, she looked up at him. 'I am so excited at ze prospect of Nicole and Ginette coming to stay for a while, I can't tell you. But I am worried about zem also,' she said, frowning slightly.

'It will all be fine, you'll see. Sounds as though they just need a bit of breathing space, until they decide what's best to do.'

As they got on the bus, Tom was saying, 'I meant to tell you, Francine has left her rag doll at home. Will she be OK without it?'

'Oh, she will be fine. Anyway she spends most of her time at Hannah's watching ze pendulum in ze grandfather clock.' Maddie took the tickets from the conductor.

Darlington Station

'Well, ah'll be buggered, ah'd have hardly recognized them. There they are, practically the first ones out of the train.' Tom was pointing through the hissing steam.

Maddie squinted to see, but it wasn't until Nicole dropped her valise on the platform, right there in front of her, that she recognized her friend.

The gasp from Maddie, as they hugged, was as much out of surprise at how lovely Nicole looked, now that her glorious dark hair had grown back, as for the tightness of the hug.

Ginette, her burgundy beret cocked to one side, allowing auburn strands of hair to escape from its hold, strode towards Tom and kissed him on both cheeks. In her broken English, she said, 'I can't thank you enough, Tom. Zis cannot have been an easy decision for—'

'Shush! Say no more about it.' Tom needed no apology.

The hissing engines, shunting carriages and blowing whistles almost drowned his voice. Quickly kissing Nicole, he shouted, 'Come, let's get off this noisy platform.'

Regardless of the noise, Maddie and Nicole managed to chat almost non-stop as they walked along, sharing the weight of Nicole's small valise.

Tom, meanwhile, had picked up Ginette's slightly larger case and followed behind, with Ginette by his side.

Glancing up at him now, she asked, 'I bet zat you know a place where we can get a coffee, no?'

'Yes I do.' He smiled. 'Just over there, look.' He nodded in the general direction.

When Tom and Ginette overtook Maddie and Nicole and headed straight for the café, the two girls followed without question, still chattering.

Twenty minutes later, refreshed and a little more relaxed, the four of them headed for the bus station to catch a bus to Bishop Auckland. From there, the three women would get a bus to Evenwood, but without Tom, who would need to go back to work for an hour or so.

On the first bus, three seats back from where Nicole and her mother were sitting, Tom, in lowered tones, said to Maddie, 'How amazing to see Nicole and Ginette looking so well. They must be so pleased that their hair has grown back. The last time I saw them there were only tufts remaining . . . What a terrible time it must have been. Well, I hope those monsters rot in hell, the lot of them!' His voice had risen above the clanking and bell-ringing on the bus.

'Shush, *mon chéri*!' Maddie linked Tom's arm and snuggled up to him. 'It is all over now, and I will never forget that if it hadn't been for you and Dominic, I would also have had my head sheared.'

'I know, but let's not get agitated, pet. It's done and we're here, safe.' He patted her hand, before adding with some concern, 'Well, I think we are, but we need to concentrate on this next hurdle now. Has Nicole said any more about it?'

'Just bits and pieces as we walked from the station . . . It seems Jacques is going to try to find out what has happened to zat brute of an uncle of Ginette's, and what he may have said to ze *gendarmes* . . . if he is still alive, of course.' Both unsmiling, they stared into each other's eyes.

Tom sighed. 'Well, we must pray for the sake of Nicole and Ginette that he is, pet.'

Bishop Auckland

'Why don't you girls have a bite to eat before you get the bus home, it'll be better than having to start when you get in,' Tom suggested, as he was about to leave them at the bus stop. '*And* it'll give everyone more time to fuss around Francine, the way that women usually do when they meet a new bairn.' Tom was proud of his own understanding of female psychology.

'But what about Francine?' said Maddie, looking at the bus station clock. 'I told Hannah that we would be back by about four o'clock.'

Tom shook his head. 'Now when have you ever known me mam in a hurry ter get rid of the bairn? She'll be in her element, and she's got Jeannie there ter help an' all.'

'Well . . .' Maddie hesitated.

'Look, pet, if it gets ter Francine's bedtime me mam'll take her back to ours and put her ter bed, she's got a key.' He shrugged his shoulders and smiled at the three of them. 'So no problem.' He pushed some money into her pocket.

'I *am* quite hungry,' Nicole nudged Madeleine.

'Me too,' Ginette smiled at Tom, 'I think it's a good idea.'

'OK, OK!' Madeleine raised her hand. 'You win, we will go to a café in the town.'

Once seated at a table, Ginette said, 'I don't know how it is for alcohol in England so soon after the war, but it would be nice to have an aperitif, don't you think?'

'If we are lucky, we might get a glass of nasty sherry.' Madeleine chuckled.

'*Nasty?* What is it, this *nasty?*'

Maddie screwed up her nose, leaving them in no doubt of the meaning of the word.

'Ha! Well, "nasty" sherry it is then.' Nicole warmed to the irony.

'It's so good to see you two in such good spirits.' Madeleine hadn't been sure what to expect.

Ginette looked at Madeleine intently, and though it was unlikely that anyone nearby would speak French, she whispered.

'I know that it must be difficult to understand how

we can be so calm after treating another human being in this way. But Madeleine,' she leaned right across the table now, 'he is not human, he is an animal . . . just like the ones who tortured us in the square in Boulogne.' The hate in her tone was unmistakable. 'We could not stop *them*, but we *can* stop him.'

'But what if he takes things further?' Madeleine failed to see how locking the man in a cellar, from which he would by now have been freed, was going to stop him.

Again Ginette leaned towards her. 'Jacques is going to send a telegram to your address, as soon as he feels that it is safe for us to return. And your *maman*,' she smiled at Madeleine, 'has kindly arranged for us to stay with your Tante Lucy on the farm, on our return to France . . . just until things calm down.'

'Maman knows?' Madeleine asked, amazed, if not a little concerned at the prospect.

'Only that we are in trouble,' Nicole answered quickly. 'We were in touch with your *maman* because she had invited us to stay at your house in Marck, as a surprise, when you were due to come home. Your *maman* thought it would do you good to see friends . . . It was a secret, Madeleine, but it wasn't to be because all this happened, and we had to get out of the country for a while.'

Madeleine stared at them, struggling to take in what she was hearing.

'Anyway,' Nicole continued, 'we wrote to your

maman, to explain that we could not come after all, but that we would be coming over to England for a while and we would spend time with you then. She was very good, your *maman*, she did not want the details of our troubles, but said that she trusted us because you do, Madeleine. She said that Tante Lucy would be happy to have company for a while. And apart from that, she could do with some help on the farm.'

Madeleine, totally taken aback by this revelation, was quiet for a moment, then suddenly spoke up. 'You will love Tante Lucy, she will make you very welcome, and she is very funny. She is the one who used to bring me the material to make all my lovely dresses, and she brought so much that I made clothes for other people too, *and* charged for making them . . .' Madeleine suddenly clapped a hand over her mouth, 'Oh, I am so sorry, how rude of me to go on like that, as if you were going on holiday or something! I didn't mean to talk about myself.'

Ginette and Nicole grinned at each other. 'Well, we will certainly look forward to meeting your Tante Lucy, Madeleine,' Ginette said. 'And once the coast is clear, we have arranged for Jacques to collect the few things we need, paperwork and suchlike, so that we can move away from that house and that town . . . We have talked, many times, of saying goodbye to the house and all its memories, so what better time than now?'

Ginette glanced at her daughter, who nodded in confirmation.

On seeing Madeleine's puzzled look, Nicole took over. 'Maman has enough money put aside to buy another house, without selling the one in Boulogne. We will worry about selling it later. For that, we must wait until the *gendarmes* lose interest in how Dugas ended up bound and gagged in the cellar. The interest, of course, will be much more intense if by any chance he has died . . .'

Madeleine couldn't help but notice how unusually matter-of-fact her friend sounded.

They took a moment to digest both the information given and, in Madeleine's case, the information received. Each sipped at her sherry, and if it *was* nasty, none of them commented.

Chapter 27

Evenwood

'Gran! Gran! The pushchair's gone!' Jeannie shivered violently, as much from shock as from the cold dampness of the swirling grey fog.

'Gone? What do yer mean, gone? Gone where?' Hannah's tone was filled with dread.

'Ah don't know where, Gran! Ah just left her outside fer a minute while ah popped into the lav, an' when ah came out Francine was gone! Ah've looked all up an' down the street.' Jeannie's mouth trembled as she fought the tears.

'Oh good Lord! Who round here would take a bairn? And in the middle of the afternoon an' all?' Hannah grabbed her coat from the back of the door. 'Come on, we've got ter find her, pet, and quick! It's getting dark already.' She glanced at Jeannie. 'Don't start blubberin', that's not goin' ter help at all, now is it?'

'What's Maddie goin' ter say?' Jeannie sounded terrified.

Even though her own heart was racing ninety to the dozen, Hannah patted Jeannie on the head in an attempt to reassure her. 'Let's hope we find her before Maddie needs ter know, eh?'

The two of them almost fell over each other as they rushed through the door and off down the street, into the thickening fog.

Bishop Auckland

Madeleine, Nicole and Ginette came giggling out of the restaurant. And even with the cloud of uncertainty that hung over not just Nicole and Ginette, at what they'd left behind in France, but over herself too now, Madeleine couldn't remember the last time she had laughed like this.

Nicole and Madeleine shared the weight of Ginette's bag this time, while Ginette carried Nicole's smaller one. They stopped at intervals to set the cases down for a moment. 'It's not far to the bus stop now,' Madeleine said.

'Let's hope not!' Ginette pulled up the collar of her coat against the fog swirling around her.

'Oh, this is nothing!' Madeleine exclaimed, seeing how cold Ginette looked. 'Wait till you get to the village, where the smoke and gases from the coal mine mingle with the fog until you can hardly see your own hand!' She stretched her arm out in front of her.

Ginette and Nicole looked at each other. Madeleine was teasing them, surely?

'You wait!' She laughed at their expressions. 'You will see for yourselves, or rather not see, when we arrive in the village, in half an hour or so.'

Feeling slightly light-headed now, helped by the sherry, Maddie sensed her long-hidden mischievous streak coming to the fore, prompting her to play on their obvious disbelief.

'You will know when we are almost there, by the smell. Sulphur, coal . . . and gases. Mmm!' she said matter-of-factly, lifting her head skywards as if thoroughly enjoying the aroma.

Chuckling to herself, and encouraged by the looks of horror on their faces, she added, even more dramatically, 'And all the village will be lit up by hot, hot *fire* streaming and roaring from the top of the tall, *tall* chimney at the mine! Men will walk around with faces blacker than coal, with only their shining eyes and wet pink mouths to be seen through the fog.'

The three of them stopped walking for a moment, then Madeleine gave Nicole a gentle shove and laughed. 'Come on then, bet you can't wait to get there now!'

Having dismissed Madeleine's portrayal of the village as sherry-fuelled impishness, they went on talking almost non-stop, even as they climbed on to the bus.

'How kind of Tom to pay for us to go to the restaurant,' Nicole said. 'He must really love you, Madeleine, because he obviously did it to save you cooking when you get home, and to cheer you up . . . and look at you, it worked!'

'Yes, it worked. I feel happy today, happy to be with the two of you, and happy to be going home to introduce you to my little girl.' There was no mistaking just how proud of her daughter she was, if the smile she flashed at them both was anything to go by.

Nicole, serious for a moment, asked, 'Maybe you'll have your baby here in England after all, Madeleine?'

'No, I want to come back with you.' She looked from one to the other. 'I love Hannah and Jack and the whole family here, but I still feel like a visitor to this country. I need to come home, to have my own family around me . . . just for a while. You understand, don't you?'

'See if you can convince her.' That was what Tom had whispered to Nicole and her mother, before they'd gone to the restaurant. But Nicole knew that no matter how happy Madeleine felt at this moment, there was no more chance of convincing her to stay in England for the birth of this baby than there had been of her coming to England before the birth of Francine.

'Of course I understand,' Nicole said with a smile.

'Oh come on, we are getting too serious. We were serious enough in the restaurant . . . well, at least until the second nasty sherry took its effect.' Madeleine pulled a comical face at her two companions, and suddenly they were all laughing again.

'Why do you look at me like that, Nicole?' Madeleine asked.

'I was just thinking how pretty you look when you are happy.' She didn't add that she'd been quite shocked at how tired her friend had looked when they'd first arrived.

Madeleine was fully aware that she had laughed more today than for a long time. Having been able to laugh and joke in her own language had been like a tonic to her.

Half an hour later, all three were shuddering as they got off the bus into the damp fog.

Madeleine looked at her two companions. 'It's not like this all the time, I promise!'

Nicole trembled slightly, as she looked around for the black-faced men with the bright eyes and the wet pink mouths. Satisfied that it had been a Madeleine-style prank, she and Ginette walked on, until they both jumped back in shock as the *whoosh!* of fire leapt from the top of the coal-mine chimney.

Madeleine laughed so much that she had to cross her legs. 'Told you!' she said.

Feeling tired and damp, they arrived at Hannah's house to collect Francine.

'*Oh merde alors!* There is no one here!' Madeleine frowned.

'Maybe Hannah has taken Francine to your house to get her to bed, as Tom said she probably would?' Ginette said cheerfully.

Nicole glanced at her watch. 'It is five thirty, and we are much later than you told Hannah,' she whispered.

'Yes, that will be it,' Madeleine answered, becoming aware of a sinking feeling in the pit of her stomach. 'Yes, of course! Hannah will have taken her home. Let's go!'

Nicole and Ginette arrived on the doorstep behind a breathless Madeleine, who with a confusing mixture of guilt at being late and a dread of impending bad news churning around inside her, had rushed silently through the foggy streets of the village until she reached home. The first thing she noticed was that the house was in darkness. Quickly she unlocked the door.

'The house is empty!' Madeleine's incredulous tone alerted the other two to the fact that this wasn't normal.

Seeing her panicked expression, Nicole dropped her case alongside her mother's, and rushed to her side. 'Look, we must stop for a moment and think rationally. Where would Hannah have gone with Francine?'

'I can't think, I can't think,' said Madeleine, wrapping her arms around her body. 'Oh, I need the toilet . . .'

As soon as Madeleine was out of earshot, Nicole said to her mother, 'There is something not right about this.' She couldn't rid herself of the thought of Madeleine's letters, telling her about the previous unexplained incidents. What if this was some kind of trick to push Madeleine even further? Or, she wondered, was her own mind playing tricks on her now?

'Let's not get ahead of ourselves, Nicole. It could be that they are at the shops or visiting a friend, *non*?'

'You saw, *maman*, as well as I did . . . the shops were closed when we passed by, and the weather is much too horrible to be out walking. Maybe she is at the doctor, or the hospital? But wouldn't you have expected Hannah to leave a note, especially as she'd been expecting Madeleine back about two hours ago?'

'You're right.' Madeleine's faltering voice came from somewhere behind Nicole. 'Hannah would have left me a note.' She rushed around the kitchen, lifting one object after another, looking underneath.

'Surely if there was a note,' Ginette said, 'it would be plain to see . . . on the table, for instance, *non*?'

'Yes . . . yes, of course,' Madeleine agreed, while still looking hopefully around her.

Finally, exhausted and at a loss as to what to do next, she sat down and looked uncertainly at the two women in front of her. 'I am so sorry about this,' she said. 'What an introduction to England and to my new home, eh? And after your long journey too. Please sit, both of you, and I will make us a cup of tea.'

'Later, Madeleine . . . when we have Francine with us, eh?' Ginette smiled in an effort to lessen the tension.

'There will be an explanation, I'm sure,' Nicole said, hiding her true feelings.

With no time to notice, let alone comment on how lovely the house was, Ginette nodded to Nicole, who took hold of Madeleine's hand. 'Come, we will go back into the village. We may find someone who can tell us something.'

Madeleine was feeling very sick. 'Yes, maybe they have just gone to visit someone,' she said, not really believing that herself. Suddenly she exclaimed, 'Madame Parkin! We will call to see Madame Parkin.' She had convinced herself now that that was where they would be.

All three rushed out once more into the fog.

But at that moment Mrs Parkin was running, running behind Hannah and Jeannie, who'd been joined by Molly and Amy. Amy had seen somebody running, and with a pushchair. She'd only noticed, she'd said, "Cause the bairn was cryin' like!'

On hearing this, Hannah's heart had almost stopped. 'Who was it, Amy?'

'Ah don't know, ah only saw the back of 'er. It was all foggy and ah couldn't see very well, but she was runnin' that way.' Amy pointed up the road towards the opening in the hedge, beyond which only farmers' fields lay to each side. The lane was nothing more than two bands of stony grey earth, deeply rutted tracks divided by tufts of green and brown weed-matted grass.

'Oh my God! Oh my God!' Hannah, mortified at the direction they were taking, could be heard calling out these words over and over as she stumbled down the stony lane, trying to move faster than her body would allow.

'Don't keep sayin' that, Gran, ye're scarin' uz!' Jeannie pleaded, as she clung to Hannah's arm.

'Take Molly and Amy and run on ahead,' Hannah called, stopping to catch her breath.

Mrs Parkin caught up with her, panting so much she could only gasp the words.

'What d'yer think ye're doin', Hannah? Are yer tryin' ter kill yerself? We can't run like this at our ages, lass!'

'Well ah'm not goin' back without the bairn, and that's a fact . . . Yer know what's at the end of this lane, don't yer.' This was a statement from Hannah, not a question. All the villagers knew that the blackening pond lay just across the wasteland.

Mrs Parkin could see that there was no point in trying to alter her mind, so she took hold of Hannah's hand. 'Come on then, pet, let's get goin'.'

Together, they followed the girls' dwindling forms as fast as they could. By the time they reached the wasteland, their breath had become so laboured that they had to stop.

Both had bent forward, their arms folded over their stomachs, in an effort to breathe more deeply and freely.

It was Hannah who straightened up first, ready for the off again, only to see, running back towards them, a blurry silhouette in the form of Jeannie, followed closely by two more that she took to be Molly and Amy. Jeannie arrived first. Her face was ashen.

'Gran! Gran!' She could hardly breathe as she pointed across the scrubby ground. 'The push . . . pushchair's in the blackenin' pond!'

Hannah felt her legs give way.

'Come . . . on!' Jeannie screamed now, as she grabbed Hannah's hand, pulling her up and dragging her over the field that sloped down to the pond.

Molly and Amy were already back there, motionless, and staring down the slope towards the water. The view came and went through the billowing fog. The outline of the pushchair handle reached out as if the buggy were pleading to be pulled free of the mud which gripped it. It was a sight that brought Hannah once more to her knees. 'Oh no! Oh nooo!'

Even more terrifying than the sight of the pushchair in the water was for Jeannie to see her gran like this. 'Gran! Get up!' she screeched. 'We have to find Francine!'

'Has the pond sucked her in?' Amy's voice trembled.

'Shush, will yer!' Molly gave Amy a hefty push, almost knocking her off her feet.

'Stay here, Gran,' Jeannie said, looking up at Mrs Parkin, her eyes begging her to do something with her gran. 'I'll go and see if ah can pull the pushchair out.'

As if she'd been hit by a torpedo, Hannah was suddenly up on her feet, and with a fierceness that Jeannie had never seen in her before, she shrieked, 'You'll do *noo such thing*, my girl! Just how many times do yer need ter be told how dangerous that water is? You girls, run back ter the village! Get somebody ter help uz!' Hannah said urgently. 'Get a move on, fer goodness' sake!'

Jeannie, Molly and Amy quickly and silently sprang to life, and all three ran off in the direction of the village.

'We need a bobby!' Jeannie shouted to the first person she came across in the street.

There was no one at home, no one at his mother's, no one at Mrs Parkin's. Tom headed off down the street, in search of *any* member of his family, in order to find out just what the hell was going on.

Since he'd received the garbled message from the girl in the office, he had become more and more frustrated by the minute. With the day's shift over, he'd been whistling contentedly to himself and looking forward to getting home. He must remember to tell Maddie how good his bait of cold beef with a spot of mustard had been. Yes, Maddie certainly knew how ter make a decent sarnie now, he was thinking, when the girl from the office had rushed out.

'Yer hav ter get yerself straight home, Tom, it's ter do with the bairn!' she'd said urgently. 'They can't find her! Ah can't tell yer any more than that, Tom, that's all ah know. Ah think it was yer da, but we were cut off.'

'What d'yer mean, can't find her?' Tom's voice had risen.

'Just get home, eh!' The girl had patted him on the shoulder, which had made it worse somehow.

The bus journey home had seemed to take for ever. Once he was back in Evenwood, he looked in all the obvious places. Trying to quell the sinking feeling in his stomach, he was still searching purposefully when the unmistakable sound of Nitty Nora's penetratingly long vowels came from somewhere behind him.

'T-oh-m.'

Cringing, he pulled up the collar of his jacket and carried on walking.

'Nooo, wait, T-oh-m!' She was getting louder.

He marched on. The last person on this earth he wanted to see was bloody Nitty Nora.

Trying to catch her breath, she caught up with him and yanked at his sleeve. 'T-oh-m, yer've got ter goo ter Jessie's, she wants ter see yer aboot summat!'

'Get off me sleeve, yer silly bitch,' he said, shaking himself free. 'Ah'm buggered if ah'm going round there right now, can't yer see ah'm busy? Tell her ter get lost!'

'But yer have ter goo, she's got somethin' for yer!'

'Not . . . now. Right?' He bent down until his face was almost touching hers.

Shocked, and afraid of the way he'd bared his teeth as he growled these words, Nora backed off and rushed into her house.

'Tom! Tom!' His dad's voice reached him now. 'Ah've been lookin' everywhere for yer! They're all down at the blackenin' pond, lad. Yer'd better get yerself down there, and quick!'

'The blackenin' pond? In this weather! Maddie's down there . . . at the blackenin' pond? Is Francine there?' Tom's voice was raised.

'Aye, they're all at the pond.' His dad grabbed Tom's arm. 'Come on, keep yerself together, we've got ter get down there. The police came ter the house just as ah came in from the allotment. Seems like Francine was taken from out of the back yard. It was me who spoke ter yer office girl, from the call box, 'cause Mrs Parkin was out like.'

'My God, Dad! Who could have done such a thing, eh? Takin' a bairn like that? 'Cause she must have been taken, she couldn't have walked away on her own, now could she.' Tom needed to think aloud to try to make sense of what had happened.

All kinds of thoughts were spinning around his head. He stopped and turned to his dad. 'Yer don't think that Jessie might have had something to do with it, do yer? Tryin' ter put the frighteners on uz like? 'Cause ah wouldn't put anything past her! She's changed, Dad, she's all bitter and twisted.'

'Nah . . . nah, rein yerself in a bit, Tom. Ye're clutchin' at straws now. As jealous as she is of you and Maddie, ah don't think even she would stoop to that level. No, this is something much more worryin'. This could be somebody that we don't even know, 'cause who in this village has reason ter take a bairn?'

Breathless from trying to keep up with Tom, Jack urged his son to go on ahead. 'Ah'll get there in me own time. The police are down there and there's two or three in the village, goin' from house ter house like, so we should know something soon.' What that something might be, he didn't dare think about.

The Blackening Pond

When Tom arrived at the pond, he saw a group of villagers huddled, shivering in the damp air. On the far side of the wet sloping bank, flashlights were moving in all directions. Police were milling around, and sticks were being poked into the thick gorse bushes; their cruel spines, protruding through the opaque fog, appeared even more vicious than he knew them to be.

'The water, why aren't they looking in the water?' he called to no one in particular. He tried to move, but his feet were like lead.

'Tom! Oh Tom!' Her voice came to him. Weak and trembling, she stumbled over the tufts of grass.

'Maddie! Maddie!' His feet freed from the spot now, he ran towards her. Trying not to crumble at the sight of her grief-stricken face, he took her in his arms.

'They can't find her . . . Francine. They can't find her. Her pushchair, it was empty, it was tipped backwards! Oh Tom! Ze 'andle . . . it was sticking out of the water!'

'We will find her, pet,' he said into her hair, as he squinted over the top of her head into the swirling fog. 'Where are the others? Where's Mam, and Jeannie?'

'Zey are all here . . . over zere.' Without looking, she pointed to somewhere over her shoulder.

'You need to get home, pet. I'll go get them, you stay here.'

'*Non! Non!* I will not go home wizout Francine!' She pulled at his sleeve.

Before he knew what was happening, she had slid down to the damp grass. Hugging her knees to her chest, she formed a tight ball of worn-out wretchedness.

She was beyond consoling. Her desolation and agony made it impossible to reason with her. It was Hannah, too tired to cry any more tears, who came to Maddie's aid.

'Oh Mam! Thank God you're here! Maddie needs ter get home.'

Maddie, oblivious to Tom's comment, said nothing.

'Surely Francine would have been right next to the

pushchair if she was in the water?' he said quietly to his mother.

'They've searched all round, it's been a right to-do. They had to lay planks down 'cause of the silt, like. Then one of the police tied himself ter the two who stayed on the bank while the one on the planks leaned in and put a rope round the handle of the pushchair to hoist it out.' Hannah hardly drew breath. 'And the carry-on with the truck that brought the planks just made things worse 'cause as it was leaving it got stuck in the soft ground, so they had ter use the planks again ter get the truck . . .'

Aware that his mam was rambling almost hysterically, Tom cut out the sound of her voice. He felt himself go cold inside. What if someone had taken Francine out of the pushchair first, then thrown her in? No . . . he wouldn't let himself go there. As he stared into the water, his heart missed a beat at the vision he had of Francine's sunny trusting smile.

If she was in there, surely she would be partly visible, he thought. The murky water looked deep, though apparently it wasn't . . . but how could anybody know that for sure? he wondered. His understanding had always been that the main danger of the pond lay in its bed of silt.

He glanced down at the boulder that lay a couple of feet in from the edge of the pond, thinking that that must be where the bobbies had rested their planks earlier to pull out the pushchair. Anybody with a decent stride could easily reach that boulder . . . say, to get closer to deeper water! His heart was quickening as these thoughts shot through his head. That's it! he thought. If the bairn *had* been in the pushchair when it went in, surely the extra weight would have sunk the wheels at the very edge of the pond? Even if you managed to get your feet on to that boulder, you wouldn't have been able to push it in far enough to leave just the handle showing when it tipped over. But if it was empty . . .

Tom's heart was pounding now. Adrenalin filled his veins and he turned quickly to Maddie. 'Come on, pet! We're leaving, we've got work to do.' Maddie recoiled as he tried to steer her away. The very thought of leaving this place without her daughter was totally abhorrent to her.

'Francine is not here! I know she isn't! Trust me?' He gripped her hand, willing her to agree.

To Maddie, he sounded harsh. She shook her hand free. 'I will not leave zis place wizout Francine. You go, but I stay here.'

With both hands, Tom took hold of Maddie's face and turned her brusquely towards him. 'Look at me, Maddie. She . . . is . . . not . . . dead! I will find her.'

Jeannie, overhearing this, wiped away her own tears with the heel of her hand. 'I trust him, Maddie, and ah think we—'

'Mr Dawson?' The bobby interrupted Jeannie's words, looking directly at Tom.

'That's right, ah'm Dawson.'

Tom's mouth was dry with fear of what he might be about to hear.

'Well, Mr and Mrs Dawson, as we haven't found anything else here, I think you should both go home.'

As Maddie tried to protest, he said kindly, 'Don't worry, missus, we will keep you informed. Some officers from the Bishop Auckland force are in the village doin' house-to-house enquiries, so we'll let you know what's what.' He glanced down at Maddie's bump. 'Too damp for her to be hanging around here in her condition. I'd get her home if I was you, Mr Dawson.'

Tom nodded. Keeping Maddie upright with his arm wrapped securely around her waist, they headed for home.

Everyone piled into Jack and Hannah's house and stood there looking hopelessly at each other. The ever-consoling cup of tea was not even thought about until Tom, getting to grips with the situation, said, 'Right, Jeannie, fill up the kettle, and get a nice hot cuppa into Maddie and yer gran and Mrs Parkin, they look frozen.' He then looked at Nicole and Ginette, and pointed to the sideboard. 'In the back there, there's a drop of whisky left.' He glanced at Jeannie, who shame-facedly looked away from him. 'Get it and put it in their drinks, will yer.' He sounded sharp, and he knew it.

Attempting a reassuring smile, he stopped, placed a hand on each of the two French lasses' shoulders, and whispered, 'Thank you.' With a nod, Ginette went to the sideboard, to search for the hidden whisky.

Back to the job in hand, Tom looked at Jack, who was stoking the fire much more vigorously than was required. 'Dad, leave that! You come with me!' Without question Jack dropped the poker and followed his son out into the back yard.

Maddie stumbled as she made to get up to follow them, but was stopped by Nicole.

'No, my dear friend, you must stay here with us . . . Tom knows what he is doing.' Far from just trying to console her now, Nicole instinctively believed that Tom was in control and had had some kind of intuition. He knew where to look.

Tom marched purposefully down the street. Someone had it in for him, and he didn't have to look far to know who.

Houses were very rarely locked in the village. Tom had no trouble getting in. No one answered his call from either the kitchen or the front room. He leapt up the stairs, two at a time.

Jessie sat bolt upright in the bed, the sheet tucked round her breasts. Staring at him full in the face, she allowed the sheet to fall to her waist. Tom, totally unfazed, didn't for a second take his eyes from hers. 'Where is she?'

'Who?'

'The bairn, that's who! Ah've seen Nora, she said yer've got something for uz . . . Now, *where is she*?' As he spat out the words, he leaned in towards her.

The menace in his voice meant nothing to her. Ignoring his question, she said, 'Come on, you know you want to.' He backed away from the bed snarling.

'If you were the last woman on earth, ah wouldn't touch yer with a bloody bargepole! So now yer have it!'

'Huh! Yer used ter have red blood runnin' through yer veins . . . sapped it all out of yer, has she? Or are yer goin' ter tell me that it's all yer experiences through the war that's changed yer?' Jessie yanked at the sheet and tied it tightly round her body before she slid off the bed and walked seductively towards him. 'Well, ah don't know where yer bairn is and ah'd like ter say ah care . . . but ah don't, so there *you* have it!'

Her smirk got right up his nose and he grabbed her by the shoulders. 'If ah find out that you've got *anything* ter do with this episode, yer'll wish that yer'd never been born.'

'Huh! Well, ah wish you hadn't, that's for sure.' As Jessie said this she knew that she was lying, but she'd say anything to hide the hurt that she was feeling at his constant rejections.

271

'Get out! Just get out!' She sounded convincing, even to herself. 'Ah have no idea where yer bairn is, and ah have no idea why Nitty Nora would have told yer that ah had something for yer either. Ah told her ah was goin' ter have a long bath, then go to bed for a while ter get rid of me headache. That's all ah've said to her today.'

As she said this, the penny dropped . . . Of course! Nora knew that I'd been trying to get Tom on his own, and she would see this as doing something good for me . . . Getting him to come round here when she knew that I was alone in the house . . . Well, the crafty little devil. Jessie couldn't help but smile at the ingeniousness of Nora's plan, coming from someone like her.

Misreading her expression, Tom growled, 'You can smile, yer bitch, but you'll get yer come-uppance soon enough, believe me.' With these parting words, he slammed out of the bedroom and raced down the stairs, calling to his dad, who was searching round the back of the house. 'Come on, Dad, yer'll find nowt down there.' In seconds he was out in the street.

He knew exactly where he was heading now.

Chapter 28

Tom tore off his jacket as he stormed down the street. He needed no restrictions, and nothing and no one was going to get in his way. From the corner of his eye, he caught glimpses of people standing under the lamp lights, fags dangling loosely from the mouths of curious faces, as they stopped to stare in disbelief.

What kind of madness, they asked each other, would cause someone to rip their jacket off in such weather? But no one approached. They knew better. Tom Dawson could be hot-headed sometimes, and this was obviously one of those times.

The thunderous banging on the front door, followed by the booming voice of a man possessed, made Nora jump up from the kitchen chair, where she had been huddled in front of a meagre fire, taking comfort from her favourite supper of bread and dripping.

When she heard the ear-splitting voice again, she

dropped her bread and fell over the chair as she ran to the corner of the room. Wrapping her arms around her head in an effort to hide from the noise, she slid to the floor, whimpering and stuttering, 'Who . . . who is it?'

'Open this bloody door *now*, yer little tart, or ah'll break it down!' came the reply.

No one spoke. Mrs Parkin, Nicole, Ginette, Hannah and Maddie were all seated around the fire, each with their hands wrapped around a mug of steaming hot, sweet tea. The house, so often full of laughter, was morbidly quiet.

Hannah had helped get Maddie out of her damp clothes and into some dry ones, and had swaddled her in a blanket. But even though she sat closest to the fire, she hadn't stopped shivering since they came in.

To see her beautiful eyes so devoid of expression, just staring into the fire as if looking for some answer there, Nicole reached over to her. Hugging her close, she whispered gently, 'It will be all right, you will see.'

'But what if it's not?' Maddie closed her eyes for a moment, then said mournfully, 'When my eyes are closed, I can feel my little girl in my arms, but when I look, she is not there . . . Where is she, Nicole, where is my little girl? I must go, I must find her.'

Nicole gently let go of Madeleine and looked towards Ginette, her eyes appealing for some help with this dear friend of hers, who she was afraid might try to sneak out of the house.

Ginette put her mug down and crouched next to Madeleine. Holding both her hands in her own, she said, 'Listen, *ma petite*, Tom is doing all he can to find Francine . . . you trust him . . . *non?*'

'Yes, I trust him, of course! But he cannot work miracles! It's all words, Ginette, all words. Words won't find my baby!' At that, she disentangled herself from Ginette, got up abruptly, dropped the blanket to the floor and ran from the room, not stopping until she reached the bedroom that had been hers and Tom's before they'd moved into their own cottage. She flung herself on to the bed and sobbed uncontrollably.

Nicole went to go after her but Hannah grabbed her arm. 'No, pet, leave her. She'll be down soon enough.'

On hearing the sobs coming from the spare room, Jeannie got herself up from her gran's bed. Feeling that the whole thing was her fault and unable to face any of the family, particularly Maddie, she'd been keeping out of the way.

Slowly, she entered the room where Maddie lay on the bed, her face pressed into the pillow.

When Maddie turned her head to see who was there, Jeannie ran over and jumped on to the bed next to her, flinging her arms around her. 'Oh Maddie! Ah'm that sorry that ah could die! Ah can't bear ter see yer sufferin' like this.' Maddie, unable to speak, held on to her tightly, and they wept together.

Downstairs, Ginette and Nicole were helping Hannah make yet another pot of tea, more for something to do than for thirst, when in barged Rene, followed closely by Rob, who'd driven her over to the village.

'What on earth's happening, Mam?' she sounded desperate. Then, suddenly realizing that she hadn't greeted the two people who were obviously Maddie's French friends, she apologized profusely and kissed the older of the two on each cheek. 'I think you must be Ginette?' Taking Nicole by the shoulders and kissing her also on each cheek, she said, 'And you are Maddie's good friend Nicole. I have heard such lovely things about you from Maddie,' and she glanced back to Ginette, 'about both of you.' She smiled.

Having understood most of what Rene had said, they returned the smile.

Hannah interrupted, 'Eee, pet! How did you get ter hear about all this anyway?'

'Dad phoned me just after he phoned Tom at work. What's happened exactly? Dad's message was a bit garbled.'

'Well ah'm not surprised, pet, we've all been in a state of shock for the last couple of hours.' Haltingly, Hannah explained everything up to the point where they found themselves now. Looking at her pale-faced daughter, she said, full of motherly concern, 'Yer shouldn't be rushin' about like this, hinny. Yer should be restin' at home after all that's happened to you.'

'How can I rest in Bishop, Mam, when all this is going on over here in the village? Has anybody *any* idea of where Francine is? And where is Maddie?'

'Maddie's upstairs, and so is our Jeannie.' Rene went to get up to go to them, but Hannah took hold of her arm to hold her back. 'Leave them a while, pet. Maddie's in a right state but ah think our Jeannie is with her. And our Tom's on to it now, pet, whatever *it* is! We don't know where he's gone, but he was pretty sure he knew where he was goin' when he left here, with yer dad.'

Jack, who'd had no chance of keeping up with Tom, arrived on Nora's doorstep gasping and holding his chest. He grabbed Tom's arm, begging, 'Hold on a minute, lad, that's no way ter get her ter come out! She'll be terrified, man! And even worse, if the bairn *is* in there by any chance, *she'll* be frightened out of her wits an' all!'

He gently shoved Tom to one side, suggesting quietly, 'Let me deal with it, eh, lad?'

Tom hesitated a moment. 'You keep her talkin' through the letter box here and ah'll go round the back of the house ter see if ah can get in. Amazingly, she's had the foresight ter lock the bloody door.' Without waiting for an answer, he bolted round the corner and out of sight.

Jack crouched down until he was level with the letter box. 'Nora . . . Nora?'

'What do yer want? Go away.'

He realized that the muffled voice was likely due to her talking with her thumb in her mouth, as he knew she was prone to do when she was ruffled or under stress. 'Ah just want ter talk ter yer fer a minute, lass, that's all.'

'Is Tom still out there? 'Cause he's very narked with me, and ah'm frightened of him.'

'Noo, he's long gone,' Jack lied, before continuing in a forced but gentle tone, 'Why d'yer think he's narked with yer then, Nora?'

'Ah don't know, 'cause ah've been a *good* girl,' she drawled in her inimitable way.

Most villagers' view was that she should have been locked up years ago, and although his own view wasn't quite that harsh, Jack had to admit that a lass like her should be somewhere where she'd be cared for, instead of just getting an occasional visit from somebody from the 'health place'.

Here she was, living in a house with hardly a decent stick of furniture to speak of. Whatever she did have were cast-offs from people in the village. Even Jessie, in her more sympathetic moments, had helped her out a bit, one way and another. That was when Nora had cottoned on to Jessie, started following her like a shadow, and spending her life trying to do things to please her.

But Jessie had soon got fed up with that, and all she did now was moan about Nora's very existence, unless of course she wanted to use her for her own convenience . . . Yes, Jack thought, that would make anybody think the two of them were the best of friends. No wonder the poor lass didn't know whether she was coming or going.

'Nora, will yer come out ter talk to uz?' he asked now, trying to remain patient.

'Ah don't know . . . ah've got somethin' ter do first.' He heard movement in the room.

'Where yer goin', Nora?' Jack was worried she'd be out of earshot if she moved.

'Just up the stairs.' She sounded far too secretive for his liking.

Before Jack could say anything more, he could hear her footsteps padding up the uncarpeted wooden stairs. 'Oh God! What's she up to now?' he mumbled while looking around, wondering where on earth Tom had got to.

Tom had found a larder window open at the back of the house and was pulling himself through it, when suddenly he heard the sound of a familiar nursery rhyme coming from somewhere above him.

'Twinkle twinkle little star,
How I wonder . . .'

Singing bloody nursery rhymes? Has she lost it altogether now and reverted back to her childhood? he asked himself.

But the next words he heard filled him with horror. '*Wake up . . . wake up, fer God's sake, will yer!*'

'Francine, oh my God, it's got to be Francine!' He hauled himself through the window, jumped down into the larder, ran through the kitchen to the hall and up the stairs, and was in the bedroom before Nora had time to think.

'You *bitch*!'

There was a resounding crack when he pushed Nora away from the hefty cardboard box that held his child, but Tom ignored it to reach down to his daughter.

He lifted her carefully from the box where she was sleeping, but when he held her tightly against him she didn't stir. He looked down and saw her pale face and bluish lips, and in utter panic he shouted, 'Oh no! Oh my God!'

Without so much as a glance at Nora, who lay motionless on the floor bleeding profusely from the head, he turned and ran down the stairs, unlocked the front door and almost knocked Jack off his feet. 'She's upstairs, see to 'er, will yer? Ah'll be at the doctor's!' he shouted.

Jack ran up the stairs, and was stopped in his tracks by the sight before him. It was the blood that struck him first, and Nora was lying beside it like a heap of rags. In turmoil as to what to do first, he went a bit closer. 'Nora? Nora . . . can yer hear uz?' Ambulance! We need an ambulance, he thought. He didn't dare touch her. He saw her eye flicker as she tried to say something.

'Wa . . . wat—!'

Understanding that she was asking for water, he said, 'Yes, yes, pet, ah'll get yer some!' He rushed down the stairs, almost tumbling over his feet at the bottom. In the kitchen he stood in the middle of the floor and turned a complete circle. Where were the glasses? He picked up a used mug off the draining board and turned the tap full on to rinse it. While the mug was filling, he noticed a bottle that appeared to have fallen over, and at the neck some kind of gloop was pooling on the draining board. For some unknown reason, he felt compelled to take the bottle. Seeing no bottle top, he quickly rinsed the neck and shoved the bottle in his pocket, before running back up the stairs with the water.

Hannah's household was still in turmoil, with Jack and Tom both gone God knows where and no one knowing what was happening. Then the back door burst open, and there in the entrance to the scullery stood Jack. Everyone looked immediately behind him, but he was alone. The expression on his face was enough to bring the whole household to a standstill, except Hannah, who ran to his side, demanding, 'What? What's happened, Jack?' Nicole and Ginette stood waiting, each with a hand pressed to her mouth, in anticipation of awful news.

'*Oh mon Dieu!*' Maddie called as she ran down the stairs, realizing that Francine wasn't there.

Jeannie was right behind her, calling, 'Where is she? Where's Francine?'

Jack put his hand up to quiet everybody. 'She's in good hands. Ah've just dropped summat off down the road, at Dr Jacobs's house, and he has driven Francine, with Tom, directly to the hospital.'

Looking straight at Mrs Parkin, he said, 'Ah need ter use yer phone, Mrs Parkin. We need ter get an ambulance, for Nora, urgently!' He looked at Hannah now.

The groan that came from Maddie as she fell made everyone jump back.

Nicole and Ginette rushed to her aid. Mrs Parkin grabbed her coat.

And Jack pulled Hannah into the kitchen, hurriedly explaining to her what had happened. He thought it better if she explained it all to Maddie, in a slower and more calm way than he could manage right now. He would more than likely get it all wrong in his haste.

Within seconds, Mrs Parkin had rushed into the kitchen and grabbed Jack's arm. Together, they ran off up the street to her house, while the others crowded around Maddie.

'Madeleine! Madeleine!' Nicole tapped her lightly on

the cheek, while Ginette pushed a cushion under her head. But it was the chiming of the grandfather clock that jolted her back to the here and now.

'Ah'll get her some medicine out of the cupboard, shall ah, Gran?' Jeannie said helpfully, but stopped when she saw the look on her mam's face. 'Ah know now that it's not medicine, Mam! Ah mean a drop of whisky.'

While Hannah poured the drink slowly down Maddie's throat, she couldn't help but think, If it wasn't for the bloody rationin', we'd have had a nice drop of brandy for her, instead of this horrible harsh rubbish.

Maddie spluttered, and as Nicole lifted her head from the cushion to help her swallow more easily, Hannah was saying to Maddie, 'Listen, pet . . . Listen to me!' To get her full attention, she turned Maddie's head towards her. Then looking straight into her swollen eyes, she continued, gently now, 'Tom found her at Nora's and ran straight to the doctor's with her. She'll be all right, she's got her dad with her. But the doctor, not bein' sure if she might have swallowed something, has driven her straight ter the hospital . . . fer observation like.'

'Ob . . . ob-ser-vation, what is zis ob-ser-vation?' Maddie was sitting up and looking around as if she had no idea what she was doing there on the floor.

'It means they want ter keep an eye on her . . . probably just for the night, pet.' She had no idea at all how long Francine would be in there, or how bad her condition was.

'But is she ill?' The panic was coming back into Maddie's voice.

'All we know is what Jack told us, before he ran out to telephone.' She hesitated a moment. 'The doctor thinks that Nora might have given Francine something to quiet her down . . . Probably ter keep her calm like,' Hannah added quietly, as if thinking aloud.

Jeannie, open-mouthed at this bit of information, cried out, her tone rising to a higher pitch with every word, 'Is it poison? Has Nitty Nora poisoned her?'

'No, pet, not exactly. It's just that in among the stuff lying around on her draining board was an empty bottle of summat called Mrs Winslow's Soothing Syrup. Yer grandda said it was lying there with the top off. But he said it was so old that it had gone all sticky, almost solid, and he doesn't think it would have poured out very well. So maybe it wasn't what Nora gave her.'

'But she could have sucked it off a finger or some such thing . . . *Oh mon Dieu!*' Maddie was now convinced that this was what had happened.

Hearing the tail end of that conversation, Rob came through from the kitchen where he'd been helping Rene. 'Wasn't that stuff taken out of the shops back in the thirties? Advertised as "Likely to soothe any human or animal". Used for quieting restless infants and small children, if I remember right.'

'Yes, it was,' Hannah answered, aiming a discreet shake of her head towards Rob. He'd picked up immediately on her meaning. He musn't say anything in front of Maddie about how the stuff had been removed from the shops because it was deemed to be dangerous. Several children had died.

Maddie had been sitting there on the floor, praying to herself, while feeling more and more hopeless. If she could scream or rant or tear her hair out, it would be better than wanting to lie down and die. Well, she couldn't do any of those things, but she *could* get out of here and go to her little girl.

The next minute, she was up on her feet and getting into her coat. 'I cannot stay here a minute longer, I am going to ze hospital.'

'You need ter stay here till Tom gets back, pet. He'll know what ter do!' Hannah sounded desperate.

'No, Mam.' Rene placed her hand on her mam's arm to stop her, and glanced at Rob. 'We'll take her, she's going to make herself ill if she stays here any longer not knowing what's going on.'

Without waiting for confirmation from Rob, Maddie was opening the door. 'Thank you, Rene . . . will you come too?'

'Of course I will.' Rene was already in her coat, but felt obliged to look briefly to Nicole and Ginette. She didn't want them to feel left out.

'Please, you go, Rene.' Nicole flapped her hand in dismissal. 'We will wait here, wiz Hannah. It is better zat it is English-speaking persons at ze hospital.'

Nicole then went to her friend and hugged Madeleine firmly.

When she came back into the room, she took her *maman*'s hand, pulling her away from the others. Jeannie noticed that they chattered quickly and seemingly urgently, in their own language.

When they returned, it was Nicole who approached Hannah. 'I have talked wiz Maman, and I hope zat you will agree. 'We would like to take Madeleine back to France wiz us, when all zis is over . . .'

There was silence for a moment, and Nicole added, 'To be wiz her family . . . you understand, *non*?'

It was Jeannie who spoke first. 'But Nicole, we can look after her here! What about our Tom an' all?'

'I know, Jeannie.' Nicole crouched beside her. 'It wouldn't be for ever, just until she is feeling stronger, *chérie*.' Nicole glanced over to Hannah, who nodded in response.

'We can do nothing, of course, until we find out what is happening wiz little Francine. If she is well, then . . .' Nicole took hold of Jeannie's hand. 'You do understand, don't you?'

'Yes, ah s'ppose so.' Jeannie looked deflated. 'But ah don't know what our Tom's goin' ter have ter say about that!'

Chapter 29

It had been three months since Maddie had gone back to France with Nicole and Ginette, and according to Maddie's last letter to Tom, little Francine was doing very well. Now that she'd started talking, she'd even managed one or two French words.

The memory of his little girl lying in that hospital bed made him want to weep. Three days she had lain there with tubes coming out of her mouth and nose! He'd watched the nurses running around like 'blue-arsed flies', making sure that the poor little mite was as comfortable as possible.

He and Maddie couldn't thank those doctors enough for what they'd done. She'd have been a goner, for sure, if they hadn't pumped her stomach empty of that bloody cocktail of old medicine and alcohol that that stupid bitch had given her, to try to calm her down when she'd started missing her mam. The very thought of it made his own stomach heave, even now.

He knew deep down that he was doing Nora a dis-
service calling her a bitch, because he couldn't imagine
for a minute that her aim had been to harm Francine, or
anyone else for that matter. But because *her* mam had
apparently given her that same medicine from that same
bottle when as a bairn she'd needed settling down –
which must have been pretty often, being as Nora
wasn't 'all there', so to speak – he could see how she
would have automatically thought it the right thing to
do. But then, when she'd struggled to get a couple of
tablespoonfuls out of the bottle because it had gone all
treacly, she'd tried giving her the other thing that her
own ma had given her if she hadn't any medicine handy,
and that had been alcohol. And the mixture had made
Francine black out.

Tom, who'd been staring, unseeing, from his seat on
the top deck of the double-decker bus on his journey
home from work, closed his eyes for a moment and
shook his head. He reminded himself, yet again, just
how lucky they were that Francine was still alive.

As the bus stopped to pick up more passengers, Tom
smiled to himself, remembering how amused Nicole and
Ginette had been by the buses in England with their
upstairs seating area. It pleased him to know that by all
accounts the two women were loving the farm life at
Maddie's Aunt Lucy's, and apparently Aunt Lucy was in
no hurry for them to leave either.

He thanked God, for Ginette's sake, that that bastard

of an uncle of hers hadn't died. Certainly not for the uncle's sake . . . no, but those two poor French lasses would have been on the run for the rest of their lives if he *had* died.

Apparently Gaston had been in a bad way for weeks. Ginette must have given him one hell of a whack with that vase. So maybe, in some sense, justice had been done. Right or wrong, Tom couldn't help but be impressed by Ginette's actions.

Anyway, Gaston would surely not be looking for Ginette any more, not after this little lot! It wouldn't be as easy to find them again either, he mused. What with the women's plans to move away from Boulogne altogether, they could change their names and lose themselves anywhere they chose.

It looked as though they were going to get away with it. He was amazed at that, mind! But it seemed that Nicole's boyfriend, Jacques, had managed, with the key that Ginette had given him, to get into the house un-observed before the police had arrived, broken down the door and turned the place upside down, looking for anything that would tell them where the occupants might be. Jacques had already taken away the women's papers and clothing, as Ginette had instructed.

And now it looked as though they were going to use the time they were based at Maddie's Aunt Lucy's farm to plan to look for a house in the South of France, close to where they'd been on holiday recently. And if he knew anything, Tom thought, he knew that a man in love wouldn't be separated from his girl for long; he had no doubt that Jacques would be following Nicole to the South of France as soon as he was able.

He'd like to meet this Jacques one day. He sounded like his kind of bloke, had spunk. Wonder if he can speak English, he mused, the thought never entering his head that maybe it would help if *he* were to study some French too.

Tom allowed himself a smile now, at the thought of the promises from Ginette and Nicole of cheap holidays for them all in the future.

But under all this musing, he was pretty fed up. The bairn was due any time, and as he sat there thinking about it now, it irked him that he and Maddie were so far apart.

He'd begged her not to go, but nothing could dissuade her from giving birth to their second child in her own country. And even his family hadn't tried to deter her this time. Knowing that the only place she'd derive any comfort, after what had gone before, was with her own family, they'd given her decision their blessing.

He knew that he'd been selfish in trying to persuade her to stay. But *three months*! It had been bad enough when she'd first known that she was pregnant and had said she wanted to be back home for the birth; then it would have probably only been for a couple of months.

But he'd seen how weak and miserable she was after the goings-on with Francine, and if he was honest about it, it *was* the best time for her to go, as she had Nicole and Ginette to chaperone her and to help with the little girl.

She'd held on until she'd heard that Nitty Nora would be institutionalized. As soon as she was sure that as far as Nora's head injuries were concerned, Tom was in the clear, she and Francine, along with Nicole and Ginette, had left for France.

It had been touch and go for about two weeks, whether Nora was going to pull through after that knock on the head. But when she finally did come round and the police questioned her, to Tom's relief she'd said that she didn't remember anything, and she wouldn't have had the nous to lie to the police about that – would she?

Anyway, the upshot of it all was that Nora, deemed unfit to look after herself, was in a home now, and he'd heard that she'd gone willingly, especially when she'd been told that she'd be given proper food every day, with no more worries about how to make a few pence just so that she could eat. He was pleased about that, as there was a part of him that felt sorry for her.

He gazed through the bus window at the pleasant countryside. Physically tired, Tom was having difficulty keeping his eyes open and could feel himself drifting away. He knew he mustn't miss his stop, but as the bus jogged along more gently now he was lulled into sleep.

One good thing to come out of all this was that Tom had felt much more relaxed since Jessie had left the village. From the day he'd received her note insisting that she'd had no part in what had happened to Francine, he'd felt a great sense of relief.

According to Jessie, Nitty Nora had thought it all up on her own. It had been her attempt to do one really big thing for Jessie, something so big that Jessie would have been her friend for ever.

Before she was taken away, Nora had confided to Tom's mother that Jessie had once asked her to get her a husband and a bairn. And Nora, Hannah realized, had taken the sarcastic statement literally. To Nora's befuddled mind, what better bairn to get her than Tom's? She'd told Hannah that taking Francine had been so easy, she couldn't believe her luck.

She'd admitted all this in such a matter-of-fact way that Hannah had had to sit down, before she fell down at the ridiculousness of the whole thing.

Nora had been walking past Hannah's back yard and had found little Francine sitting in her pushchair, all on her own. She knew that Jeannie was in the lav, and at first she just intended talking to the little girl, to keep her company. Then, to use Nora's words, 'It was as if a light had come on in me 'ead.' Not only could she bring Jessie a bairn, but she could upset that French lass of Tom's at the same time. After all, Jessie hated her, didn't she? It was too good to be true. She took the pushchair and just walked away, as simple as that!

'Why on earth did yer go ter the pond? Why not straight home, that's what I want ter know?' Hannah had found her tongue at last.

'Ah went ter the pond ter get rid of the pushchair, of course! Ah had nowhere ter hide it at home!' Nora said this as if it should be blatantly obvious. 'And when ah was standin' down there, in the fog, holdin' the bairn in me arms, it struck me that folk might think that the bairn was in the water an' all, so nobody would be lookin' for 'er like.' Hearing this mixture of innocence and pure wickedness coming out of Nora's mouth, Hannah had no idea how to respond.

When she related all this to the family, they had agreed that somewhere in Nora's twisted mind it must have all seemed logical. And now she was gone from the village, and so, thank God, was Jessie. But so was Maddie, and there was Tom without a clue as to when she was intending to come back, or even *if* she would come back.

'It'll all work out, pet. These things are sent to try us,' had been Hannah's comforting words to Tom that morning, when he'd popped in on his way to work.

'Tom! Tom!'

'Wha— Oh, hello there, mate!' Tom stretched and yawned loudly. 'Ah didn't see yer get on the bus, ah was miles away.'

'Miles away? Yer were sound asleep!' George, his

long-standing mate, was laughing at him. 'Ah just got on at the last stop like. Anyway, budge over, ye're tekkin' up two seats there. Ah've got some news that ah think'll bring yer nicely back ter the here and now.'

Tom moved into the window seat and George sat down next to him.

'Come on then, don't keep uz in the dark.' Tom nudged George playfully, eager to know his news now that he was fully awake.

'Well, yer know that ah've been seein' Maisie for quite a while now?'

'Of course ah do, seein' as it was me that introduced the pair of yer!' Tom grinned.

'OK! OK! And ah'll never be able ter thank yer enough fer that.' Tom could see that George's gratitude was genuine.

'Anyway, we're goin' ter get hitched . . . well, engaged first like. Can yer believe it?'

'Ay, mate, ah'm that pleased for yer.' Tom slapped him hard on the back. 'She's a lovely lass. And yer know ah would have been interested meself, if it hadn't been for the fact that ah love my Maddie so much.' Tom grinned at George, joking, 'Shame she's had ter settle fer second best though.'

'Aye, well, that might be.' George's smile was broad, then he added more earnestly, 'But we get on really well, man. Ah think this is it fer me, there's nowt else ah need . . . except for gettin' some money together of course, and . . .'

'Money?'

'Ah was just goin' ter say, that's where you come in like.'

'Me? Ah've got no money, mate, yer know that.'

'Aye, but aren't yer savin' fer a motorbike?'

'Aye, I—' He stopped mid-sentence when the penny suddenly dropped. 'Ay, don't tell me ye're thinkin' of sellin' yer Royal Enfield?'

'The very same . . . and ah'm offerin' it to you at a good price.' Noticing that Tom was doing sums in his head, George said, 'Yer can pay on the never-never, ter start with like, as long as ah've got some money ter put away each month . . .'

George hadn't even finished the sentence before Tom was saying, 'Done! It's a done deal!'

'Hang on, we haven't even discussed how much yet!'

'No need, ah trust yer, Georgie lad. Ah know yer bike and ah know you, and I also know that yer wouldn't diddle me, and if, as yer say, ah can pay on the never, it'll be no problem!'

Tom didn't even try to hide his excitement. 'Yer know what this means? It means that ah can get a sidecar fitted and get over ter France ter bring me wife and bairns back! 'Cause it will be bairns in plural by then! Ay, Maddie'll be made up!'

All thoughts of Maddie possibly not wanting to come

back had disappeared in no more time than it had taken him to say, 'Done deal,' and all he could think now was that she'd be as excited as he was. And it would mean he could tell her she'd be able to return to France a bit more frequently, once they had the bike . . . Not too frequently of course, because she really would have to try to settle in England if things were going to work out.

It was two days later, while Tom was completing the deal on the motorbike in England, that Maddie was screaming their son into the world in France.

Hannah, Jack, Rene and Jeannie had just sat down to tea when the telegram arrived.

Tom, you have a lovely little boy – stop – All well – stop – Please phone Martine's number at her work 5pm English time – stop

That was all it said, but it was enough to put the whole family in a whirl. Everyone seemed to be talking at once, while Jeannie nodded, her mouth full, as she added another boiled potato to her plate.

'Ah wish our Tom would hurry up, ah can't wait to see his face when we tell him he has a son.' Jack was pacing around with a permanent grin on his face.

'Well, what with his new motorbike *and* a new bairn, he won't know which way to turn!' Jeannie piped up, helping herself to another slice of ham along with a dollop of pease pudding.

'Well, I know exactly which way he'll turn,' said Rene. 'He'll be on that bike and over to France before we can draw breath.' Looking at Jeannie now, she said, 'Are you starving or something? You've not stopped eating since you sat down.'

'It's all this excitement, Mam, it makes me hungry.' She was too embarrassed to tell her mam the real reason she was eating so much. But she just had to fill out and grow some curves before Ian same back. And she only had till next weekend!

'Leave her be, pet.' Hannah patted Rene's hand. 'Ah like ter see her eat, she's as skinny as a rake!'

'Oh, she'll fill out soon enough. She's growing up far too fast for my liking. In fact, in that school in Bishop all the girls seem to be far too grown up for their own good.' Rene said this with some concern.

Before Hannah could comment, Tom came rushing in. Throwing off his jacket and hardly able to contain his excitement, he said, 'Come on, all of yer, come and see it.' Full of pride, he led the way to the motorbike, which stood, gleaming, against a backdrop of the red-brick wall in the back yard.

'And guess what! Ah've got a sidecar arranged an' all!' He was obviously pleased with himself for having arranged it so promptly.

'That's handy then,' said his dad, holding him

back for a second, 'cause ye're gonna need it now.'

'Ah know, Dad, ah'll be needing it soon enough.' Tom carried on walking while the others had all stopped.

'Ah mean, ye're gonna need it right now, lad . . . Yer have a son!'

The shock, evident in his flushed face, stopped Tom in his tracks, while his mam and Rene came rushing over to him.

'Oh Jack, that was no way ter tell him such news!' Hannah admonished.

'No, Mam, it's all right.' Tom stood very still, trying to get his head round it. 'A son, eh? Ah've got a son! How's Maddie? Is Maddie all right?' He looked from one to the other, panic setting in.

'Maddie's fine, lad,' his dad answered.

'Let's get back in the house, we can see the bike later.' His mam put an arm around him, turning him about.

'Well, *I'm* goin' ter have a look at the bike, 'cause we can't see the new bairn at the moment, can we!' Jeannie wandered off in the opposite direction, which made Tom laugh out loud.

'A son, ah've got a son! This calls for a celebration. Dad, have we still got some of the hard stuff in that cupboard?'

'What! Yer mean the magic bottle that keeps fillin' itself up?' said Jack.

Marck

Despite the aching tiredness coursing through her body, Maddie was sitting up in bed in the room where she, her brother and sisters and little Francine had all been born.

Her envious sisters, and her *maman*, had spent hours sitting on and around the bed, happily chatting about this and that. Even though a week had gone by, still, whenever they had the chance, they were taking turns to hold and coo over the new baby. Francine, now sleeping peacefully in the bed alongside her mother, was happy enough just to give him a sly poke, whenever the opportunity presented itself.

Right now, at last Madeleine was having a moment alone. Martine and Simone had gone down the road to the dairy, where the old lady, Madame Gertrude, would ladle fresh milk from the giant urn into their tin jug. And if they were lucky, they would bring back some freshly made butter to spread on the crusty bread that her *maman* had made that morning. The aroma of it, for a while, had taken her right back into Hannah's house.

And now, Maman, who'd hardly left her side since the birth, had rushed off to answer the hammering on the front door.

As her health had improved, Madeleine's longing to see Tom had increased dramatically. She could only guess at how he might be feeling, and what he might be doing. Absently, she picked up the pillow, and hugged it to her, and for a brief moment it was as if he were there in her arms.

Her thoughts wandered over the Channel, to England. In her mind's eye she was able to draw the route, and in her head she meandered up through the right-hand side of England, until eventually she reached Bishop Auckland, from where she allowed her mind to take her on the bus to Evenwood.

Once there, she could see the mine, smell the fumes, and see the smiling black-faced men with a twinkle in the eye, as they walked home from their shift at the pit. She wandered from the bus stop through the village, towards Hannah's house. She could see Hannah on the doorstep, dressed in her best pinny, arms outstretched, welcoming her and enfolding her into the warmth of her home full of love.

With a jolt she was back in her bed, still holding tightly on to the pillow, and it was at that moment that she realized she was feeling homesick. Homesick for the place that, not so long ago, she'd wanted so desperately to leave. All that time in England wanting to be in France, and now I am here, I want to be back in England! Her mind was working overtime, confusing her. She sighed, long and hard. '*Oh mon Dieu!* Where do I belong?'

She slid down under the covers, but not to sleep, because she knew she wouldn't sleep. She just lay there staring at the ceiling, and half listening to her *maman*'s distant and muffled voice.

'*Une minute! Une minute!*' Maman called impatiently, as she unlocked the front door. '*Oh mon Dieu!*' She clapped a hand over her mouth, as there before her stood Tom, grinning from ear to ear.

'Oh Tom!' she cried. Dispensing with the usual kisses on each cheek, she flung her arms around him and hugged him as tightly as she could. 'She will be so pleased to see you . . .' Then suddenly releasing him, she grabbed his sleeve. 'But she cannot travel yet!'

'No, no, I am not here to take her back to England . . . not yet, anyway. I am here to be with her and Francine, and to meet my son.' He smiled, relishing those two words, *my son*.

Maman, having to take a guess at what he'd just said in English, took his hand and led him through the reception room, to the bedroom on the ground floor at the front of the house. She opened the door and gently pushed him through, closing the door behind him, while she rushed off to fetch Papa from his workshop. Then she would make a pot of coffee for all of them, which she had a feeling was going to be much needed.

For a moment they just looked at one another, Maddie with her mouth open. What she saw before her was surreal. Had she fallen asleep after all, and was she dreaming? During the split second it took for those thoughts to go through her mind, Tom, without a word, tears welling in his eyes, stepped towards her, his arms opening.

Maddie reached out to him, and as soon as she felt his arms securely around her body, she knew, she knew without doubt, it was him, it actually *was* him, and not the pillow she'd hugged only minutes before. She buried her head in his chest and the tears fell freely. Tom murmured something into her hair, she didn't know what and she didn't care. He was here, he'd come all this way to be with her.

Still holding on to her, he leaned over to the cot alongside the bed and his heart was full. 'My son!' he said.

'Our son.' She smiled.

'Can I hold him?' he asked warily.

'But of course. You will have to get used to that, so you may as well start now, eh?' she mocked.

'Oh God! He's so small.' Tom's hands could have belonged to a giant, he felt so awkward holding his tiny son.

'He won't break, *mon chéri*, you will get used to him soon enough. Anyway, it's not that long since you were holding Francine at that size,' she reminded him.

He smiled, and looking towards his sleeping daughter on the bed now, he asked quietly, 'And Francine, is she OK with her new brother?'

'Yes, but she tries to hug him a little too tightly, so we have to watch her.'

'Little monkey.' He grinned, then added more seriously, 'but she's been all right since all the trouble in England?'

'I don't think she is aware that anything unusual happened . . . I think often of that girl, Nora . . . and what the outcome of her actions could have been.'

'We don't have to worry about Nora any more, pet, or Jessie. They're both gone . . . I have to tell you, my darling, that Jessie pushed a note through our letter box before she left. Among other things, she told me to "get the coal hatch fixed, as anyone could get in there".'

'Why would she be interested in our—?' Maddie stopped mid-sentence, suddenly realizing why Jessie would have said that. 'Oh no! It was *her*? Her doing all those things?' Maddie shrieked. 'My bicycle, the running tap, the salt in the stew, the radio coming on all by itself, and all the other things which no one believed?'

Tom hugged her to him. 'I am so very sorry, my darling, that we thought it was your imagination. We all knew how homesick you were, and wrongly, very wrongly, we put it down to that. Oh God!' he whispered, as he hugged her more tightly to him, full of remorse. 'You must have felt so alone.'

Tom had been overrun by guilt when he'd read the note and realized what must have been going on all that time. And he was embarrassed now to even ask the next question of Maddie. 'Can you forgive me, pet? Can you forgive all of us?'

Still raw from all those happenings in England, the only answer that Maddie could give right now was to hold him close.

Happy with this response for now, Tom quickly changed the subject. 'Everything will be different when we get back, my love. We can start afresh.' He pushed her hair from her forehead and kissed her furrowed brow.

Maddie looked up at him, her eyes momentarily filled with fear. 'I am not strong enough to travel yet, Tom.'

'Shush! Shush! I know that, I'll wait until you're ready.'

'But your work, what about your work?'

'I can go back to England if necessary, and then come back for you.'

'But the money! Where will you get the money to travel, and how will we all get back to England . . . and the luggage?'

'Ah well!' He smiled. 'Mam, Dad and Rene clubbed together and have helped me out with money for this trip, it being a special occasion and all that. And as for how we will all get back, when the time comes, I have that covered too. We, my darling . . . are the proud owners of a motorbike *and* a sidecar!'

'Oh!' Maddie clapped a hand over her mouth. 'You 'ave a motorbike?'

'Yes, my darling, and a very essential sidecar.'

'But is it big enough, zis . . . 'ow you say . . . sidecar?'

'It's big enough for two small bairns *and* a suitcase in the back, two at a push.' He grinned, then, knowing how much stuff Maddie liked to cart around, he added quickly, 'But only small ones, mind!'

'But is it safe, zis . . . sidecar? Can it fall off? How is it attached?'

'Let me worry about that, pet. I wouldn't do it if I didn't think it was safe fer our bairns, now would I.' He hugged her close. 'It's just like . . . a little car. Anyway, are you well enough to get out of bed, 'cause you can see it through the window. It's just outside.'

'Yes, help me up . . . I want to see.' Tom helped her out of bed and led her to the window.

Together they stood there, staring out at this marvellous contraption. Seeing Tom's face, so full of pride at his acquisition, Maddie swallowed hard, continuing to gaze in wonderment at the bike and sidecar. He has done this for me, she thought. *Oh mon Dieu!*

Tom spoke. 'Of course you know what this means now, my pet.'

She looked up, her eyes smiling into his. 'I hope it means that we can come back here to France whenever we can afford it, and maybe then I will think that my family is not so far away?'

'You got it, pet! That's exactly what it means.'

'Oh Tom,' she held him tight, '*je t'aime, mon chéri*. I do love you.'

She needed no more words from Tom. His wide grin, and the deep love in his eyes, said it all.

ALSO BY FADETTE MARIE

From the battle-weary fields of northern France
to the bleak village industries of north east England,
Northern Girl takes you on an unforgettable journey
– a journey of all-consuming passion, heartbreak,
and family shame and ultimately to a destination
that no one could have expected.